D0935059

THE RETREAT

Also by Patrick Rambaud

THE BATTLE

Patrick Rambaud

THE RETREAT

Translated from the French by

William Hobson

Atlantic Monthly Press
New York

First published in English in 2004 by Picador,
an imprint of Pan Macmillan Ltd., London, England

Originally published in 2000 as *Il neigeait*
by Editions Grasset & Fasquelle, Paris

Published simultaneously in Canada
Printed in the United States of America

FIRST AMERICAN EDITION

Library of Congress Cataloging-in-Publication Data

Rambaud, Patrick.
    [Il neigeait. English]
    The retreat / Patrick Rambaud ; translated by Will Hobson.
        p. cm.
    ISBN 0-87113-877-8
    1. Napoleonic Wars, 1800–1815—Campaigns—Russia—
Fiction. I. Hobson, Will. II. Title.
PQ2678.A455153 2004
843'.914—dc22   2004050281

Atlantic Monthly Press
an imprint of Grove/Atlantic, Inc.
841 Broadway
New York, NY 10003

04 05 06 07 08   10 9 8 7 6 5 4 3 2 1

To Tieu Hong for ever

To The Unknown Soldier

To Captain Fasquelle and his crew
who, I'm certain, are delighted to welcome
you aboard this flight 1812 to Beresina

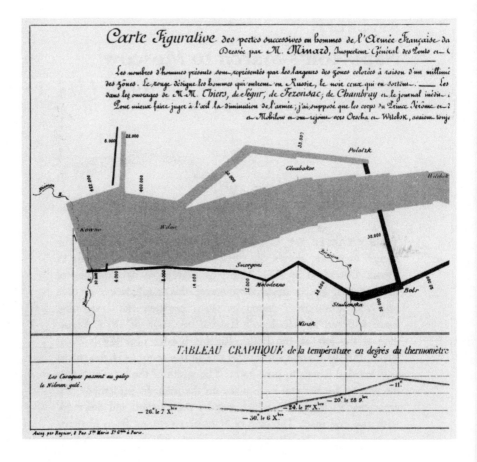

Translation of caption

Map representing successive troop losses sustained by the French army during the Russian campaign, 1812–1813. Drawn up by M. Minard, Inspector General of Public Works retired. Paris 20 November 1869.

The number of men present at any particular time is represented by the width of the coloured lines, to the ratio of one millimetre for ten thousand men [at original size]. Numbers are also written at an angle to the

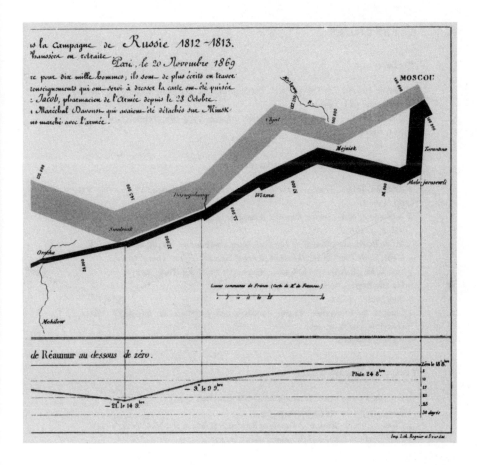

us la campagne de Russie 1812 ~1813.

Paris, le 20 Novembre 1869

MOSCOU

de Réaumur au dessous de zéro.

lines. Red [grey tint here] designates men entering Russia; black those leaving. The sources consulted for this map are the works of Messrs. Thiers, Ségur, Fezensac, Chambray and the unpublished diary of Jacob, an army pharmacist from 28 October. In order to represent the army's losses more clearly, I have treated the troops under Prince Jérome and Marshal Davout, who in fact were diverted to Minsk and Mikilov and only rejoined the others at Orcha and Vitebsk, as if they marched with the main army throughout.

'ON 20 MARCH 1811, sir, I was in Paris. It was a Wednesday. I was hugging the walls as usual . . .'

'Did you have the Imperial police on your tail?'

'Not a bit of it, but Paris's streets were still narrow, filthy affairs in those days; the drains ran into them, people emptied chamber pots out of their windows, and one was always within a whisker of being flattened against a corner-post by some passing carriage or other. Anyway, suddenly, at ten o'clock in the morning – I'd just consulted my fob watch – I stopped dead in my tracks.'

'In the middle of the street? With all those hazards?'

'The carriages weren't moving, the passers-by had fallen silent, all of us were straining our ears.'

'To hear what?'

'The cannon.'

'Were we going to war?'

'Oh, no, the Invalides's little cannon was firing blanks.'

'I see! A ceremony.'

'Better than that, much better. We were counting the reports, ten, eleven, twelve . . . When it got to twenty-two, everyone all over Paris started shouting and singing and applauding like crazy. It was a boy. The throne had an heir and the Emperor had a son.'

'Ah. And this warranted such an outpouring of joy, did it?'

'Yes, because it meant continuity: if the Emperor were to die, a regency would succeed him, we would be spared further upheaval, and believe me sir, we had had too much experience of upheaval.'

'But I was told that Empress Josephine couldn't have any more children . . .'

'My poor friend! That's why Napoleon divorced her. After defeating the Austrians at Wagram, he married their monarch's daughter, a Habsburg, the great-niece of Marie-Antoinette. And this royal princess had just given him a blond, pink cheeked, chubby son who was created King of Rome in his cradle.'

'What if it had been a girl?'

'She would have become Queen of Venice, but . . .'

'I understand. With a boy, the dynasty was assured and the French reassured.'

'Exactly. From then on the Emperor need not be so preoccupied when he left Paris to pursue the unification of Europe. He already governed a hundred and thirty departments of an enlarged France; he controlled Germany, Prussia, Holland, his father-in-law's Austria and all the kingdoms and duchies which he had persuaded to enter into alliances with him.'

'By force, once again.'

'Napoleon wanted peace, finally, he said, but England opposed French domination of the Continent. The Emperor hadn't managed to invade that island; in fact he had lost his fleet to it at Trafalgar.'

'So, if I'm following you correctly, he hoped to neutralize England, but how?'

'By a blockade of its merchandise. If the English were

no longer able to sell their goods in Europe, their factories would shut and their merchants go bankrupt, food shortages and unemployment would run rife – in short, London would have to capitulate.'

'I understand the plan, but in practice?'

'Alas, the Continental blockade had a perverse effect. It may have put England in an awkward position, but it was the other European countries that had to pay the real price: staples grew scarce, factories shut for lack of imported raw materials, there was no cotton, no sugar, no fabric dyes, everyone was at the mercy of a bad harvest . . .'

'And the Europeans resented it.'

'Exactly. The Russians in particular. The Tsar had sworn friendship to the Emperor, but the rouble was falling, the merchants were bemoaning their predicament and, as you might expect, the English seized on the opportunity to intrigue. They were constantly in St Petersburg, winning the Tsar over: "Open your eyes!" they'd say. "Napoleon rules from Naples to the North Sea, now he has Elba and is threatening the Russian borders – where will he stop? And what about Poland? Doesn't he want to make it a kingdom at Russia's expense?"'

'We still had the Grande Armée . . .'

'Hardly! Our best troops had been wearing themselves out for years in Portugal and Spain. They were no longer invincible.'

'So, in a nutshell, we were heading for war.'

'And no sparing the horses. This was common knowledge in Paris, in Vienna, in Berlin, all the more so because the Tsar, by opening his ports to British contraband, had broken the blockade. Tension was mounting, everyone was raising armies.'

'The eternal spiral, then?'

'In June 1812, with more than five hundred thousand men, Napoleon crossed the Niemen and entered Russia. He was confident; he thought the matter would be settled in twenty days.'

'There he was mistaken, but how did this rapid victory of his turn to tragedy?'

'Let me tell you . . .'

One

MOSCOW, 1812

Captain d'Herbigny felt ridiculous. Swathed in a pale cloak that floated on his shoulders, one could make out a dragoon of the Guard by the helmet enturbanned in navy calfskin, with a black horsetail on its brass crest, but astride a miniature horse he had bought in Lithuania, this strapping fellow had to dress his stirrups too short to stop his boots dragging along the ground – except that then his knees stuck up. 'What in Heaven's name do I look like?' he grumbled. 'What sort of a sight must I be?'

The captain missed his mare and his right hand. The hand had been hit by a Bashkir horseman's poisoned arrow during a skirmish: the surgeon had amputated it, stopped the bleeding with birch cotton because there was a shortage of lint, and dressed the wound with paper from the archives for lack of bandages. As for his mare, she had bloated after eating rain-soaked green rye; the poor thing had started trembling and soon she was hardly able to stand upright; when she stumbled into a gully, d'Herbigny had resigned himself to destroying her with a bullet behind the ear; it had brought him to tears.

His batman Paulin limped behind him, sighing, dressed in a black coat covered with leather patches and a crumpled hat, and with a cloth bag slung over his shoulder filled with grain he'd gathered along the way; he was leading by a string a donkey with a portmanteau strapped to its back.

These two fine fellows were not alone in railing against their ill fortune. Lined with a double row of huge trees similar to willows, the new Smolensk road they were trudging along ran through flat, sandy country. It was so broad that ten barouches could drive down it abreast, but on that grey, cold September Monday, as the mist lifted it revealed an unmoving crush of vehicles following the Guard and Davout's army. There were goods wagons in their thousands, a mass of conveyances for transporting the baggage, ambulance carts, masons', cobblers', and tailors' caravans; they carried handmills and forges and tools; on their long wooden handles, scythe blades poked out of one dray. The most exhausted, victims of fever, let themselves be carried, sitting on the ammunition wagons drawn by scrawny horses; long-haired dogs chased in and out, trying to bite each other. Soldiers of all arms of the army escorted this throng. They were marching to Moscow. They had been marching for three months.

Ah yes, the captain remembered, they'd been a mighty fine sight in June when they'd crossed the Niemen to violate Russian territory. The procession of troops across the pontoon bridges had lasted for three days. Just imagine: cannon by the hundred, over five hundred thousand fresh, alert fighting men, French a good third of them, with the grey-coated infantry rubbing shoulders with Illyrians, Croats, Spanish volunteers and Prince Eugène's Italians. Such might, such order, such numbers, such colour: one could spot the Portuguese by the orange plumes of their shakoes, the Weimar carabineers by their yellow plumes; over there were the green greatcoats of the Württemberg regiments, the red and gold of the Silesian hussars, the white of the Austrian chevaux-légers and the Saxon cuirassiers, the jonquil jackets of the Bavarian chasseurs. On the enemy bank, the Guard's band had played 'Le Nouvel Air de Roland', 'Whither go these gallant knights, honour and hope of France . . .'

The moment they crossed the river, their misfortunes began. They had to tramp through desert wastes in intense heat, plunge into forests of black firs, suffer sudden freezing cold after hellish storms; countless vehicles got bogged in the mud. In under a week the supply trains, heavy, slow-moving wagons drawn by oxen, had been left far behind. Resupply posed a grave problem. When the vanguard arrived in a village, they found nothing. The harvests? Burned. The herds? Moved. The mills? Destroyed. The warehouses? Devastated. The houses? Empty. Five years earlier, when Napoleon was conducting the war in Poland, d'Herbigny had seen peasants abandon their farms to hide in the depths of the forests with their animals and provisions; some secreted potatoes under their tiled floors, others buried flour, rice, and smoked bacon under the firs and hung boxes full of dried meat from the highest branches. Well, it had begun again, only much worse.

The horses gnawed at the frames of mangers, ate the straw in mattresses and the wet grass; ten thousand died before a Russian had even been seen. Famine reigned. The soldiers filled their bellies with a porridge of cold rye; they devoured juniper berries; they fought over the water in the mires, since the peasants had thrown carrion and dung down their wells. Dysentery was rife; half the Bavarians died of typhus before seeing action. Bodies of men and horses rotted on the roads; the stinking air they breathed

made them nauseous. D'Herbigny cursed but he knew he
was favoured; officers had requisitioned other army corps's
rations for the Imperial Guard, which led to brawls and no
lack of resentment towards the privileged men.

As his horse plodded along, the captain crunched a
green apple that he had taken from a dead man's pocket.
With his mouth full he called to his batman:

'Paulin!'

'Sir?' the other said in a barely audible voice.

'Heavens above! We're not moving at all now! What's
going on?'

'Well, sir, I wouldn't have the foggiest.'

'You never know anything!'

'Just give me a moment to hitch our donkey to your
saddle and I'll run off and find out . . .'

'Because, on top of everything else, you see me leading a
toy donkey, do you? You complete ass! I'll go.'

They could hear swearing in front. The captain threw
away his apple core, which was immediately fought over by
some yapping, raw-boned mongrels and then, with a noble
flourish, he steered his minute mount left-handed into the
bottleneck.

Skewed sideways across the road, the covered vehicle of
a canteen was blocking the traffic. A chicken, tied to the
cart's frame by its feet, was shedding feathers as it struggled
to escape; a band of dirty conscripts leered at it with spit-
roasters' eyes. The canteen-woman and her driver were
bewailing their luck. One of their draught horses had just
collapsed; some voltigeurs in torn uniforms had put down
their arms to take it out of the shafts.

The captain went closer. The carcass was now unharnessed but the soldiers, despite their number and their efforts, couldn't push it onto the verge.

'It'd take two good sturdy carthorses,' the driver was saying.

'There ain't none,' a voltigeur was replying.

'A strong rope will do,' d'Herbigny suggested as if stating the obvious.

'What then, sir? The animal's going to be just as heavy.'

'No, dammit! Tie the rope round the pasterns, and then ten of you haul it together.'

'We're no stronger than the horses,' replied a pale young sergeant.

D'Herbigny twisted up his moustache and scratched the wing of his long, proud nose. He was preparing to direct the road-clearing operation when a great clamour stopped him. It came from up ahead, towards the horizon, where the road curved. The clamour was persisting, taking hold, a fearsome, unremitting barrage of sound. Slowed by the canteen's accident, the throng now stopped dead. Every face turned in unison towards the uproar. It didn't sound warlike, more like a song bursting from a thousand throats. The cries were growing louder as they came nearer, passing along the column, rolling, echoing, swelling, growing distinct.

'What are those devils yelling?' the captain asked no one in particular.

'I think I know, sir,' said Paulin who had caught his master up in the crowd.

'Well, out with it, then, you halfwit.'

'They're shouting *Moscow! Moscow!*'

*

At a bend in the monotonous road, the first battalions had emerged onto the Hill of Salvation, and from there, spread out below them, they saw Moscow. It was a vision of the Orient at the end of a desolate plain. In the ranks, noisy shouts of joy gave way to a stunned silence; they gazed at the measureless city and the grey sweep of its river. After flushing its brick walls, the sun was glinting on the gilded domes of a clustered multitude of churches. They counted the blue cupolas spangled with gold, the minarets, the pointed towers, the palaces' balconies; they were astonished by the mass of cherry-red and green roofs, the brilliant splashes of orangeries, the tangles of waste land, the geometry of kitchen and pleasure gardens, the ornamental lakes glittering like sheets of metal. And radiating out from the crenellated walls stretched suburb after suburb, each a village enclosed by a simple epaulement. Many of them dreamt they were in Asia. Grenadiers who had survived Egypt feared a mirage, feared that, like a terrible memory, Ibrahim Bey's savages might suddenly appear again, chain mail under their burnooses and black silk tassels on their bamboo lances. The majority, who'd seen less service, anticipated a reward: Caucasian women with hair the colour of straw, something to eat, too much to drink, a night between clean sheets.

'What a sight, eh, Paulin?' said Captain d'Herbigny when it was his turn to crest the hill. 'More impressive than Rouen from St Catherine's Hill, wouldn't you say!'

'Certainly, sir,' replied the servant, who preferred Rouen, its belfry and the Seine.

Unfortunately for Paulin, his was a loyal nature; he followed where his master led. D'Herbigny stood as his guarantor whenever, with a soldier's wartime licence, he stole, and, since wars followed one after the other, Paulin's savings were growing; he hoped to buy a tailor's shop, that was his father's trade. If the captain was wounded, he pitied him – whilst discreetly rubbing his hands together, quarters nearer the ambulances were always better – but the respite never lasted. D'Herbigny had the constitution of an ox; even when he lost a hand or took a bullet in the calf, he quickly recovered and his spirits never wavered, since his devotion to the Emperor was bordering on the religious.

'Still,' grumbled the manservant, 'why come such a long way . . .'

'It's because of the English.'

'Are we going to fight the English in Moscow?'

'I've told you a hundred thousand times!'

The captain launched into his habitual lesson. 'The Russians have been trading with the English for a century, and the English want our downfall.' Then, more heatedly, he continued, 'The Russians are hoping to get money from London to improve their ships and dominate the Baltic and the Black Sea. And the English are having a whale of a time, naturally! They're turning the Tsar against Napoleon. They want an end to the cursed blockade that's stopping them flooding the Continent with their goods and so driving them to ruin. As for the Tsar, he takes a dim view of Napoleon extending his conquests. The Empire is pressing on his borders; the English point out the danger in that; he's swayed by their arguments, seeks some incident, provokes us and the next thing you know, here we are, outside Moscow.'

Will all this ever end? Paulin thought about his shop and the London cloth he'd like to cut.

A squadron of Polish lancers charged past, roaring

orders which they had no need to translate; flourishing their lances adorned with multicoloured pennons, they moved the inquisitive crowd back to clear a sort of terre-plein. Recognizing the white greatcoats and the funnel-shaped black-felt shakos of the Imperial escort, the regiments covering the hillside raised their hats on the points of their bayonets, saluting His Majesty's arrival with wild cheers; d'Herbigny shouted himself hoarse in unison. Napoleon rode by at a fast trot, his left arm hanging slackly at his side, a beaver-fur bicorne pulled down over his forehead, followed by his general staff in full uniform – plumes, gold lace, broad fringed belts, spotless boots – riding well-fed chestnuts.

The cheers redoubled when the group halted on the brow of the hill to study Moscow. The Emperor's blue eyes lit up fleetingly. He summed up the situation in four words: 'It was high time.'

'Ah yes, sire,' murmured the grand equerry, Caulain-court, jumping down from his horse to help the Emperor dismount. Napoleon's mount, Tauris, a silver-grey Persian Arab that was shaking its white mane, had been a present from the Tsar, when the two sovereigns held each other in high regard, intermingled with curiosity on the part of the Russian, and pride on that of the Corsican. In the first rank behind the lancers, d'Herbigny stared at his hero: with his hands behind his back, grey and puffy-faced, the Emperor seemed as broad as he was tall because of the very full sleeves of his grey overcoat which allowed him to put it on over his colonel's uniform without first taking off the epaulettes. Napoleon sneezed, sniffed, wiped his nose and then took from his pocket the pair of theatre glasses that never left his side now his sight was beginning to deteriorate. Several of the generals and his Mamelukes had dismounted and were standing around him. Outspread map in hand, Caulaincourt was describing Moscow; he indicated the triangle of the Kremlin's citadel on a rise, its winding walls flanked by towers following the line of the river; he pointed out the walls that bounded the five districts, named the churches, listed the warehouses.

The army grew impatient.

Apart from the officers' conference, it was unnervingly silent. Everyone held their breath. Nothing, they heard nothing, barely even the wind: no birds, no dogs barking, no echo of voices or footsteps, no clop of hooves, no creak of cartwheels on Moscow's cobblestones, none of the usual hum of a substantial city. Major General Berthier, his telescope to his eye, scrutinized the walls, the mouths of the deserted streets, the banks of the Moskova, where a number of barges were moored.

'Sire,' he said, 'it's as if there's no one . . .'

'Your good friends have flown, have they?' the Emperor snarled at Caulaincourt, to whom he had been unfailingly unpleasant since his return from the embassy to St Petersburg: this scion of an old aristocratic family had made the mistake of liking the Tsar.

'Kutuzov's troops have carried on past it,' the grand equerry replied glumly, his hat under his arm.

'That superstitious oaf Kutuzov refuses to engage, does he? We gave him a good hiding at Borodino, then!'

The officers of the general staff exchanged impassive glances. At Borodino they had lost far too many men in terrible hand-to-hand combat, and forty-eight generals, one of whom was Caulaincourt's brother. The latter sank his chin in the folds of his cravat; he was smooth-skinned, with a straight nose, close-cropped brown hair and mutton-chop whiskers. Created the Duke of Vicenza, he may have had the manner of a maître d'hôtel, but he did not have the matching servility; unlike most of the dukes and marshals, he had never hidden his disapproval of this invasion. From the start, when they had crossed the Niemen, he had been telling the Emperor in vain that Tsar Alexander would never give in to threats. Events had proved him right. The cities had gone up in flames; all they took possession of was ruins. The Russians slipped away, laying their country waste. Sometimes a party of Cossacks attacked; they swirled about, fell on a marauding squadron and then vanished. Often in the evening they'd see Russians bivouacked; they'd prepare themselves, post men on watch, but by dawn the enemy would be gone. There were brief, bloody bouts of fighting, but no Austerlitz or Friedland or Wagram. At Smolensk the Russians had resisted long enough to kill twenty thousand men and set the city on fire; most recently, a few days earlier, near Borodino, ninety thousand from both sides had been left dead or wounded on a field riddled with shell holes. The Russians had been able to withdraw towards Moscow, although they didn't seem to be there now, or at least not any longer. After half an hour without moving, Napoleon turned to Berthier. 'Give the order.'

*

The sky-blue gunners of the Old Guard were waiting for the signal to light the match; they fired the shot that triggered a great rush amongst the scattered men. Troopers mounted, squadrons re-formed, infantrymen fell in in their battalions and the drummers played. Reinvigorated by being so close to his Emperor, d'Herbigny had no intention of lagging behind with the baggage. 'I'm going on,' he said to his servant. 'Find me at the Guard's camp tonight.' A look of panic crossed Paulin's face; to reassure him, the captain added, terrifying him still more, 'I can still run these Mongol pigs through with my left hand!' He touched the flanks of his kind-of pony with his whip and disappeared into the tide of troops.

Barely had he caught up with his brigade, General Saint-Sulpice's, than all over the hillside officers, half turned towards their men, raised their bare sabres. Yelling, the troopers broke into a gallop, the cannon and caissons followed at full tilt, sending up showers of sand, and the voltigeurs and grenadiers set off towards the city at a run. Everyone bawled at the tops of their voices; the axle-trees creaked; a hundred thousand men tore downhill and in moments none of them could see a thing; a storm of dust blotted out the sun. Blinded, this throng came to a halt at the gates of the suburbs. Youngsters fell to their knees from so much running, gasping, coated from head to gaiters in yellow sand. Captain d'Herbigny spat out a mouthful of grit, like everybody else, while his horse shook the dust from its long mane.

Exhilarated by ten minutes' headlong stampede, the soldiers' anxiety gradually began to return. The Russians still weren't showing themselves. The captain dismounted and stretched expansively, cutting a swagger; with his good hand he took off his coat, folded it loosely and strapped it behind his saddle. To one side he saw troops taking up position on the plain for as far as the eye could see, to the other he saw the last of Murat's uhlans passing between the two forty-foot-high obelisks that flanked the gates of Moscow. In the suburb the dragoons had reached, low, mud-walled cottages pressed up against pine isbas. The street leading to the river and the bridge was as wide as the Smolensk road, which it continued, a dusty thoroughfare unrelieved by vegetation except for a few grey bushes dotted here and there. The captain checked his pistol and, just in case, tucked it through his belt like a corsair. He had fallen in again with the troopers of the 4th Squadron, who he knew by name and whose horses he envied – skeletally thin perhaps, but at least they were a decent size. As he was gazing covetously at Trooper Guyonnet's worn-out old Rosinante, its rider suddenly stared wide-eyed, 'What is that? King Carnival?'

'Eh?'

'The other side of the bridge, sir . . .'

D'Herbigny looked around. Over on the right bank of the Moskova, a frenzied figure was shaking a three-pronged pitchfork. It was an old man sporting a sheepskin; he had long, greasy hair and a white beard that spilled over his chest and down to his belt. With Guyonnet following, the captain set off towards him. The old moujik gesticulated, threatening to run through anyone who dared to enter the city. D'Herbigny drew closer; the tramp grasped his fork with both hands and dashed at him; he stepped aside. Carried along by the momentum of his charge, the old man went flying. The captain helped him on his way with a kick, toppling him into the water; the strong current caught him and dragged him under.

'You see, Guyonnet,' the captain said, 'one can fight with one hand and a judicious kick in the backside.'

As he turned back towards the dragoons, d'Herbigny saw the Emperor; thin-lipped, hunched forward in his saddle, he hadn't missed a thing; a turbaned Mameluke was holding his Arab by the bridle.

*

As he was already on the threshold of the city, d'Herbigny was detailed to reconnoitre it to bring back some Muscovites, or at least some information. He took command of thirty cavalry of the Imperial Guard, choosing them from amongst those riding small, wild horses, so he wouldn't feel inferior on his diminutive model. Of consequence again, the captain entered Moscow at the head of his column, by the stone bridge spanning the Moskova, a river he'd imagined as broader and deeper, less of a rushing torrent. The patrol found itself again in city streets, narrow but cobbled with stones from the riverbed — touchstones, madrepores, ammonites of different sizes — in which the horses caught their hooves. They passed fountains, glasshouses and wooden houses painted green, yellow and pink with carved verandas and facades as intricately wrought as ironwork. Then the streets broadened out and the scenery changed. They rode alongside white stone edifices, palaces of brick and thickly wooded gardens overrun with wild flowers, with winding avenues, extravagant rockeries, gazebos and brooklets. The tread of the horses was the only sound to be heard in this rich, dead city that so unnerved the dragoons. They were jumpy, wondering where the nasty surprise was going to come from — the sniper's bullet, the Russian howitzers trained on them as they turned the corner of an avenue. Of course Murat's cavalry had been through before them in force, but still misgivings remained, the vague sense of a trap. The captain thought he glimpsed the silhouette of a man at the bottom of a palace's steps; it was just a bronze statue holding up a candelabra containing twenty unlit candles. Now they were skirting a lake lined with large houses; each had a landing stage with small, brightly coloured boats made fast to its piers. Further on, on the square of a colossal church topped with a slate dome, screeching and the sound of flapping wings made them look up: a bird of prey had flown into the gilt chains strung between the church's little towers; the more it struggled, the more entangled it became.

'That looks just like the brigade eagle,' a dragoon commented.

'Only way you can free that is kill it,' said another, raising his musket.

'Silence!' the captain cut in angrily. 'And you, you bloody imbecile, lower your weapon!'

'Listen . . .'

Straining their ears, they made out a vague tramp of feet; some people must be marching in a band; every sound reverberated through those lifeless streets. The captain had his troopers dismount and take cover under the trees in a garden, ready to take aim. A procession came out onto the crossroads.

'Civvies . . .'

'They're not armed.'

'Who speaks Russian?' asked the captain. 'No one? Come on, look sharp, let's go!'

They emerged as one from the thickets, muskets levelled at the townsfolk, of whom there were about twenty, apparently harmless; they were waving at the soldiers and quickening their pace. A portly, bald fellow with greying side whiskers called out in a reedy voice, 'Don't shoot! We're not Russians! Don't shoot!'

The two parties met in the middle of the square.

'What are you doing here?'

'These gentlemen are French like me,' said the rotund individual. 'Those are German and he is Italian.'

He indicated his companions in dark frockcoats and laced shoes, with watch chains looped across their waistcoats like garlands.

'We work in Moscow, sir. My name is Sautet, Monsieur Riss is my associate.'

The associate doffed his otter-skin hat in greeting. His skull was as smooth as his colleague's, whose portliness, florid complexion and choice of apparel he also shared. Sautet continued ceremoniously, 'We run the most extensive French booksellers in the entire Empire, sir. And this is Monsieur Mouton, a printer, Monsieur Schnitzler, renowned in the fur trade . . .'

D'Herbigny interrupted the introductions to question the speaker. Where in the devil's name were the inhabitants? Were there any boyars he could take back to the Emperor? And what of Kutuzov's army?

The army had crossed Moscow without stopping; officers had been seen weeping with rage. That morning, before dawn, the governor, Rostopchin, had organized the exodus of the population; an almighty throng of civilians with icons at their head, chanting hymns and lamenting and kissing crosses. There had been terrible scenes that Sautet hinted at but dared not relate: 'Monsieur Mouton will tell you what he has endured.'

'It's a miracle I am alive,' the man in question spoke up,

trembling. 'On the pretext that I had made insulting remarks about the Tsar, policemen dragged me before Count Rostopchin. I wasn't the only one. There was also a young Muscovite whose father was an acquaintance of mine, a merchant. Well, he was accused of having translated one of the Emperor Napoleon's proclamations; actually, I know this for a fact, he had only translated extracts from the *Hamburg Correspondent* and these included, among other things, the famous proclamation – I read it myself, I'm a printer after all . . .'

'We know . . .'

'Well, he was the son of nobility, this young man, even if he did belong to a sect of German Illuminati whose name I have forgotten . . .'

'Come to the point,' d'Herbigny said impatiently.

'The young man was handed over to the crowd, they were madmen, sir, the thought of it still makes me shudder, look . . . and he was torn to pieces, flayed alive like a rabbit, and then fanatics tied a rope round his corpse to parade it through the town, and all they found in the end was a hand with three fingers.'

'What about you?'

'I was terrified . . . I thought they were going to tear me apart in their frenzy, but no, not a bit of it, I simply had to put up with a lecture from Count Rostopchin. He wanted me to tell you what I just have, the treatment traitors and miscreants can expect from patriots in Russia.'

'Well, that's that, then,' concluded the captain, who had stopped being affected by stories of atrocities long before and preferred to enquire about the city's resources and inhabitants. 'Where are the dignitaries?'

'Gone.'

each carrying two casks of Chambertin, and field kitchens preceded by the major-domos and cooks on mules.

'Paulin!' said the captain. 'We know him, he's from Rouen.'

'Who, sir?'

'That whippersnapper, thin as a lath, who's getting out of the secretaries' berline.'

'It looks like the Roques' son.'

'He is, I am almost certain. I thought he was a solicitor's clerk in rue du Gros-Horloge.'

'It's been so long since we've seen Rouen,' the manservant remarked plaintively.

As the cavalry of the Old Guard was taking the Moscow road, d'Herbigny didn't have time to confirm his impression. But it was indeed Sebastian Roque who was stepping out of the secretaries' berline behind Barons Ménéval and Fain, both of whom were now inseparable from their recently acquired, embroidered rapporteurs' uniforms. He was twenty years old, with blue, almost purple eyes, a black hat with a broad brim and cockade, and an ample cape of equal blackness with a plethora of collars, piled atop one another. His father owned a cotton mill in Rouen, but after the English maritime blockade, merchandise couldn't travel any more, and like the other manufacturers of the region he had been forced to cut his output by half. With no immediate future in his father's business, Sebastian had started working for Maître Molin, a solicitor, instead. He would gladly have settled for that life, peaceful as it was to the point of boredom, since he had very little ambition of any kind: a young man ill cut to the cloth of his age, with no passion for soldiering, he knew he had little talent for war; he preferred a civilian life without glory, but with both his arms and legs and no shell splinters in his stomach. The only people still living in the country were widows, cripples and little boys; battles were devouring all the men. To Sebastian, the world was a chaos that had to be shunned.

He had shown considerable perseverance in his attempts to avoid being called up. Thanks to the offices of a cousin, a porter at the Ministry of War in Paris, he had become first a supernumerary, then a titular, clerk under the little-liked General Clarke, who ran central administration a long way from hostilities. Unlike most people, Sebastian was fond of this curly-haired general, with his round head perched on a stovepipe collar, who protected him from the fighting. For a year his life had been one of irresponsible, comfortable routine until one day the previous spring – a Wednesday he vividly remembered – when his fine handwriting had played him a nasty trick. One of the assistants to Baron Fain, the Emperor's secretary, had fallen ill. A replacement had to be found urgently. The Ministry's clerks were assembled, given a passage of dictation and the results were collected. Since he formed his letters so elegantly, Sebastian Roque was chosen. And that is how, by trying to avoid war, he'd ended up in the heart of it . . . He was looking at Moscow's gleaming domes when a voice called him.

'Monsieur Roque! This is no time for daydreaming.'

Baron Fain took him by the arm and pushed him into an open barouche. He squeezed in between a lugubrious major-domo and the chef Masquelet. His Majesty was making arrangements; he would spend the night in the suburb, but he was sending members of his household ahead to prepare for his occupation of the Kremlin. Baron Fain, therefore, was dispatching his clerk with the job of setting up a secretariat as close as possible to the Emperor's apartments, within range of his voice. Several barouches filled up with staff with similar tasks. A detachment of elite gendarmes opened the road for them.

*

The Kalitzin mansion, with its colonnade, was modelled on a Greek temple, like the English Club on the Stratsnoi Boulevard. At its magnificent entrance, two vast dogs with spiked iron collars were barking; muscles bulging, they strained at the chains attaching them to wall-rings and threw vicious looks with their yellow eyes, slavering and baring their fangs. D'Herbigny, arm outstretched, was aiming his pistol at the first one's mouth when one of the double doors opened on a bewigged major-domo. He wore livery and held a whip: 'No, no! Don't kill them!'

'You speak French?' the captain asked in amazement.

'As is customary in polite society.'

'Let us in and get these wild beasts of yours under control!'

'I have been waiting for you.'

'You're joking?'

'These are not the most conducive circumstances.'

He cracked his leather strap. The mastiffs sank into sphinx-like poses, but continued growling quietly at the back of their throats. D'Herbigny, Paulin and a group of dragoons mistrustfully followed the major-domo into a stone-flagged hall. His master, Count Kalitzin, had left that morning with the family and servants, entrusting him with the task of handing the house over to an officer to prevent it being looted. The same arrangement existed in most of the large residences that had been abandoned; the owners hoped to recover them unharmed as soon as the two

Emperors came to an agreement. It seemed self-evident that the French and their allies couldn't stay in the city for ever.

'Which is why, General, I place myself, wholly and without reserve, at your service,' the major-domo explained.

The captain threw out his chest like a bantam, neither correcting the flattery, nor even suspecting a trace of irony in the fulsome declaration. From a glance at the lighter patches of different sizes on the wallpaper, he knew that the paintings had been taken away, along, no doubt, with the main valuables. There wasn't much to loot in the hall, apart from an unwieldy chandelier and some tapestries. The dragoons were waiting in the gloom for permission to inspect the pantry and cellars, since their throats were as dry as dust, when they heard dogs' howling and roars of laughter. The captain went back out under the colonnade, the major-domo at his heels. Keeping well back, some chasseurs were goading the mastiffs with a piece of broken glass stuck on the end of a pike; the animals were choking on their chains, snapping, biting on nothing but glass, blood dripping from their lips; they were becoming crazed, pawing the air.

'Stop those idiots!' d'Herbigny bellowed at a pock-marked sergeant.

'They're as high as uhlans, sir!'

Shouting, d'Herbigny laid into the guffawing chasseurs with the flat of his sabre to chase them off, but they were very drunk and one of them, still laughing, fell flat on his backside. The major-domo tried to quieten the dogs with his whip, but the pain in their mouths and the general commotion only made them more agitated.

The avenue was filling with soldiers of the Guard

looking for alcohol, fresh meat, loot and the girl of their fantasies. A drum-major in full uniform gave directions to his musicians who were carrying sofas. Brandy flowed in a stream from the staved-in door of a shop; a squad of gendarmes with their peaked caps were bringing out barrels and rolling them over to a handcart. Another gendarme, whose yellow cross-belt could be seen under a stolen coat lined with bear fur, was clasping in his arms a ham, a big vase, a pair of silver chandeliers and a jar of crystallized fruit; the jar slipped from his unsteady grasp and shattered on the ground, the soldier skidded on the crystallized fruit and went sprawling; some grenadiers instantly grabbed the ham and ran off amid a hail of abuse.

The captain wasn't in a position to put a stop to these unruly removals operations – in fact, he rather fancied a piece of them himself. As he was smiling at the thought, the major-domo asked very anxiously, 'You are going to protect our house, aren't you?'

'You mean *my* quarters, I trust?'

'Exactly, your and your men's residence.'

'Very well, but first we'll go over it from top to bottom.' Turning to the sergeant, he ordered, 'Post sentries at the gates.'

'That won't be easy.' He gestured to the dragoons already scattered about the neighbourhood; a chain of them were passing tables, armchairs and bottles out of the windows of a little pale-green pine lodge.

'What now?' exclaimed the captain, his sabre hanging by its sword knot from his left wrist.

Shadowlike figures with wild hair and beards and rags flapping at their legs were coming onto the avenue; they were carrying pitchforks. D'Herbigny turned towards the major-domo, who was wringing his hands. 'And they are, in your opinion?'

'Yes...'

'Convicts? Madmen?'

'Something of both.'

*

In the streets of Moscow, Sebastian Roque had already encountered similar mobs, which the gendarmes had broken up with musket butts, but when his barouche entered a narrower thoroughfare, a moujik with a bristling black beard, long locks and glaring eyes, ran up and violently grabbed his arm. Masquelet and the other passengers tried to make the brute let go by hitting him on the head, but the gendarmes had to beat him almost senseless before he toppled over backwards, blood matting his hair. He got to his feet instantly, leaping at the horses as the coachmen whipped them; the horses knocked him back down, he rolled under the barouche; they heard his bellows, bones cracking; the carriage jolted heavily. Huddled together on the ground, packs of vagabonds considered this spectacle impassively, a look of dazed stupor on their faces. They were a frightening sight, these savage-looking moujiks, but as well as finding their freedom, they had also discovered sizeable stores of brandy and it had sapped them of all their strength. They didn't even move as their maimed comrade writhed on the cobbles. Sebastian was as white as a Pierrot, he felt hot and cold, he looked at the ground, his teeth chattered and he rubbed his aching arm.

'A genuine cannibal, your attacker,' joked the chef. 'He'd have gladly devoured your whole arm!'

'They're bears, not humans,' the major-domo pronounced with a learned air, a single finger raised.

What seemed a banal, everyday event to the other servants terrified the young man. From the moment Baron Fain had given him a mission, and he had had to leave the Imperial entourage, he mistrusted everything. Danger prowled around armies. Die young? What sort of glory was it that did not allow one to enjoy its benefits? The Opera – ah, now that was brilliant, and if he had had a voice ... Dash it! Sebastian wanted to experience the seasons of his life consecutively; youth he saw as a winter, he was hoping for spring, when, with age, one's energies could be deployed. Heroism held little fascination for him: in any case, where were the heroes? The officers thought only of their promotion; the men hadn't come to Russia of their own accord, many had joined up simply to eat. In France, wheat was becoming scarce and the poor were given rice thrown into water-gruel, which satisfied no one. Robbery was on the increase. Unemployed labourers were dying of starvation. In Rouen, the only bread to be found was made from pease-meal flour, and in Paris the Emperor spent extravagant sums to keep the price down to sixteen sous for four pounds to avoid unrest; financiers speculated on grain, exacerbating the famine to make themselves rich. The most confirmed optimists had believed it would be a quick war and that the Grande Armée would enter St Petersburg in July, but it hadn't turned out that way, and at times the weary men had longed for defeat so that they could be done with it all. Now they were taking their revenge on Moscow.

The cortège of Imperial staff finally passed through the

fortress's pseudo-gothic gate, amidst a tide of soldiers lugging furniture to set up their quarters. Behind its high red walls, the Kremlin was an amalgam of monumental styles: cathedrals with minarets and bulbous towers, monasteries, palaces, barracks and an arsenal where they had just discovered forty thousand English, Austrian and Russian muskets, a hundred-odd cannon, and lances, sabres, medieval armour and other trophies recently seized from the Turks and Persians in which the soldiers were dressing up around their bivouacs on the great esplanade.

Prefect Bausset, hands on hips, face as pale as if it was powdered, had started up the stone staircase that stretched the length of the palace's facade ahead of his staff: 'Those gentlemen in His Majesty's personal service, follow me.' He climbed the Venetian-style staircase to a vast terrace overlooking all of Moscow, onto which the Tsars' apartments opened their shutterless and curtainless French windows. Sebastian Roque, Masquelet the chef and sundry valets and upholsterers entered what were to be the Emperor's quarters as if paying a visit, removing their hats. They walked through an interminable reception room, which was divided in two by pillars and three-legged braziers, before reaching the bedchamber, a long rectangle with windows directly over the Moskova, tarnished gilt mouldings, a baldachin and French and Italian paintings from previous centuries. There were logs in the fireplaces. The clocks were working.

'The valets will take the next-door room, there, to the left. The dividing wall is very thin, His Majesty will not have to raise his voice to call you.'

'The secretaries?' asked Sebastian.

'They could set up their office in the adjoining reception

room, but the Tsar's apartments are the only ones that are furnished – everyone must shift for themselves.'

It was the same old story. They often slept on the floor, in the open, on stairs, in antechambers, barns, anywhere, always fully dressed and ready to respond immediately.

'The kitchens?'

'In the basement, I think.'

'The Emperor loathes his dinner being cold,' the chef complained. 'If I have to climb three flights of stairs, then walk three leagues of corridors, he'll throw his fricassée in my face!'

'You'll find a solution, Monsieur Masquelet, Tsar Alexander doesn't exist on cold food either.'

Everyone set to. Sebastian asked about a desk, Masquelet a stove; one bright spark brought in wolf skins he'd purchased from a corporal to make up a bed on the parquet floor; on Bausset's orders, a valet took down the portraits of the Tsar and his family, which would have irritated the Emperor. A small, silent group on the terrace were casting an eye over the city and the white marble statues of the Pascov Palace by the ramparts.

'There's a whole stack of furniture in the cellars,' a valet said to the Intendant. 'A grenadier has just passed it on.'

'Well, what are you waiting for?' said Bausset.

'Coming?' Masquelet suggested to Sebastian. 'You're bound to find your desk down there.'

Striding briskly along the corridors so as not to waste time, the expeditionary party of Roque, the chef and a number of valets enlisted several grenadiers who were guarding empty rooms or playing cards on a drum. The most heavily moustachioed fellow had put his bearskin on a plaster goddess, which he had taken down from its plinth;

he was pawing the statue and declaring, 'My pay to anyone who finds me a real Russian beauty!' The presence of these veterans, Napoleon's old 'grumblers' who'd seen hell a hundred times, comforted Sebastian, but where was the entrance to these cellars? They hurried down a grand staircase, wandered through deserted reception rooms and along passageways, pushed open doors, asked other soldiers who had no idea and eventually found another, worn stone staircase, narrower and cruder, that led to enormous rooms with vaulted ceilings, like chapels, that were so dark that one of the grenadiers went back upstairs to look for torches. They waited. The walls and floor smelled of damp. From one torch they lit several more and started to explore. Openings in the walls appeared in the darkness; they ventured through them, even if it meant not being able to find the way back. The torches smoked, their eyes stung; their misshapen shadows stretched across the pillars and vaults, flickered over the ceilings; with his cape with all its collars, Sebastian's silhouette looked like a vampire's (alone in that situation, he would have scared himself).

'There's something at the back,' said a grenadier.

'Crates . . .'

'Give us some light, but not too close,' ordered Masquelet, 'What if it's munitions, eh? You there! Come and open this with your bayonet.'

The lid of a crate sprang open with a splintering sound; the chef fearlessly plunged in his fist and brought up a handful of powder.

'Hold your torch up, here, over my palm, so we can see what we've got . . .'

'No need,' answered the grenadier. 'You can smell it.'

'I can't smell anything.'

'You haven't got a nose, sir. It's snuff.'

'Well, well,' said a lackey coming over.

'You're right,' agreed the chef and took a large pinch, which made him sneeze and the torchlight flicker.

There was a mountain of other crates like it; Roque and Masquelet had to chivvy the grenadiers and lackeys as they filled their pockets with snuff. Next they found a stack of bales and rows of barrels, the former containing wool, the latter star anise, which disgusted the chef.

'I can't do anything with those spices; they're only fit for their barbarian's food. If I used aniseed in his macaroni, His Majesty would be furious!'

'Here it is, your furniture's this way,' interrupted a grenadier who'd ventured into an adjoining room.

The torches lit up a collection of chests of drawers, armchairs and bed frames; they just had to help themselves from the hoard. Sebastian spotted a little roll-top desk, which would be ideal for taking down the Emperor's correspondence in full flow, but to get it, a massive cupboard had to be pushed aside and a path cleared between a tangle of sideboards and footstools.

'These cushions are mouldy,' a valet declared disconsolately.

'Come and give me a hand over here instead,' asked Sebastian.

'Hold my torch,' said a grenadier. 'I'll see to your desk.'

Just as Sebastian took the torch and held it up at arm's length, a man stood up behind a wooden sideboard that glinted red where the light caught it; the apparition wore a Roman centurion's helmet and a toga thrown over one shoulder. Everyone stopped their foraging. One of the grenadiers drew the bayonet he had tucked into his sword-belt.

'Ah! Gentlemen! I could hear that you are French,' said the apparition, 'and now I can see your glorious uniforms!'

'Who are you?' Sebastian asked him.

'What's that? Who am I? The lighting is poor, I grant you, but even so!'

In the flickering torchlight his expression turned to a grimace. Hand on heart, the costumed figure began to declaim:

'Until our age, Athens and Rome
Doubted a man could create a throne
To rival their dominance.
But now their pride fades, is muted
All their conceit stands refuted
By the sovereign of France . . .'

Everyone was dumbfounded by this performance, apart from one grenadier, less literate, perhaps, or less susceptible to blandishments, who frowned and said threateningly, 'Answer Mr Roque or I'll give you a good thrashing!'

The soldier started climbing over the furniture to grab hold of the old ham, who swept on, 'You see before you the Grrrreat Vialatoux, who has carried our authors, classical and not quite so classical, to the furthest corners of the Empire! Comedian, tragedian, singer – the theatre, don't y'know! All the arts in one sole, unique form!'

Other figures stood up behind him and a bossy, high-pitched female voice cried out, 'Damn and blast it! Long live the Emperor!'

'Show yourselves,' ordered the chef, who hated complications and still hadn't got his extra stove. There were three of them stepping from one piece of furniture to the next down to the cellar's beaten-earth floor: a thin boy who was clasping a set of tinplate medieval armour to his chest, the overacting Roman and a woman of forty or more, rather round-shouldered, the manageress of this travelling company.

'Thank goodness you weren't any longer,' she said. 'We couldn't take any more in this horrific hiding place! Look what we've been able to salvage: Joan of Arc's armour, Brutus' helmet, Caesar's toga and nothing else, nothing!'

'Why are you in this palace?' Sebastian asked wide-eyed.

'For the past week we've been rehearsing the historical fantasia composed by Mme Aurore for Count Rostopchin,' said Vialatoux. 'He had lent us a room in the Kremlin, and then events stopped us in the middle of the third act.'

'What do you mean?'

'It was terrifying,' the boy with the armour continued. 'There was a stampede, everyone was petrified, we had to find somewhere safe; there was no way of getting back to the house we're renting from an Italian merchant behind the bazaar, everywhere people were in a frenzy, weeping, moaning . . .'

'And then?' Sebastian again asked.

'We had to bury ourselves away here,' explained the Great Vialatoux, hitching up the toga, which was slipping off his shoulder. 'Too dangerous outside for French citizens.'

'You hadn't sensed anything looming?'

'Only our performance,' exclaimed Mme Aurore, shocked by the tactlessness of such a question.

'How is that possible?' Sebastian asked in amazement.

'Art is enough for us, young man,' boomed Vialatoux.

'All we thought of were our parts,' murmured a young girl at the back. 'Acting's very absorbing, you know.'

'I don't, actually,' said Sebastian, trying to see her better in the shadows. 'But even so! This is war.'

'We were concentrating on the play.'

Sebastian was still holding the torch. He cast more light on this ingénue, whose voice fascinated him. As he looked at the actress from head to toe, he felt himself grow short of breath. Mlle Ornella was dark-skinned with curly hair, oblong, very dark eyes, and long eyelashes. Sebastian immediately thought of the actress who had enraptured him in *The Triumph of Trajan* at the Opera, the unattainable Mlle Bigottini who was showered with ducats by a Hungarian Maecenas. Her counterpart here wore a short-sleeved over-blouse with an old-fashioned cotton cambric skirt and lace-up leather boots that came to above her ankle. Because the torch was trembling in Sebastian's hand and he was about to set a chest on fire, the grenadier took it back from him and asked, 'Do you want your desk, then, Monsieur le secrétaire?'

'Yes, yes...'

*

The Emperor was irritable. His mood hovered between fury and exhaustion. At six in the evening, he had picked half-heartedly at some cutlets, sitting outside on his red morocco-leather chair, his feet resting on a drum. Now he was silently watching the servants taking his iron bed and folding furniture out of the leather slings in which they were carried by the mules. On the doorstep of the one passable inn in the neighbourhood, where he was going to spend the night, he saw Roustam, his chief Mameluke, cleaning the pistols with Medusa-head grips, which he only used to shoot crows. Night was falling; bivouac fires were being lit under the ramparts and on the plain. After drinking his glass of Chambertin diluted with iced water, Napoleon was seized by a dry cough, which shook him in his armchair. Dr Yvan, as ever, was not far away; as soon as the fit passed, he advised immediate rest and a course of hot baths once they were in the Kremlin. The Emperor's health was deteriorating. On the eve of the battle near the village of Borodino his aide-de-camp Lauriston had applied emollient poultices to his stomach; not having recovered his voice since the stop at Mojaisk, His Majesty had scribbled hard-to-decipher orders on pieces of paper. He was growing stout. He walked less because of the oedemas in his legs. More and more often he slipped a hand under his waistcoat, pressing down as spasms stabbed him between his stomach and bladder; he was in pain relieving himself, passing muddy urine, drop by drop. His physical decay made him aggressive. Like Robespierre. Like Marat. Like the tubercular Saint-Juste. Like Aesop, Richard III and Scarron, the hunchbacks.

'Come along, Monsieur Constant,' he said to his valet, 'this cursed charlatan must be obeyed . . .'

Thus described, Dr Yvan helped him stand; they followed Constant into the inn and climbed a rudimentary staircase without a banister. Upstairs the Emperor found his campaign furniture, two high stools, a writing desk with a lamp and several candles, and his bed with its green silk curtain. Constant helped him out of his overcoat; his armchair was brought up, he threw himself into it, tossing his hat on the floor. He had a plump face, smooth as ivory, the delicate and determined features of a Roman, according to their statues, and thinning hair, a lock of which curved like a comma over his forehead. With a weary gesture he dismissed his attendants. He loved power, not men, with an artist's love, as a musician loves his violin; it was an exercise of absolute solitude and mistrust. Who could understand? The Tsar perhaps: Alexander had also surrounded himself with sycophants, libertines, villains and mercenaries who bombarded him with dangerous advice; English and émigrés mingled with these prophets of doom. 'Napoleon's Europe is cracking,' they said, and they were right. Marmont had just let himself be crushed near Sala manca. Out of pure jealousy, Bernadotte, his old rival, had instigated talks between Sweden and Russia. Who should he rely on? The allies? Oh, they were a fine bunch, the allies! The Prussians detested Napoleon. Half the Spanish battalion had been shot for indiscipline. The thirty thousand Austrian soldiers sent in exchange for some provinces kept as far away from the fighting as they could; anyway, Russia and Austria had a secret understanding. The allies! Old enemies waiting for the chance to betray him. And the marshals themselves were complaining: they said that by extending its territories France was going to become diluted, that a Europe under coercion was ungovernable. The Emperor believed in nothing anymore except destiny. Everything was written. He knew he was invulnerable but still the image of Charles XII haunted him.

Every evening he'd return to Voltaire's description of that young Swedish king's disastrous undertaking; a century earlier he had lost his army and his throne on the road to Moscow. He'd experienced the same inconclusive battles; his artillery and wagons had become mired in the same marshes, the dragoons of his vanguard had been similarly weakened by surprise attacks from the Muscovite rearguard. People had called him invincible too, but he'd ended up fleeing to Constantinople on a stretcher. Was that repeating itself? It was unthinkable. And yet there were coincidences that troubled Napoleon. A little while ago, when he saw one of his captains throw a moujik armed with a pitchfork into the Moskova, he had remembered a story told by Voltaire at the end of the first part of his *History of Russia*. An old man dressed entirely in white, holding two carbines, had threatened Charles XII in the same fashion; some Swedes had cut him down. The peasants had mounted a revolt in the fens of Mazovia; they had been captured and forced to hang one another. But then the King had pushed deep into desert wastes chasing Peter the Great's armies, who kept on retreating, drawing him on, leaving nothing but scorched earth behind them ... The Emperor stirred nauseously in his armchair. 'Constant!'

His valet, stretched out in front of the half-open door, an ear cocked, stood up, straightening his uniform.

'Sire?'

'Constant, my son, what a terrible musty smell!'

'I will burn some vinegar, sire.'

'It's unbearable. My coat.'

Constant draped a slightly worn sky-blue coat with a gold embroidered collar over the Emperor's shoulders; he'd worn it in Italy and since then whenever he was under canvas. He went downstairs treading heavily, one step at a time, disturbing the secretaries, officers and servants; they were spending what they anticipated would be a short and uncomfortable night on the stairs. Immediately outside Napoleon found Berthier and some generals engaged in animated conversation.

'Fire, Your Majesty,' said the major general, pointing to a glow in the city.

'Where?'

'Barges caught fire on a branch of the river and then the wooden piers and a brandy warehouse,' explained an aide-de-camp who that moment had come back from Moscow.

'Our soldiers can't work out how to light the Russian stoves,' Berthier said ruefully.

'Get a bloody move on! Those *coglioni* had better not torch my brother Alexander's capital!'

Two

THE FIRE

HIS BRAWNY HANDS resting on one of the Byzantine crenels of the Kremlin's parapet, old Marshal Lefebvre was watching the blue flames rising in the distance from the alcohol warehouse. 'My eye!' he stormed. 'Vat are they shilly-shallying for, those bluudy sapperrrs!? It's not that complicated, pourrring riverrr water on a shack!' He took a deep breath and said to the officers of his staff, 'I haf seen some firrres in my time, some devilishly big ones, as a materrr ov fact.' Lefebvre was starting to repeat himself, endlessly chuntering on about his past exploits. Decent fellow though he was, he was about to launch into a story that was all too familiar to his staff when, wrinkling his potato-shaped nose, he caught sight of Sebastian.

'You'rrre still herrre?'

'To obtain your permission, Your Grace . . .'

'Still your agtors? Can't you see I'm busy vatching these insects in uniforrrm who can't even put out a campfirrre on the Moskova?'

'Yes, Your Grace, but . . .'

'My dearrr sirrr, concerrn yourself with copying out His Excellency Barrron Fain's notes in ink and imparrrting an elegant turn ov phrase to His Majesty's vords; ve all haf our worrrk. Aparrrt from those in the Emperror's service,

therrre's no kvestion of me prrroviding quarters for civilians. Do you underrrstand?'

'Yes, Your Grace, but . . .'

'He's stubborrrn, the little nitvit,' grumbled the marshal,
crossing his arms.

'Can I at least borrow a barouche to drive them back to
their neighbourhood?'

'Do whateverrr you so please, monsieur le segrétaire,
but I don't vant to see your band of jackanapes in fancy
dress loiterrrring anywhere near me! Do you vant my
infantry to trample your leading ladies underrfoot?'

'No thank you, Your Grace.'

As Sebastian was leaving, the marshal shrugged his
shoulders and sighed, 'They're all the same, these civilians,
they haf no idea. And that other lot, over there, not bloody
able to put out a chit ov a firrre! Where are they vrom?
Not vrom my part of the country, at any rate – a rrreal
peasant can put a burrrning barn out vith a glass of vater!'

Son of a Rouffach miller, whose accent he had inherited,
husband to a laundress of whom the hereditary nobility of
the Court made fun, and yet the first to be rewarded by
Napoleon with an imaginary duchy, Lefebvre took pride in
recalling his humble origins at every possible opportunity.
But today, his officers thought, even armed with a bucket,
his ideal peasant wouldn't have had any luck: that was a
mighty blaze raging on the other side of the city.

*

At ten o'clock in the evening, an open army barouche
equipped with lamps that reached only as far as the horses'
hindquarters left the Kremlin and headed towards the
north-east corner of the city. Mme Aurore's entire troop

was crammed into it: the Great Vialatoux had agreed to take off his centurion's helmet and one of Joan of Arc's greaves was sticking out of the door. Sebastian had positioned himself on the box next to the postilion, Intendant Bausset having given him permission to escort his protégés, and he kept on turning round in his seat to try to see Mlle Ornella's silhouette in the darkness. This furtive contemplation was complicated by the omnipresence of Mme Aurore, who knew the way by heart and was an outspoken guide; standing in the middle of the carriage, despite the bumpy road, she pointed out the short cuts to their rented lodge.

'To the right, down there, we're going to drive round the bazaar . . .'

The carriage turned where the manageress said.

'It would be shorter going through the bazaar,' the chatterbox carried on. 'But the cellars' trapdoors open right in the middle of the street and, just look at that scrimmage . . .'

The carriage passed narrow streets of single-storey brick houses with porticoes. Finally rid of their officers, the soldiers were stocking up, squabbling over barrels of honey or a scarf woven with silver thread. This was the Chinese quarter; Lan Tchu's merchants dispatched goods here from all over Asia. They came from beyond the River Amor, from places where one no could be sure where Russia finishes and China begins. Their caravans left the Silk Road north of the Caspian and travelled up the Volga and the Don to Moscow to sell white silk from Bukhara, engraved copperware, sacks of spices, sticks of soap and blocks of pink-veined salt. Hanks of hair swung in the shop windows, lit up by lanterns of the pillagers of the Guard. Uniforms disappeared under garishly coloured brushed velvet, shakoes were swapped for Tartar caps with earflaps; they pilfered objects made from walrus tusks and draped yellow- and violet-striped fabrics from Hissar round themselves as capes. The men poured out of the bazaar in unrecognizable bands and the carriage had to fight its way through; the horses were reduced to a walk. The journey seemed endless but Sebastian was growing more and more thrilled, the longer he spent in the presence of Mlle Ornella, who seemed to him to possess all the virtues of heaven and earth, when an explosion made him jump. On their left a bazaar stall was on fire. Blurred figures were running in all directions, shouting. The postilion whipped up the horses, which broke into a smart trot in the chaos, sometimes hitting a grenadier or a voltigeur as they came rushing out of the Chinese quarter; one of them hung on and climbed onto the footboard. 'It blew up when we broke the door down!'

The soldier had knotted a piece of silk round his neck and donned a wolfskin jacket, and he was saying accusingly, 'You'll see, we'll end up roasting in this filthy town!'

'Hold your tongue,' Sebastian said with an authority that was new to him. 'You're scaring these ladies.'

'Ladies aren't the only ones who get jittery. If I could play the bird, I'd fly away from here pretty damn quick, I can tell you!'

'It's on fire the other side as well,' said Mme Aurore. 'Past the Foundling Hospital. It must be the Solenka.'

'The what?' asked Sebastian.

'The salt fish-sellers' street, Monsieur Sebastian.'

Mlle Ornella had just spoken to him. All that registered was the soft musical lilt of her voice and he clean forgot

about those countless fires which no longer seemed fortui-
tous in the slightest.

*

Captain d'Herbigny had claimed Count Kalitzin's scantly,
but nonetheless welcomingly, furnished apartments for
himself and was studying a candlelit painting of bathing
nymphs that had been spared in the upheaval. He would
have preferred real women to these plump, dimpled figures,
so out of step with the tastes of the day, but unable to sleep,
with a touch of imagination and the prompting of his
memories, he was bringing the scene to life and peopling it
with young Russian wantons. Paulin had found dinner
services emblazoned with the family crest but not much to
serve on them: some dried fruit and a brown, sickly sweet
jam. The captain held out his glass and his servant filled it
with birch wine, which he drank down in a single draught.
'This really isn't anything like champagne,' he said, smooth-
ing his moustache. He had exchanged his dragoon's uniform, waistcoat and shirt for a fox-fur-lined, vermilion
satin coat and was picking at the food, eating the jam with
a spoon. Paulin, meanwhile, was making the bed, using
tablecloths instead of sheets. At the front of the house, the
chained mastiffs started barking again.

'I should have cracked their skulls, those babbling
hounds. Paulin, go and see.'

The servant opened the casement window, leant out; he
reported to his master that some unknown civilians were
talking to the sentries.

'Go down and find out what's happening, at the double!'

The captain filled a glass to the brim and gazed at his

reflection in the mirror on the wall facing the table. He liked the look of himself this evening, decked out like a Muscovite, without a helmet, glass in hand. 'To my very good health,' he said, saluting himself. The decor, these vast, bare rooms, reminded him of growing up near Rouen in the d'Herbigny chateau, a big farmhouse, really, on an estate which his father farmed. The bedclothes were crawling with insects; the guests who wouldn't leave ate all the food, because there were always visiting neighbours, a relative who was a parish priest or some other impoverished member of the decayed nobility. In winter everyone huddled round the only fireplace that worked. D'Herbigny had enlisted in the National Guard very young, and learnt the profession of soldiering in the field; after that he was only good for killing, charging at the sound of the trumpet and collecting medals. He'd encountered death so often that everything seemed to be its due. One day he'd buried his sword in a little pipsqueak's guts who cut him an insolent look. Another day, at a toll barrier, he'd beaten the life out of a customs officer who'd intended to levy a charge for entering Paris. And that fight at Vaugirard between the dragoons and chasseurs when they clashed in the middle of the open-air cafes; he was laughing at the memory of it when Paulin appeared.

'Sir, sir . . .'

'Your report, you brute!'

'Strolling players, they're asking for shelter.'

'No room for bohemians in my palace.'

'They're French, sir, they were living in the green villa opposite which our men have ransacked.'

'Well, let them sleep on the ground, it's very good for your back. Got to bring 'em to heel, that sort.'

'I thought . . .'

'Who pays you to think, fool?'

'There are young women . . .'

'Pretty?'

'Two or three.'

'Bring them to me so I can choose.' He twisted up his moustache. 'Unless I take the whole batch.'

The captain was splashing himself with an eau de cologne he'd rooted out from the countess's bedroom when the batch, as he put it, entered behind Mme Aurore; her voice like thunder, she was pushing a dragoon in front of her and pummelling him in the kidneys. Brandishing a shawl with her other hand, she called out to the captain, 'Are you the officer in charge of these good-for-nothings?'

D'Herbigny opened his mouth but didn't have time to answer the actress before she stormed on, 'Will you explain to me why I found my shawl tied like a belt round his belly?' She hit the sheepish dragoon harder in the stomach. 'I know why! It was your soldiers who ransacked the house we've been living in for the last two months! I demand . . .'

'Nothing at all,' said the captain, getting up from his chair. 'You have no demands at all to make! The entire city belongs to us! Whoa there, you! What on earth are you up to?'

The Great Vialatoux had put his centurion's helmet down on a console table and was trying on the captain's, which was too big for him.

'Don't touch my things!' yelled d'Herbigny.

'Did you have any scruples about ours?' said Mme Aurore, not at all impressed by this sort of flashily dressed swaggerer.

'We are members of the Emperor's intimate circle,' added Vialatoux. 'By the offices of one of his private secretaries. He brought us here personally.'

'A much more agreeable boy than you,' said a redhead, accentuating the mocking tone of the soubrettes she was used to playing.

The captain recovered his temper as he let his eye dwell on this young lass who he anticipated would not put up great resistance. 'Well ... You've got to understand how soldiers are, for a start, and then we can come to some agreement, can't we ... compatriots, what? There's plenty of room here. Paulin! Put up our new friends. Mesdemoiselles, my room, where a count slept, is at your disposal.'

'Do you come with it?' Mlle Ornella asked ironically, knowing that she had been singled out.

'Ah well, we'll see ...'

D'Herbigny retrieved his helmet and Paulin led the rest of the band to the stairs, with a lamp; the two chosen ones sat on the edge of the big bed, whispering things and making each other laugh. The captain stayed stranded in the middle of the room; to interrupt the chorus of mockery, he asked them their Christian names.

'Jeanne,' said Mlle Ornella, who was called Jeanne Meaudre offstage. 'She's Catherine.'

'Catherine? Ah hah, that rhymes with libertine! Not so?'

The two girls burst out laughing again. 'And what does Jeanne rhyme with?'

'Now let's see, let's see ...'

Embarrassed by the question, the captain frowned to show he was thinking, unable as he was to come up on the spot with any rhyme other than 'man' or 'handstand'.

'Oh!' exclaimed Catherine the redhead. 'Your right hand.'

'My right hand?'

He raised his stump, which was trussed up in a shirt tail like a sausage.

'My right hand has stayed somewhere in Russia, my pretty ones, but I often get the feeling that the fingers are moving.'

Since his two guests had stopped giggling and were listening with new interest, the captain described the amputation. To show his courage and tease them by scaring them a little, he explained how Dr Larrey, Surgeon to the Guard, had applied fly larvae to the open wound, since he'd discovered that, in the process of breeding in colonies, maggots could prevent gangrene. Then he recited his wounds, each linked to a valiant feat of arms, which he listed at random, becoming more and more stirred. 'At Wagram I was burnt when the artillery set fire to the crops. At Pratzen I had a horse disembowelled beneath me by a shell. I was almost swallowed up by a peat bog in Poland. With the English on my tail, I all but drowned swimming across a torrent near Benavente; at Saragossa my skull was split open by the butt of a musket and the day after that, a mined house fell on my head! I've often thought I was dead, I've seen blood bubbling out of my mouth, that was in the convent of San Francisco – and here, look, I was shot in the hip . . . Hey!'

The girls had fallen asleep during the catalogue, snuggled up together.

'Ah no, my darlings, that would be too easy!' grumbled the captain, his shirt unbuttoned to the waist to show his glorious, pinkish scars, and going closer, he listened to the girls' rhythmical breathing. With a knife he slit the laces of Mlle Ornella's half-boots, who did not wake up, and he was working his way through all the little flibbertigibbets' buttons, braids and ribbons when a knocking disturbed him. He ran to the door in a fury, tore it open and bumped into Paulin, who was red in the face, with dragoons holding lanterns standing behind him.

'Paulin! I want to be left in peace! What is it? Our travelling circus's bothering you, is it? Well, they can go to hell!'

'They're fine, sir . . .'

'Well?'

'You should come and see, sir,' said one of the dragoons.

'It's serious,' Paulin added to convince his master, who glanced at the sleeping women, both of whom were snoring gently, before shutting the door behind him and letting himself be guided by the intruders to another staircase, at the back of the Kalitzin house. At the bottom, Paulin showed him oil on the steps.

'It smells of camphor; at least, it did smell of camphor, your eau de Cologne is rather overpowering . . .'

'Is it camphor?'

'Spike oil, sir, look . . .'

The glistening trail continued and further on a wick was floating in it; the wick went out into the street through a hole in a low, double-glazed window which, the captain could have sworn, had been made by a pistol ball.

'Someone was planning to light this wick, sir and roast us alive.'

'*Someone?* The major-domo, you mean! That Russian,

where is that Russian? Search the house and bring him to me so I can blow his brains out!'

*

A hand brusquely kneaded his shoulder; Sebastian opened his eyes on a floral-patterned sleeve and heard Baron Fain saying, 'It's all very well having such a beatific smile on your face, Mr Roque, but up you get, His Majesty won't be long now.' Sebastian realized that he had fallen asleep in the Kremlin: a moment earlier he had been smiling as he dreamed that he was in Rouen with Mlle Ornella; through a window in his father's house in rue Saint-Romain, he was showing her Saint-Maclou's gothic spire, and then he was putting horses to the charabanc to take her for a drive to the Forêt-Verte ... He got up from the sofa, mechanically buttoning up his waistcoats, gathered up his black overcoat and his cockaded hat, which he kept in his hand, and then, eyes silted over with sleep, joined the Baron who was leaning his elbows on a window, looking out. The Guard's camps were lit by a white light coppered by the glow of the fires that hadn't yet been brought under control. The shadows of soldiers were moving in the courtyards, smoking around bivouacs or stretched out on the ground wrapped in blankets; some, squatting on their heels, were lighting their long pipes with brands picked from the embers; others could be seen staggering about, looking for their muskets or saddle cloths, and the empty bottles strewn everywhere accounted for their state.

Baron Fain turned away, catching hold of Sebastian by the arm. 'Show me the arrangements.'

'This way, my lord, is His Majesty's chamber, our desks could go in this reception room . . .'

Overnight, the apartments and their annexes had been refurbished. Valets had fitted Napoleon's bed with lilac sheets; the portrait of the King of Rome, his son, painted by Gérard and received from Paris a week before, hung in place of that of the Tsar. Baron Fain stopped in front of the painting. In his crib, the heir to the Bonaparte dynasty was playing with a sceptre as if it was a rattle. On the eve of Borodino, which the Emperor in his bulletins preferred to call Moskova to emphasize that it had been fought before the holy city, the painting had been exhibited on a chair outside the imperial tent; the army had paid it homage before the battle.

'We won't be around when he mounts the throne, Monsieur Roque.'

'If he mounts the throne, my lord.'

'You doubt it?'

'We are so used to the improbable that one can't foresee a week ahead . . .'

'Keep your sentiments to yourself, my lad.'

'We are devoted to the Empire but the Empire should protect us, Jean-Jacques said . . .'

'Spare us your Rousseau for one moment! The Emperor no longer shares his thinking and you were only a brat under Robespierre! As for the classical authors whose volumes you lug around in your bag, they lived in a saner age. If you wish to grow old and make your fortune, keep your peace, Monsieur Roque.'

The commotion redoubled around them, heralding the Emperor's arrival. News spread about his mood; he had slept poorly, not enough, Constant had burnt aloes-wood and vinegar all night to purify his room, he had hardly been able to breathe; in the morning the coat he had slept in had been infested with lice. Chattering away, clerks were bringing in ill-assorted desks and chairs, paper, sharpened pencils, crow's feather quills and ink wells and setting them out according to an unvarying ritual when trumpet calls answered one another from courtyard to courtyard: Napoleon strode past the columns of comatose grenadiers without giving them a glance. He slowly climbed the monumental staircase between the major general and Caulaincourt, his aides-de-camp following. Contrary to his entourage's pessimistic expectations, he was delighted by his Moscow apartments; the fact that on his way to them he hadn't encountered anyone apart from his army didn't seem to trouble him. He grew voluble gazing at the tall column of Ivan's tower with its cupola and giant cross. 'Make a note that the Invalides's dome needs regilding,' he said to Berthier. Then, to everyone else, he declared, 'We have arrived at last. Here I will sign the peace.' As he spoke, he was thinking, 'Charles XII wanted to sign peace with Peter the Great in Moscow as well.' Satisfied, he turned towards the church where the Tsars had their tombs and barely reacted when he heard that the treasures in the Arsenal had been removed, the crowns of the kingdoms of Kazan, Siberia and Astrakhan which it would have amused him to wear, the diamonds, the emeralds and the equerries' silver axes which he would gladly have squeezed into his bags.

In a corner of the reception room crowded with officers and uniformed administrators, his hands behind his back, he then listened to reports. He learnt that two nights previously, Governor Rostopchin had had horses put to all the fire engines, a hundred or so, to take them out of the city. The wind was spreading the fire, and water was in short supply.

'Find the wells, divert the river, draw water from the lakes!' the Emperor ordered. 'I've come from the Foundling Hospital which I visited with Dr Larrey and what was there in the main courtyard? A fountain with a storage tank that supplied water from the river to the whole building! What else?'

'From foreign merchants, sire, we know that a chemist, a Dutchman, or an Englishman . . .'

'An Englishman, if the aim is do me harm!'

'An Englishman then, Smidt or Schmitt, was preparing an incendiary balloon . . .'

'Oh, what rot!'

'On board, a crew of fifty people would launch projectiles at Your Majesty's tent . . .'

'What utter bloody rot!'

'An Italian, a dentist in Moscow, has informed us of the whereabouts of Smidt's hideout, six versts from the city.'

'Well, go and have a look! What else?'

'It appears that the Russian nobility would like to stop the war,' said a Polish colonel. 'And Rostopchin and Kutuzov loathe one another.'

'That's more like it!'

'This is what Russian prisoners claim, sire; we don't know it for certain.'

'Berthier! Killjoy! I tell you that Alexander will sign the peace!'

'Otherwise?'

'Our quarters are secure. When the fires have been put out, we will winter in this capital, surrounded by enemies, like a ship caught in the ice, and we will wait for the summer months to resume the war. To our rear, in Poland, in Lithuania, we have left more than two hundred and fifty thousand men in garrison who will resupply us and secure communications with Paris; this winter we will levy fresh contingents to reinforce us and then we will march on St Petersburg.' Napoleon closed his eyes and added, 'Or India.'

His audience stiffened, some were open-mouthed with astonishment, but no one dared heave a sigh.

*

There wasn't a street at the back of the Kalitzin residence, as d'Herbigny had thought, but a high-walled courtyard of stables, without straw or horses, and outhouses where the carriages were kept. The captain posted himself there after discovering the wick hanging from a hole in the low window; he planned to catch the incendiary in the act, make him talk, and then kill him. His troopers had gone through the house room by room, or so they said, but no luck; the major-domo had vanished. There must be nooks, hiding places, secret compartments in the walls like in Paris, in the days of Fouquier-Tinville's tribunal, those double partition walls behind which aristos and their spies used to escape the Terror.

When day broke, d'Herbigny continued his surveillance hiding in the shadow of the stables. Worn out by an agitated, watchful night, he sat on a stone corner post by the gate; he hadn't taken off his red fox-fur-lined coat. All of a sudden he saw a parish priest in a soutane coming out of the house, very calm, his face hidden by a woman's mantilla, and a second, taller figure whom he thought he recognized as the famous major-domo by the powdered wig and livery. He gripped one of the pistols stuck in his sword-belt. The gawky pair were casually strolling about, passing a bottle back and forth between them and drinking from it in turn: one of them must be about to produce his tinderbox and light the wick snaking across the ground, mustn't he? But no. They walked past it without paying it any attention; they didn't even look down, just carried on pacing up and down the courtyard, chatting away and taking swigs from the bottle. The captain may have been one-armed but his eyesight was excellent; he could see boots and spurs under the soutane. What then? An officer of the Tsar's disguised as a priest? He raised his pistol, stepped out into the yard and, in order not to shoot his enemy in the back, called out, 'Show yourself!'

The major-domo turned round. It was Sergeant Martinon; his eyes had a glazed look. The captain stamped on the cobbles. 'You inbred idiots! I could have killed you!'

'Me too?' asked the bogus curate, pushing back his mantilla.

'You too, Bonet!'

'Sir, as you can see, we've laid our hands on this Russian's clothes . . .'

'An entire wardrobe,' added Trooper Bonet, shaking out the skirts of his soutane.

'The major-domo?'

'Nothing to fear on that score, sir,' said Martinon. 'He's been asleep all this time in the apartments on the second floor with the troupe of actors, that's why we couldn't find him.'

'Take off that tawdry finery and follow me, you utter incompetents! Do you think you're at a masked ball?'

The captain tucked his pistol back in his belt and grabbed the bottle of brandy, which he finished in a single draught. Then the three troopers set off up the main staircase, almost at a run, but in the middle of the first landing the captain gestured at them to slow down: a couch had been dragged up the steps and a Russian cuirassier was sprawled on it, muttering incomprehensibly in his sleep.

'No danger, sir, he's no more Russian than we are and he's drunk.'

'Maillard!' roared the captain, hoisting the sleeper like a sack of grain.

Maillard didn't wake up either when d'Herbigny tore off his white tunic with its black facings or when he dropped him back onto the tiles. In a fury, the captain urged on his dragoons, still dressed as a parish priest and a servant; on the next floor he kicked open the reception room's double doors and discovered the actors' dormitory. Each of them had made a bed with furniture from the other rooms. Mme Aurore, the manageress, had been entitled to the softest sofa, the others had unhooked curtains and pushed chairs together. They woke up together, squealing; amongst them, a tall, shaven-headed figure in a collarless linen tunic, who was propping himself up on one elbow when the cuirassier's wig and uniform hit him in the face. 'Get up,' cried the captain. 'And confess!'

'Confess what, sir?'

'That you're no more a major-domo than I am!'

'I have been in Count Kalitzin's service for fifteen years.'

'False! You've got the cropped hair of the Tsar's soldiers!'

'To make my wig easier to wear.'

'Liar! And this uniform?'

'It belongs to the count's eldest son.'

'This good fellow has not left our side,' Mme Aurore

put in, hoping to calm d'Herbigny, who was turning bright red.

'It's an alibi! He's just waiting for his moment to burn us alive!'

'By all the saints in heaven, it's not true,' said the Russian, crossing himself.

'Get up!'

'A little peace and quiet wouldn't go amiss. It is morning, after all,' observed the Great Vialatoux, emerging from under a blanket.

'Silence! I know about war and I've got a nose for this sort of thing!'

'You have got a nose, a long one, but you don't condemn someone just on a hunch,' said the juvenile lead, who had spent the night on a bed of Oriental rugs, his tinplate armour by his side.

The Russian agreed to get up. He didn't look at his accuser but at the door instead; he opened his mouth slightly, probably to speak; the captain took this as an opportunity to force the barrel of his pistol down his throat. Then he pulled the trigger. As the major-domo collapsed, spewing blood, they heard voices shouting 'Fire!' Thick grey smoke was seeping in from the landing, spreading across the floor.

'Take what you can and get out!'

'We should have cut the wick, sir . . .'

'You could have thought of that, Martinon!'

'I didn't have any orders.'

Mme Aurore, her actors and the dressed-up dragoons, one of whom had hitched up his soutane and tucked it into his belt, rushed in a panic to the stairs; they couldn't see the steps any more.

'You too!' the captain said to the juvenile lead, who was on all fours in the reception room, his face in the low, dense smoke.

'The man you have murdered . . .'

'Executed!'

'Fell on our Joan of Arc armour and flattened it.'

'If you want to burn like Joan of Arc, that's your affair!'

'No, no, I'm coming.'

They caught up with the others on the half-landing; the smoke was up to their waists and the Great Vialatoux almost lost his balance.

'Hang onto the banister!'

'I've trodden on something soft.'

D'Herbigny bent down, groped around in the smoke, felt a body at his fingertips, sat it up; it was Maillard, as asphyxiated now as he was drunk and weighing a ton; he grabbed him by the collar and dragged him down the stairs. The rest followed, choking in a cloud of smoke, their eyes stinging; they covered their noses and mouths with their clothes, a handkerchief or a scarf. Paulin had come out of the count's bedroom, struggling with the portmanteau and pushing Catherine and Ornella in front of him, wrapped in tablecloths, rubbing their eyes and coughing themselves hoarse. 'Quick!' d'Herbigny told his men and they tore down the stairs, suffocating, not even thinking to be afraid; on the ground floor he saw flames curling under a door that was cracking as it burnt. 'Quick! Quick!' he repeated and they rushed towards the hall door but outside on the steps the chained dogs lunged at them, trying to bite. Suddenly bursting from the back of the building, the fire was already catching the long curtains. The captain laid Maillard down on the flagstones, shot one of the dogs with his second pistol, then had no time to reload – anyway, what with? As for Martinon and Bonet, those imbeciles had mislaid their weapons when they were getting dressed up. Paulin, kneeling next to Maillard, reported, 'This one's dead, sir.'

'He won't be causing a stir in any more henhouses, bloody idiot!'

The captain picked up the body by an arm and shoved it at the other guard dog, which sank its teeth into it as if it was a quarter of beef.

'Make a dash for it!' d'Herbigny commanded the fugitives, who ran to the avenue, where the rest of the troop were having trouble quieting their horses as they pranced and jostled, terrified by the spreading fires.

*

Sebastian waited, his pencil in the air. The secretaries never knew if the Emperor was going to want to dictate just one or several letters at a time, so they were always ready to take notes, in pencil; in either case, His Majesty's quick, rushed delivery gave them no chance of taking down entire sentences in a clear hand. So Baron Fain, following his colleague Méneval's lead, had devised something like a code of practice: it was a matter of catching the key words as they spilled forth, using them as aides-memoires with which to reconstruct a coherent text and then copying this out in ink, polishing the language in the process and adding the customary civilities. At first Sebastian had dreaded the exercise, the risk that he might misrepresent Napoleon's thoughts, but Fain had reassured him, 'His Majesty never re-reads what he signs.' Today, therefore, the secretaries were waiting at their desks facing the wall, a position which made dictation harder for them because they couldn't decipher difficult words by reading the Emperor's lips. Hands behind his back, he was pacing up and down, mumbling, delivering streams of invective or grumbling. Napoleon wanted to send a message to the Tsar proposing peace; the secretaries had been told this, to make it easier for them to improvise on the final draft. A letter had to be dashed off that was at once majestic, amicable and conciliatory – so much for the tone. But the content? They were still waiting when the major general entered the salon unannounced with some grenadiers of the Old Guard in long grey greatcoats, who were escorting a moustachioed man in a big bearskin coat.

'Berthier, you're bothering me!' said the Emperor.

'Sire, I beg you.'

'I'm listening,' the Emperor sighed, dropping into a chair and jabbing at the armrest with a penknife.

'And looking, I trust – this is what we found on this bandit.'

'A muff? A cushion?'

'A powder hose, sire. This brute was trying to set the palace roof on fire.'

The Emperor took the well-sewn canvas object thoughtfully; he slit it with his penknife the way one guts a fish, and black powder spilled onto the floor. The prisoner was laughing noiselessly.

'Are you convinced, sire?'

'That this Russian wanted to set this whole damn place on fire? Oh yes, Berthier, but why is he laughing, the devil?'

'Because "sire" in his language means "cheese",' explained Caulaincourt, who had joined the group with Marshal Lefebvre.

'Very amusing!' Turning to Lefebvre, he asked, 'Have you questioned him, Your Grace?'

'Ov corrrse.'

'Well?'

'He sit nawthing.'

'But under his bearskin,' said the major general, 'look, he's wearing the blue jacket of a Cossack officer.'

'It is an isolated attempt.'

'No, sire, a premeditated crime.'

'A trap,' added Caulaincourt.

'Yor orrrdrs?' asked Lefebvre.

'My orders? Guess, *è davvero cretino!*'

Lefebvre signalled to the grenadiers. 'Have this incendiaarry shot!'

'He is not necessarily alone,' continued the major general.

'Send out patrols, suspects are to be shot, hanged, exterminated, understood?'

The Emperor stood up and pressed his forehead to the pane of a French window. The Chinese quarter was burning again but this time in different parts. Fires were breaking out in remote suburbs towards the east, and the wind was rising, carrying the flames towards the ramparts.

*

From the Kremlin, the Emperor could not see the fires that were starting beyond the bazaar, they were obscured by a ring of churches, but all the glass in the windows of the Kalitzin house had shattered and flames were belching out of them and blackening the facade; the curtains, net and hangings had been torn loose and were flapping in the wind. Beams started snapping, one after another, and then the roof collapsed with a crash as if the house had sucked it into itself. The surviving watchdog, which was still chained up, had abandoned Maillard's barely touched corpse and was barking frenziedly; when the fire rolled onto the steps, it would burn alive.

At the head of his men, with Mme Aurore close on his heels, d'Herbigny kept to the middle of the thankfully broad avenue, while his dragoons pulled their mounts behind them by the bridle; the horses had been blinkered so they wouldn't see the lurid light of the fires, but still the oven-like heat and the smells of charred wood, tar and black smoke made them step nervously. The troupe of actors followed, indistinguishable from the bizarrely dressed soldiers. Mlle Ornella limped, barefoot, on the hot cobbles; in one hand she carried her half-boots with their slit laces and with the other she held her friend Catherine Hugon-net's arm. Both of them were barely dressed, with embroidered damask tablecloths draped over their shoulders, and they cursed that swine of an officer who had set about slitting, ripping and taking their clothes apart stitch by stitch the minute they'd gone to sleep. They watched him up there in front, strutting along like a cock of the walk, even though his troopers were laden with furs and trinkets as if they were about to perform an opera. Still, they thought to themselves, at least they were alive; destitute but alive. They had looked on miserably as their green chalet had burned to the ground, but the wooden houses in this part of town had been spared and, at the end of the avenue on an untouched square, there stood a church – or perhaps cathedral – with blue domes. They had nearly reached it when the dragoons' horses refused to go any further. At the foot of a clump of trees, a pack of large, silent dogs was staring up into the branches; they had powerful chests and grey coats. The party came to a halt; the captain's voice rang out, 'These nags are a little afraid of fire, but dogs give them the mortal terrors, is that it?'

At the sound of this voice, the dogs in question quit their trees and glanced over at the stationary group. They had slanting, green eyes and flat heads.

'Those aren't dogs, sir,' said Trooper Bonet, 'they're wolves.'

'You've seen wolves, then, have you?'

'Oh, I've seen them close up, in the Jura. There was one that ate a woman from my village and attacked a whole score of other people. Dangerous, they are. They love war: the more dead and carrion and snakes there are, the more wolves you're going to get.'

No one had interrupted the trooper. They were all standing stock-still, observing the wild beasts. Were they going to attack? Those who still had sabres unsheathed them. No need. At that moment, a band of red-uniformed hussars came riding past the great church's porch, leading two moujiks with their hands bound. Too many men, too much risk: the wolves ran off.

The hussars led their prisoners to the trees. D'Herbigny called to them and a lieutenant rode over at a gentle trot and asked, 'Do you understand French?'

'Captain d'Herbigny of the Dragoons of the Guard.'

'Forgive me, Captain, but I wouldn't have guessed . . .'

'I know!'

'Sir's uniforms are in that portmanteau,' said Paulin, pointing to the baggage strapped to his donkey.

'We've just escaped a fire by the skin of our teeth,' said Mme Aurore.

'I wouldn't stay out in the open, if I was you. Take cover in that church; it's good solid stone, a fair old distance from any wooden buildings, there shouldn't be any danger of it going up.'

'Do you think I'm just going to stand around twiddling my thumbs, Lieutenant?'

'Captain, drunken convicts are swarming all over this neighbourhood, spreading the fires with these . . .' He threw a lance at d'Herbigny which the captain studied closely. 'They stoke them with tarred lances like that,' the hussar reiterated, then rejoined his companions who were stringing up two of the alleged incendiaries.

When d'Herbigny and his troop rode round the copse before taking shelter in the church, they saw a dozen or so hanged men: dinner for the wolves. Ornella looked down and didn't look up again until they were inside the church and, as it seemed to her, in another world: in the side aisles, between each of the pillars and in front of the choir, hundreds of candles gleamed in bulky candelabras. Lit by whose hands? It didn't occur to her to ask. Instead she clung tighter to her friend. She would have liked to have fallen asleep and woken up a thousand leagues from Moscow, in the wings of a Parisian theatre. She and Catherine had known each other for ages, sharing the stage countless times from their debuts in minute roles – non-speaking or one-line perhaps – to *Monsieur Vulture*, when they had played opposite the wildly, fabulously famous Brunet, and Mme Aurore had remarked upon them, the dark-skinned woman for her style, the redhead for her freshness. They were hired and enjoyed an unbroken run at the Délassements, in the faubourg du Temple, until the day came when Napoleon decided to close most of Paris's theatres to prevent competition with the eight houses he subsidized. To get any work, they had to leave France and tour abroad, playing to expatriates or cultivated Europeans who understood French. Aurore Barsay's wandering troupe had been acclaimed in Vienna, St Petersburg, and, for the last two months, Moscow – Moscow, where they were at the mercy of fire and soldiers, without audiences, roubles, luggage or costumes.

'Oh, Catherine,' said Ornella. 'I've had enough . . .'

'Me too.'

'I'm going for supplies!' d'Herbigny announced. 'Get yourselves set up in that side chapel. Martinon, you, and you, follow me. The rest of you, tether the horses to the altar rails.'

'The what?'

'There, you ignoramus! Those things in gilded wood!'

*

The captain kept his weariness and doubts buried deep inside him. One-handed for the rest of his life, scars all over his body, he stifled his true desires by gripping the hilt of his sabre. Sometimes there rose up in him a paradoxical yearning for a peaceful, rural life, or he'd imagine himself as an innkeeper, since he liked people and wine and fattened pullets on spits, all golden and tender and juicy. He dismissed the image of roasting birds which jarred on that September afternoon in Moscow overrun by wolves, convicts and fire. Instead, stomach rumbling, he put on one of his green coats and buttoned up a pair of grey linen over-breeches at the seams – his helmet had stayed in the ruins of the Kalitzin house, crushed and melted – and set off prowling with his ragged men.

Apart from several churches, the neighbourhood they found themselves in consisted predominantly of small, pitched-roofed houses, like Swiss chalets, two-storeyed, with little gardens in front enclosed by low picket fences: d'Herbigny thought it would be darned surprising if they couldn't find something to eat. They were preparing to work their way through the houses systematically — a dragoon had raised the butt of his musket and was about to stave in the lock of a door — when lancers came galloping down the street. One of them slowed and shouted at d'Herbigny, 'Watch out for the doors! They've booby-trapped their hovels!'

The dragoon stopped, his musket poised in midair, his mouth open.

'You heard, didn't you, you blockhead? Through the window.'

They tore off a shutter and smashed a window pane; the captain climbed through the window, inspected the room: a bench, a stool ... He took a few steps. Twigs snapped under his boots. He looked down. The former inhabitants had made a pile of sticks and wood shavings in front of the door. He saw a musket tied to the lock: if they'd broken down the door, the impact would have depressed the trigger, the flash of the charge would have set fire to the pile of dry wood. Sergeant Martinon poked his nose through the window. 'Captain, we've gone over the garden with our sabres and found a chest.'

The troopers had dug up the chest, which opened easily. It contained crockery. They continued their search in the other houses. With extreme care, they tested the ground with their sabres, turned the soil, went down to the cellars; they found a shell in one stove and a number of other booby-trapped doors. It took them the whole day to muster a barrel of brandy, some root vegetables and a smoked sturgeon.

*

A strong easterly wind was gusting hard, pushing the fire towards the Kremlin. Soot was raining down on its court-yards and clouds of eddying smoke wreathed the tops of its towers. The spectacle was making Sebastian feverish. On the sofa in the large salon, where he was failing to get any sleep, he struggled to shake off terrible visions: Ornella walled in by flames, her hair burning like a torch, her running – but no, Mme Aurore knew Moscow, its twists and turns, its shortcuts and traps, she would never let herself be cornered by the fires. With such arguments he tried to convince himself. It was night but one could see without a lamp because of the conflagration. He stood up, burnt his hand on the glass of the French window and went out onto the terrace. Half the city was ablaze. He inhaled ashes, bitumen and sulphur, heard the wrought-iron roofs of the shops in the bazaar exploding, went back into the salon covered in sweat, and caught his breath.

His Majesty was asleep. The letter to the Tsar had been adjourned. Napoleon had gone to bed early, wanting to make up for his trying night in the filthy inn at Dorogom-ilov, and no one had taken it upon himself to inform him of the situation. How were they supposed to ask him to leave the city? Berthier, Lefebvre, Caulaincourt and various other decorated generals were holding a conference about this problem at the other end of the salon. Eventually Duroc, the Marshal of the Imperial Household, sacrificed himself; he tended to be insulted less than his colleagues.

Nevertheless shouting could still be heard through the door of the imperial bedchamber. How were they to persuade their sovereign to abandon the Kremlin, which was now under threat, and evacuate his troops to the surrounding countryside because no one could check the fire? How was he going to react? Badly, they guessed. Berthier, as was his wont, bit his fingernails, Caulaincourt looked at the door, Lefebvre the floor, until their emissary returned to announce that the Emperor was being dressed by his valets.

Then he appeared, surly and irritated, with Constant helping him into his overcoat as he strode out of his room. He went up to the windows and grimaced at the sight of the inferno. 'The savages! Savages like their forefathers! Scythians!'

'Sire, we must leave Moscow without delay.'

'Go to the devil, Berthier!'

'We're there already.'

Napoleon shrugged his shoulders contemptuously, then clamped his theatre glasses to his eyes. Below, in a lurid orange glare, gunners were trying to smother the showers of sparks falling from the sky. Already the wads from a number of caissons thoughtlessly parked in a courtyard were starting to catch fire; men were trampling on them: four hundred ammunition chests could explode at any moment. Above, on the Kremlin's iron roofs, soldiers of the Guard were sweeping hot ashes blown by the wind. He could see others at the windows of the Senate, throwing out archives so as not to fuel the fires in the building, and the papers fluttered down, sometimes catching fire and burning before they landed. Fresh fires were breaking out in the west of the city now, and nearer, in the palace stables and one of the towers of the Arsenal. The alarm was being sounded. Windowpanes clattered to the ground; the wind was gusting twice as hard.

'Let's go and see,' said the Emperor, taking Caulaincourt's arm.

Wrapping rags round his fingers, so as not to leave any skin behind, Roustam the Mameluke opened a French window. The air burnt their throats. Stepping into clouds of ash, the cortege left the imperial apartments by the large front staircase. Some knotted a handkerchief round their necks to cover their noses and mouths; others pulled their cloaks up over their heads. Grenadiers in grey greatcoats with fixed bayonets surrounded Napoleon and his suite. Sebastian jammed his broad-brimmed hat down over his forehead, turned up his collars and followed at their heels. They hurried, beating their clothes to shake off the falling cinders that burned holes in them. A grenadier's bearskin caught fire; its owner took it off and beat it on the steps. Down on the esplanade, grooms and stable boys were putting horses to the vast number of carriages that belonged to the commissariat; having just been brought out of the stables where the roofs looked like they were about to collapse, the horses were hard to control, whinnying and rearing and refusing the harness, stamping their hooves on the cobblestones. It was becoming clear they were evacuating; everyone was chaotically making their preparations. Shouts, panic, agitation; commissaries in black uniforms were loading cases of wine and snuff, statuettes and violins into their carriages. A colonel arrived at the double, out of breath, before the Emperor. 'A wall has collapsed on the north side!'

'Sire, we must cross the Moskova as soon as possible!'

'By the main gate,' said Berthier.

When the gate's two leaves were pushed open, a wall of fire sealed off the colossal square. The narrow streets leading to the river on the right were covered with a vault of flames. Entire walls of houses were collapsing, making it even harder to get through.

'There, sire, where the fire is weakest, there is only one cordon of fire to cross.'

'Sire, we will wrap you in our cloaks and carry you.'

'Let us go back,' said the Emperor, unnervingly calm. His overcoat had been scorched in several places.

Sebastian had joined the cortege so as to be one of the first to leave Moscow before the fire spread to the entire Kremlin, and now he followed the party back across the esplanade, his face black with smoke. He stopped at the foot of the towering staircase, which the Emperor was climbing to return to his terrace. The young man's legs felt weak, numbed. All around, civilians of the administrative staff, commissaries and members of the household were continuing to pile mounds of goods from the palace's cellars, bottles especially, into their carriages, even onto the roofs. Brushing at the glowing ash falling constantly on his cape, Sebastian walked along the line of overloaded barouches and berlines. Baron Fain was holding a bunched-up cloth over his nose, but Sebastian recognized him by his uniform.

'My lord!'

The carriage door was shut and the Baron, who was drowsing between a white marble goddess, a stack of rugs and other pieces of luggage, couldn't hear him. Sebastian knocked on the window, the door opened and Fain said reprovingly, 'What on earth are you doing here, Monsieur Roque?'

'I was with His Majesty . . .'

'But no longer! You were taking the night watch, were you not?'

'Yes . . .'

'Deserter! To whom will His Majesty dictate his correspondence if he is so minded? Off you go! No, wait a moment. What has the Emperor decided?'

'He has gone back up to his apartments with the major general, that's all I know.'

'Cut along now!' said Baron Fain, brusquely, and uncharacteristically, slamming his door shut.

*

Like many soldiers who enjoy obeying because it spares them having to think, d'Herbigny was a simple man of animal pleasures and commonplace tastes: inactivity sent him into a sharp decline. Rest was out of the question: mulling over familiar, persistent memories would only make him bitter; he needed to be constantly on the go. It is also fair to say that he could not stand Mme Aurore and the affected little princesses and appalling old hams of her troupe a moment longer. His exasperation had reached a pitch when the manageress had dismissed his forage as woefully meagre, and called him, in so many words, useless. Grumbling, he had given her his part of the sturgeon, a mouthful, to shut her up, and then gone to perch at the top of one of the pinnacle towers of the church in which they had taken shelter. From there he studied the situation. Day was breaking, not that one could tell. Ceaselessly fed by the infernal fires, the smoke was banked up in a thick black pall that covered the entire city. Pillars of flame soared into the sky like tornadoes. The captain could barely make out the ramparts of the Kremlin on its hill, overlooking neighbourhoods that had been utterly laid waste. The fire, however, had not yet reached the northernmost districts; d'Herbigny thought they could make their way back to the citadel through these, along the banks of the river, and meet up with the rest of the brigade. He rounded up his dozen or so troopers, none of them very presentable, and gave Sergeant Martinon, who was still in valet's livery, another earful. They walked their horses out of the church; not even the ring of their hooves on the flagstones woke the actors, who had collapsed with exhaustion in the side chapel.

The dragoons headed north by guesswork, assailed by searing fumes, skirting conflagrations that were straining to spread out. Passing through a stone arch with a green slate roof, they rode down a street of log houses and came out onto a patch of waste ground. Starving dogs with protruding ribs were rooting around in a pile of corpses: moujiks who had been bound hand and foot, blindfolded, shot against a wall and left pell-mell in the dirt. Interrupted by the sudden appearance of the dragoons, the animals began barking, the fur bristling on their backs, their muzzles smeared with blood, strips of flesh hanging from their mouths. One of them leapt at the captain's horse; using his good hand he slashed at it with his sabre, but it wouldn't back off and kept trying to bite him. Fearing for his horse, d'Herbigny dismounted to set about the dog, at which the rest of the pack advanced and were met by a volley of musket fire. Cut to pieces, the dogs in front distracted those behind, who began greedily lapping at their blood, and the dragoons took their chance to slit the dogs' throats with their sabres or stave in their skulls with their musket butts. Then they rode off without giving a thought to the gnawed

Russian corpses. Further on they passed other incendiaries swinging from posts; one of them was dressed in the uniform of the Cossack regulars and had a clipped moustache; his body was riddled with bullet holes and nobody had closed his white eyes.

'Sirrrrrrr!'

Muttering, d'Herbigny reined in his horse. Behind him Paulin was thrashing the hindquarters of his stationary donkey with a switch. The captain drew a breath, assumed a weary air and retraced his steps. The donkey was refusing to set one foot in front of the other and the beating was only making it more stubborn.

'Don't leave me on my own in these hostile streets, sir!'

'It's my uniforms I don't want to leave on their own! You'd be quite capable of getting yourself robbed.'

'The only people we've seen have been dead . . .'

'They're quick on their feet, your dead,' said the captain.

He had just seen two or three furtive shadows with bundles on their backs in an alley of battered isbas. He forgot his servant to plunge into the higgledy piggledy little thoroughfare. No sign. Wait, there, in a small yard, the shadows were scurrying past. He urged his horse on and blocked in three Muscovites under an outside staircase. The man wore baggy trousers under a long, tight-waisted coat, the two women aprons and headscarves knotted under the chin; they dropped their bundles. With the tip of his sabre, the captain slit one open and foodstuffs spilled out, a sack of flour, a cabbage and a ham which made his mouth water. Other dragoons came to his assistance, staring wide-eyed at the ham.

'Split that in two and give half back to these people,

they don't look like convicts and they're scared to death.'
He asked the Muscovite, 'The river? This way?'

'Ver?

'The Kremlin, do you understand?'

'Kreml! Kreml!' the man repeated, pointing.

'Help!'

D'Herbigny saw his servant being carried off by the donkey in the direction the Muscovite was indicating. Paulin was holding his hat and yelping; the other dragoons were following at a smart trot, laughing.

'What's the matter with that donkey?'

'I gave him a little pat with my tinderbox, Captain,' said Trooper Bonet.

'Mount up, you two!' d'Herbigny commanded the dragoons who had cut up the ham and were stowing the pieces in their saddlebags. Paulin was setting a fast pace; the captain had to overtake him to steer his ass. In a short while the group came out onto an avenue. To their left they heard the roaring of the fire. Veering southwest, the wind was blowing through the broken windows of a big brick house, creating an in-draught and fanning the flames that were belching forth, first from the small basement windows and then from wherever they could. They had worked their way round to the north of the Chinese quarter. Paulin's donkey stopped dead.

'I've had enough of your donkey,' shouted the captain. 'Is there any blasted thing it is good for?'

'Sausages?' suggested Martinon.

'I'll listen to what you have to say when you're wearing something presentable!'

The captain turned: convicts were roaming about on the

outskirts of the bazaar, led by one of Rostopchin's policemen, who held up a torch, making no attempt to hide his
uniform. D'Herbigny flew at him whilst his men shot at
the moujiks at random, wherever they seemed thickest, like
starlings. The captain and the policeman squared off. An
able swordsman, even with his left hand, the captain darted
in sideways and severed the incendiary's wrist along the
line of his jacket's red cuff. Unconcerned by the gushing
blood, the Russian was picking up the torch with his other
hand when d'Herbigny's sabre ran him through the throat.

Gusts of wind were lifting burning fir joists into the air;
firebrands were crashing to the ground like missiles. The
fire was converging on the end of the Chinese street,
devouring everything in its path, driving soldiers in Turkish or Persian robes from store to store, their arms full of
ill-assorted plunder, fur-lined boots, hides, sacks of tea or
sugar, the entire contents of an ironmonger's shop; Muscovites driven from their basements, brigands and drunken
moujiks darted amongst them, with the same design in
mind. These silent bands were tossing furniture and bolts
of silk and Oriental muslin into the middle of the road; a
few fellows could be seen caught in two minds, putting
down sacks of coffee to pick up a mirror with a carved
wooden frame instead. The luckiest bunch had got their
hands on a cart; uhlans from a regiment of the Vistula,
they were thrashing a team of Russians they'd yoked like
cattle with their riding whips. 'They slaughtered all my
family in Warsaw!' a lieutenant was bawling.

The dragoons left their horses on the avenue with
Paulin, who was protesting wildly, and dashed after
d'Herbigny into one of the bazaar's porticoed alleys. 'Watch
out!' cried the captain, jumping behind a butcher's stall.

Molten lead was running off the caved-in roofs in boiling streams. 'This way! This way!' They changed course, clambering over a barricade of lacquered furniture. With a creaking noise, a japanned iron roof collapsed a few metres from them; they took cover under the porticoes where pillagers were breaking down the doors of shops, oblivious to the crackling flames and falling beams, so busy amassing their treasures they didn't even feel the soles of their boots burning, but kept on forcing open crates and levering up cellars' trapdoors.

A young lad with blond hussar's locks poking out from under a tricorne, who was squeezed into the sort of currant-red dressing gown the Kalmuks wear, was taking bottles which were being handed up to him from a cellar, and stacking them in a chest on casters. The dragoons surrounded him. 'We'll help you shift that lot,' said the captain, putting a heavy hand on the chest.

'If you want some, you can take your pick,' the hussar said. 'All these cellars are crammed full of wine.'

'But your bottles are the ones we've taken a fancy to.'

A few paces away, flames were curling out of a grating. Alcohol wasn't the only thing stored in the cellars; they also contained resin, oil and vitriol and d'Herbigny had no intention of dawdling. The hussar was defying them, calling for help from his comrades. A bloated face appeared through the trapdoor in the smoke, a strip of cashmere wound round his head. Martinon caught him full in the face with a spur, knocked him back down the steps and flung himself into the basement after him; there was a sound of breaking glass and shouting voices. Martinon reappeared almost immediately, moving slowly and jerkily, like an automaton. He had been run through with a sword;

the tip was sticking out of his stomach and he was oozing wine and blood; he gave an inane smile before falling over.

The whirlwind of flames drew closer.

*

Surrounded by officers, the Emperor left the Kremlin in the afternoon. Berthier had come up with the decisive argument: 'If Kutuzov's cavalry are to turn the fire to their advantage, they will attack the army corps on the plain. How will you be able to intervene from here?' Napoleon left by a postern gate, which opened onto the bank of the Moskova, and crossed a bridge that sappers had been dousing with buckets of water since the previous day. The suburb opposite was in flames and red-hot cinders were blowing across the river, falling in a constant rain on the bridge's wooden roadway. Caulaincourt had organized the horses. All the staff had been given the order to evacuate; only a single battalion would remain to guard the citadel and attempt, with the rudimentary means at its disposal, to contain the fire. Sebastian wandered from one courtyard to the next, his bag over his shoulder. Columns of carriages were waiting in a boulevard at the rear of the Kremlin. No one was listening to the contradictory orders any more; they were all wondering how they were going to escape. Most of the coachmen were drunk, and still drinking, and the horses were stamping their feet. Sebastian was trying to find a place in one of the berlines crammed with baggage, plunder and sweating, drawn-faced administrators, but no one would have him.

'On your way!'

'There isn't room for a needle in here!'

A postilion refused to let the young man come and sit

on his bench. Vexed, Sebastian asked a groom, 'What are you waiting for?'

'For the wind to change.'

'And then?'

'We'll drive over the ashes, of course! Isn't that better?'

'That avenue over there is clear.'

'But that leads us away.'

'Away from what? Ye gods!'

Sebastian didn't persevere, disheartened by this drunkard's reasoning. He cursed his fine handwriting, which had brought him to Moscow; he missed the ministry in Paris, so peaceful, where war was waged with a quill. He couldn't envisage any way out of his predicament and hated the whole world. I was born at the worst possible moment, he thought to himself. A plague on it all! Why? Why on earth am I here? I couldn't give a hang about the Russians! I'm so weak and small! A puppet! How many cretins envy me my position with Baron Fain? Well, it's theirs! Why did I accept — but how could I refuse? Do I lack courage? Oh yes, I lack courage, I dream too much, I hide away in my head, I barely exist! Ah, if I was English, I would be walking without a care through the streets of London now, or I'd be setting off on a trader to buy cotton in America! This filthy age! And what about Mlle Ornella, whose image clouds my mind, paralyses me? The devil take her! Idiot that I am! Did she pay me any attention? She doesn't care, actresses don't become attached, everyone knows that, and yet I worry, I eat my heart out with nothing to hope from her — and why, just for the pleasure of adding this misfortune to the store of misfortune I already possess? Why don't I think of saving my own skin? Idiot!'

This last word he had said out loud, and a coachman had heard. 'And why am I an idiot, my good sir?'

Sebastian didn't answer, but flew into a passion and walked back along the line of coaches trembling with rage. In this respect, however, he was alone; all around him a crowd of civilians in cockaded hats waited in a state of utter resignation, as if the flames would obligingly recede at an order from the Emperor before so much as licking her shoes. A wagon ventured down a street of which only one side was on fire; it had barely started before they saw it catch alight. The neighbouring streets were choked with furniture.

'Don't they want none of you?'

Some gendarmes had pitched a bivouac against the ramparts. They were heating punch in a silver bowl.

'It's Jamaican rum and sugar,' a gendarme said to Sebastian. 'Before burning to a frazzle on the outside, don't you fancy a bit of the same on the inside? It'll brace you, help you stick it out.'

Sebastian dropped his bag, squatted down on his heels, took the silver-gilt ladle which the jovial gendarme was holding out to him, plunged it in the rum and drank the concoction in little sips. It seared his tongue and throat and seemed to hollow out his whole body. On the second ladle he forgot about the black smoke and the coal dust falling on his hat and shoulders. On the third he took an aesthete's delight in the beauty of the fire. On the fourth, he had trouble getting back to his feet. He thanked the gendarmes who were slumped around the punch; they smiled with blissful expressions, screwing up their bloodshot eyes. He dragged his baggage over the cobbles as if it was an obstinate animal on a leash, taking great strides, in all but a straight line, and swaying, but still managing to keep his balance. The commissariat's barouches were blocking the whole avenue. A fat man was mopping his forehead with his handkerchief; he was quarrelling with a fellow passenger in a carriage laden with flour, wine and violins. It was Monsieur Beyle, one of the resupply commissaries; they knew each other vaguely from having argued one evening about Rousseau, whom they interpreted with significant differences. Sebastian stopped, unsteady on his legs, his sight blurred.

'Ah,' said Monsieur Beyle, seeing him. 'A man who can read! Providence has sent you, Monsieur le secrétaire. I almost had to travel with these chimpanzees in uniform!' He took Sebastian's arm. 'Take a look at what I've looted from that pretty white house there, you see? A volume of Chesterfield and the *Facéties* by Voltaire. It's spoiled the Complete Works, I grant you, but still, these books are better in my pocket than in the flames. Do you have a carriage?'

'No...'

'Me neither. My servants have stuffed it with baggage and I've been forced to invite that tedious fellow Bonnaire along. Do you know who I mean?'

'No...'

'Auditor to the State Council and a crashing bore to boot!'

'I'm not really in a fit state to chat...'

'I understand, I understand. We're surrounded by boors. This fire is a grand and beautiful spectacle, but one needs to be alone to truly enjoy it. What a pity to have to share it with people who'd belittle the Colosseum and the Bay of Naples! And what's more...'

'Yes, Monsieur Beyle?'

'I have an appalling toothache.'

He held his cheek. Sebastian moved off without a word, heading nowhere in particular except further on, his mind clouded by the punch. Administrators were trying to squeeze into packed berlines, arguments were breaking out, tussles, insults; office colleagues were hurling home truths in one another's faces. Nerves were fraying through fear. It was all taking too long. In the glow of the fires devastating Moscow, groups of troopers were riding alongside the column of carriages while others set off on reconnaissance to clear a path for the convoy. Sitting on his bag, his chin in his hands, Sebastian Roque closed his eyes; the punch hadn't affected his memory, words of his dear Seneca came to him: '*All things must be made light of and borne with good humour; it is more human to laugh at life than bewail it.*' How human I am, he thought to himself, hiccupping. The hiccup became a giggle, then the giggle uncontrollable laughter and the berlines' passengers looked at this young man overcome by mirth. 'The poor lad has gone mad,' sighed a coachman. 'Lucky blighter,' like an echo, answered a passenger leaning on his carriage door.

*

A tingling sensation made Sebastian jump. His sleeve was on fire. He stood up, slapping his arm. How long had he been asleep, his head on his bag? The carriages had gone, no one had bothered about him, he was alone on the boulevard; he had shooting pains in his head and a stiff neck. He heard hammering – no, it was hooves and wooden wheels echoing on the cobbles. He saw riders outlined against the smoke. The light of the fires accentuated the outlandishness of their headgear. The one leading the way, a strapping great rogue, was wearing an enormous fur hat, the others Tartar hats, Cossack regulars' caps or brass helmets. They rode closer, their getups becoming clearer. Russians were they, with those boots some of them wore that turned up at the toe? A detachment come to put the finishing touches to the disaster? The one at the front had a long nose, a pale, walrus moustache, a green Guard's coat; an abbot in a hitched-up soutane followed, then men in long embroidered coats with scimitars at their belts. They were towing a chest on casters; their little long-maned horses were laden with booty. This motley troupe stopped in front of Sebastian, who stood up, thinking that they were going to kill him. 'And I don't even care! It must be the punch, or fatigue . . .' Two of the troopers were whispering in each other's ear, and then their leader said, in French, 'Don't stay there, Monsieur Roque, you'll brown like a side of beef.'

'You know my name?'

'Rouen, the spinning-mills . . .'

'You're from Normandy?'

'Herbigny, does that ring any bells? Herbigny, on the way to Canteleu, just before Croisset.'

'I know the chateau, yes, with the limes, the meadow slopes down to the Seine . . .'

'That's my name, and that's been my house since the death of my father who knew yours.'

'So you are d'Herbigny, goodness!'

'Paulin! Put Monsieur Roque's bag with my portmanteau and you, Bonet, give him your nag. You'll walk, that'll teach you to play the parish priest!'

'I can walk,' said Sebastian.

'So can he. Shall we get on with it, Bonet?' To Sebastian,

he added, 'I needed to do something to that good-for-
nothing, his soutane is putting me to shame.'

'What about Martinon's horse?' said Trooper Bonet.

'You think it hasn't got enough already with our cloth
and provisions? Anyway, it's an order, for Heaven's sake!'

They set off at a walk again though passable streets,
taking the long way round to skirt the fire and get out into
the countryside. The sound of flames and crashing roofs
was accompanied by the howling of guard dogs which, as
was customary in Moscow, were chained up outside many
of the palaces; forgotten, they were burning to death.
Sebastian saw some under a peristyle. Driven into a frenzy
by the heat, the creatures were scrabbling at their scalding
chains but the metal wouldn't give, the fire was surrounding them, holding them prisoner, they were darting in
every direction to try to stop the pads of their feet from
burning. Beams were crashing to the ground, showering
them with sparks, their coats were catching fire, and they
were howling themselves hoarse one last time before they
roasted alive.

Then the troopers followed the banks of the Moskova,
passing charred bridges; the piles were breaking off and
smoking and spitting in the water. They took a stone
bridge, which had withstood the fire in that suburb; below,
the river washed along blackened timbers. The road was
lit by the blaze. In the plain, homelier fires marked the
bivouacs of Davout's army corps.

They turned their backs on the torrid city and set off
towards Petrovsky, which the Emperor had retired to. The
road was narrow (it cannot have been more than three
metres wide), so they were unable to pass a berline that had
stopped in the middle, taking it up completely. The captain

dismounted grouchily, intending to give some postilion in a drunken stupor a good shake, and walked round the berline. An open barouche had overturned on the verge; the occupants of both vehicles were straining to get it back on its wheels with a lot of panting and shouts of 'Ho!'

'Excellent timing,' exclaimed one of the passengers, who was brick red and running with sweat, his waistcoat unbuttoned and his sleeves rolled up; he was mopping his forehead with a lace petticoat.

'Anybody hurt?' asked the captain.

'Just some bumps and spoiled flour.' He pointed to the torn sacks in the ditch. 'I know this damned road is difficult, but if the coachman hadn't drunk so much ... It is not as if you can complain about the light!'

His cheeks quivered as he looked at Moscow. Somewhere a grating melody began which set their teeth on edge; suddenly downcast, the man exclaimed, 'It's Bonnaire! He thinks he can play the violin.'

'Monsieur Beyle?' asked Sebastian.

'Ah, it's you, is it, Monsieur le secrétaire? Bonnaire, yes, Bonnaire, the stupidest, most timorous spoilt child I have ever met! Hey! You there, stop him murdering Cimarosa! That's what he claims to be doing, Monsieur le secrétaire – playing Cimarosa on an out-of-tune violin he stole a moment ago!'

At a signal from the captain, Trooper Bonet marched up to the violinist who was mangling Cimarosa's 'Secret Wedding' and grabbed his instrument. 'Confiscated!'

'Leave me alone!' cried Bonnaire. 'What gives you the right?'

'Our ears! These gentlemen don't like your noise.'

'Noise? Boeotians!' Bonnaire protested, hitting the dragoon with the bow. Bonet parried the blows with the violin, which he held like a racket; a string broke with a crack and whipped Bonnaire in the cheek, who began yelping, then sniffling, tears pricking his eyes, before running off and shutting himself in the berline to sulk in earnest. Bonet threw the violin onto the plain, then rejoined his companions and helped them set about righting the barouche. Even with the extra pairs of hands, it took a long time before they got the carriage back on its wheels. Then, dog-tired, they continued on their way together in silence. It was eleven o'clock at night.

As they pulled away from the city, they saw the moon shining above the canopy of smoke. Bivouacs began to proliferate in the plain; they were approaching Petrovsky. The troops grew denser. Massed in the middle of fields, soon they formed a vast camp around a column of sofas and pianos looked from palaces that rose up like a pathetic obelisk. There was no way of carrying on through that horde of soldiers at rest. D'Herbigny and the others had to abandon their carriages at Prince Eugène's Italian cantonments, which surrounded the chateau. The dragoons went off to find their brigade, so they said, but in fact they were looking for a good spot to eat their ham and sleep off their wine. Sebastian fetched his bag and gave Bonet his horse back; when he dismounted, his boots sank into a thick mire, which explained why the soldiers had spread straw on the cold, wet ground, laid planks on the straw and covered the planks with furs and material. They were feeding their fires with window sashes, gilt-handled doors and billets of mahogany as they sprawled, with exaggerated languor, in armchairs upholstered with tapestry. Resting on their knees were silver dishes of black mush baked in the ash, which they pushed around with their fingers, rolled into balls and tossed into their mouths between bites of bloody, half-cooked chunks of horsemeat. Sebastian's stomach heaved.

'Not hungry any more, Monsieur le secrétaire?' joked Henri Beyle.

'These people spoil my appetite.'

'I have some figs, some raw fish and a poor white wine from the cellars of the English Club. For someone from supplies, this seems pretty pitiful, I know, but do let's share it, if you fancy, and let's not wake Bonnaire up, for pity's sake.'

Sebastian accepted the invitation. They took a chest out of the berline to sit on and a basket of the aforementioned provisions and started to eat, looking pensively back at the city. Sebastian chewed the sticky, tasteless flesh of a freshwater fish, and found himself involuntarily thinking of Ornella. It exasperated him, but how could he get her out of his mind? He saw her in the Kremlin's cellars, in the barouche, he heard her saying 'It's the saltfish-sellers' street, Monsieur Sebastian...' He sighed, his mouth full. He would have liked to talk about his anxieties, but with whom? This Henri Beyle? He spat some bones onto the ground.

'What are you thinking about, Monsieur le secrétaire?'

'The burning of Rome,' lied the young man.

'Let's hope Moscow's won't last nine days! When I think people have blamed Nero for starting it!'

'There's no doubt Rostopchin organized Moscow's fire, Monsieur Beyle.'

'This Rostopchin will either be a scoundrel or a hero. We'll have to see how his plan turns out.'

'The Russian historians will accuse Napoleon, the way the Latin historians accused Nero.'

'Suetonius? Tacitus? Those aristocrats who hated an Emperor who was too well liked by the people? Add the slanders of the victorious Christians and you have an odious reputation to last for centuries.'

The two Imperial functionaries drank their lukewarm white wine out of Chinese porcelain cups, and spoke about the destruction of Rome as they gazed on that of Moscow. That night they needed to escape into the past in order to feel they belonged to history.

'Did Nero really have nothing to do with it?' asked Sebastian.

'Listen ... The fire caught at the foot of the Palatine in some sheds which were used to store oil. The wind was blowing from the south. The conflagration, like today, spread quickly through a town made up of little wood-frame houses jammed up against one another. Nero returns from Antium, where he has been resting, sees his capital devastated, its treasures from all over the world in flames – his library, the former Temple of the Moon, Romulus's sanctuary, the great amphitheatre of Statilius Taurus ... And what does the Emperor do? Rejoice? Not a bit of it! He organizes emergency relief, takes care of the refugees, constructs temporary shelters, distributes food to those who have been impoverished by the fire, lowers the price of corn for everyone else, posts guards around burnt-out houses to prevent looting. At one point, exhausted and bitter, he takes up his lyre and sings a dirge. His enemies immediately twist this to their advantage: Nero, they say, has set Rome on fire to have a subject for song.'

'Nevertheless, he did blame the Christians ...'

'Forget Suetonius and the other scandalmongers. The Emperor ordered an inquiry, and it was the Roman people who indicted the Christians. Throughout the catastrophe, the leaders of the sect just laughed at Rome's misfortunes! The Christians weren't persecuted for their religion but for their refusal to abide by the laws, their constant cavilling. The reprisals were severe but brief. Fewer Christians were killed under Nero than under the clement Marcus Aurelius...'

'And us? What will they say about us, Monsieur Beyle?'

'Horrors, no doubt, Monsieur le secrétaire. Would you like another fig?'

*

Moscow was still burning the following morning. Sebastian Roque had resumed his duties in the Petrovsky Palace, the Tsars' baroque summer residence, a brick and tile castle with Greek towers and Tartar walls. In the middle of an immense circular room, under a dome that gave light, Napoleon had had his great wax- and ink-stained map of Russia laid out. The chubby, dishevelled figure of Baron Bacler d'Albe, head of the Topographical Department, had gone down on all fours to stick coloured pins in the map indicating the positions of the two camps. The Emperor was considering the enemy armies' possible movements.

'We are only fifteen marches from St Petersburg,' he said eventually. 'Our scouts assure us the road is clear.'

'Winter is on its way,' said Berthier. 'Are we going to seek it further north?'

The major general and the officers were concerned. The Emperor pressed on, 'The Tsar dreads our offensive. He has had his archives and treasures evacuated to London.'

'We have that from the Cossacks, but how do they know? Aren't they trying to trick us?'

'Be quiet! Murat's reports should steady us, you bunch of cowards! The Russian army is disheartened, their soldiers are deserting before the King of Naples' eyes, the Cossacks are ready to go over to him!'

'The Cossacks admire the King of Naples' courage, sire, but you know him . . .'

'Go on!'

'Murat is easily convinced because they flatter him.'

'And then,' Duroc broke in, 'the King of Naples has only encountered their rearguard. Where has Kutuzov's army got to?'

'Carried straight on, no doubt about it, he's to the east of us.'

'We're not certain of that, sire.'

'I know how he reasons, that one-eyed oaf!'

'What if he had gone down south, which is fertile country, to restore his strength?'

'Where?'

'Towards Kaluga, perhaps.'

'Show me this Caligula!'

'Kaluga, sire, under your left foot . . .'

'Conjecture!'

The Emperor got down on all fours like his topographer; he moved pins around, commentating as he did so, 'The Viceroy of Italy's divisions will make quick time along the Petersburg road, here, while the other corps pretend to follow but in fact only give support . . . Understood? The rearguard will hold Moscow's environs. In the plains, our columns will effect a circular movement, like this, to link up with Gouvion-Saint-Cyr's Bavarians and take the Russians in the rear . . .'

'Bravo, sire!' exclaimed Prince Eugène de Beauharnais, Viceroy of Italy, with his clipped moustache and sparse hair.

'Oh no, sire, if it does turn out that Kutuzov is going down towards Kaluga, then he is trying to cut off our return route.'

'Berthier! Who is talking about returning? *I cannot retreat!* Do you want me to lose face? I will go and seek the peace at St Petersburg!'

'If he wanted to negotiate, the Tsar would not have destroyed Moscow.'

'Alexander holds me in high esteem, and he didn't give the order to burn his capital!'

'Sire,' intervened Count Daru, who was in charge of the Imperial commissariat, 'in any case, we should retire before winter. The men are exhausted.'

'They are not men, they're soldiers!'

'Even soldiers must eat . . .'

'As soon as this wretched fire is brought under control, we'll search the cellars, we'll find leather, hides for winter.'

'Provisions?'

'Those too! If need be we'll have them brought from Danzig!'

Crouching lower, his hands flat on the floor and nose buried in the map, the Emperor grew fervent. He created a Russia to suit his convenience, running roads through marshes, bringing in imaginary harvests, launching cavalry charges, snapping up victories. Advancing in this whirlwind fashion on St Petersburg, he bumped heads with his geographer, let out a yell and abused him in Corsican dialect. No one had the heart to smile. The fate of a hundred thousand men depended on a word; for once, everyone knew that reality would not yield to one man's whims.

*

The fire was laying siege to the stone church in which the actors had taken refuge. The cobblestones of the square insulated the building from the burning houses, and, having nothing to feed on, the fire stopped well before it, but the heat was suffocating as soon as you left the nave. Wrapped in their tablecloths, Ornella and her friend Catherine had ventured a little way outside, onto the scalding steps, before quickly retreating, drenched in sweat. They may have been hungry, like their companions, but, above all, they needed water; their tongues and throats were parched, even their saliva had dried up. When he'd gone, Captain d'Herbigny had left them the keg of brandy, but alcohol staves off thirst rather than quenches it and they had no way to escape to the river or the lake Mme Aurore knew of in the west, where the wind was coming from. In the middle of this fire, if they didn't die in the flames, the actors were going to die of thirst. The Great Vialatoux had been caught with his head in a stoup, lapping at the brackish water, and was now doubled up on the flagstones with a vicious stomach ache. Mme Aurore had had to stop her juvenile lead chewing the candles, lest he exacerbate his thirst. They hoped for a miracle, for rain, for the fire to die down for lack of fuel. Could they hold out without drinking? They waited for a storm, they called one down, but all they heard on all sides was the din of buildings crashing to the ground, the crackle of beams, the spit of flames, the howls of men and animals trapped by the fire. A stained-glass window, its lead lattice melted clean away, shattered at the foot of a pillar; a splinter of blue glass cut Ornella in the shoulder.

Mme Aurore rationed out the grain alcohol by the cup, the half cup, the quarter cup. They had to moisten their lips; at least the fumes allowed them to forget their plight or to distort it. Was it day? Was it night? A charcoal sky blocked out the rays of the sun and moon alike; only the restless orange light of the fire shone through the rose window, rearranging the shadows on the walls and wrought-silver icons. The candles had gone out. The actors were subsisting in a sallow half-light, drained of all their strength, lying on the ground. Curled up in a ball, hugging her knees to her chest, Ornella stared at the relief portrait of a heavily bearded saint; his face stood out against a background of precious stones; he had almond-shaped eyes, a stern expression. She thought she could see his lips moving, as if he was going to say something to her, a prayer, and then step out of his frame and take her away. The hallucinations were starting. She thought she was in hell. The ribs of the vault swayed like branches; the pillars rose like stacks of tree trunks. She caught sight of a black giant in a pale bearskin hat and a gilded coat with epaulettes that made him seem even broader-shouldered. The demon came closer, and closer, and picked her up without her reacting and carried her out, his heavy, resolute footsteps echoing down the nave. His name was Othello, this tall Negro who Murat had brought back from Egypt and taken into his service as a groom. In a landscape of embers and ashes, the King of Naples sat his horse on the smoke-filled square, a fine-looking figure with his long, curly hair under a plumed Polish hat, his green coat fringed with silver, the tiger skin under his seat and his yellow boots. The *velites* of his guard surrounded him.

Three

THE RUINS

'In society, it is reason that gives way first. The most sensible people are often swayed by the most foolish and eccentric personage: they study his weaknesses, his temper, his whims, and accommodate themselves to them; they avoid thwarting him and everybody gives him his way; if his countenance shows any sign of serenity, he is heartily praised; he is given credit for not always being insufferable. He is feared, considered, obeyed and sometimes beloved.'

La Bruyère, *The Characters*

ON THE THIRD DAY, heavy rainfall checked the fire without dousing it completely; pockets sprang up again under the rubble. The Emperor often went up onto the terrace of the Petrovsky Palace, a hand under his waistcoat, clamped to his painful stomach. He meditated, staring at the devastation. He had abandoned the idea of throwing his army on St Petersburg, over three hundred leagues of bad road in the middle of marshes, which a handful of peasants could render impassable.

As soon as he was able, Sebastian attached himself to the Emperor's immediate entourage. He had changed: the fire had made him more egotistical. In a catastrophe, everyone looks out for themselves; his death would not have affected anybody – even Baron Fain, whom he'd thought of as his protector, would have left him to cook in Moscow. He had no friends. The other clerks? Too silly, too ignorant. Monsieur Beyle? He hardly knew him, but what a wonderful idea, evoking classical history amidst a scene of modern desolation. In an age when death seemed the rule, people were easily moved to tears; an academic lecture, a counsel's plea reduced the most hardened listeners to sobbing wrecks; Napoleon himself admitted to crying while reading *The Trials of Sentiment* by the bombastic Baculard d'Arnaud. Bucking fashion, Sebastian resolved to remain dry-eyed. He swore there would be no more reaching for his handkerchief while leafing through *The New Héloïse*; instead he would remain true to Rousseau's disillusioned side: 'I go with secret horror into the vast desert of the world . . .'

From then on, Sebastian cultivated a fabricated zeal. He wanted His Majesty to notice him – him, the scribbler, the valet who blended into the furniture. I lack substance, do I? he thought to himself. Well, let's turn that to my advantage. With cold dedication, he applied himself to mastering the courtier's profession, from which he hoped to acquire a more elevated position, an income, and even a title, an estate, his own box at the principal Parisian theatres – in other words, security and the kind of love that gold and fame arouse in young women.

On occasion Sebastian left the palace. Since the downpour, the encampments on the plain were awash with mud and he always returned begrimed, but it gave him a chance to see d'Herbigny again, his neighbour from Normandy.

Following army practice, the effects of missing soldiers were put up for auction for the benefit of their wives and children, or their regiment if they were unmarried, and not having been paid yet, the soldiers indulged in the most anarchic forms of bartering. On one of Sebastian's visits, d'Herbigny was auctioning off the belongings Sergeant Martinon had strapped to his horse: nothing really, a tobacco pouch made out of a pig's bladder, a hatchet for chicken, a grain sack which he'd used instead of a hooded greatcoat when in bivouac.

'And a tinplate mess kettle!' the captain announced, waving the object. 'Any takers for this nearly new mess kettle?'

'All right,' said a pudgy fellow in a blue suit.

'A barrel of beer?'

'It's not worth that much. A sack of peas – for the lot.'

The bidding did not go higher. It seemed a fair enough trade, and the buyer went off to fetch his side of the bargain.

'Who is that?' Sebastian asked the captain.

'Don't you know Poissonnard? He's an old fox who's getting rich out of all this.'

'How's that?'

'He hoards things, sells them on – he's well placed for it, the sly dog!'

Poissonnard worked in the provisioning section of the general administration; he was one of six comptrollers in the commissariat service in charge of meats, and never hesitated to take advantage of his position. When shops near the Kremlin were going up in flames, he had pulled out sacks of rye, nuts and peas, barrels of beer and Malaga, sugar, coffee, and candles. He had taken his cut, which he was now openly hawking. Sebastian gave him one of his waistcoats for a long Russian sabre that he would take home as a souvenir and prop for invented deeds of derring-do.

He hadn't forgotten Mme Aurore's troupe but he dismissed Ornella's image from his mind; he would have been upset, or anxious, he would have pined for her, and that didn't correspond to the new role he saw himself playing at court. Although Napoleon preferred military men to civilians, Sebastian was racking his brains for ways to win him over, without thus far coming up with the slightest self-evident or reasonable idea of how to qualify for his favours.

*

Before the end of the week, the equinoctial gale had stopped rekindling the embers of the fire and it was possible to re-enter the destroyed city. Everything was black and grey in the ruins of Moscow. Black, the smoke that hung motionless overhead, the squalling ravens that hovered in dense clouds, the charred trees that stretched out their branches like arms, the broken peristyles, the brick chimneys emerging here and there like towers from the wreckage of fourteen thousand houses. Grey, the ashes covering the ground, the shattered walls, the misshapen furniture, the remnants of carts and belongings scattered through the rubble; grey, too, the wolves that had come out in packs to tear at the human and animal carcasses.

The Imperial Guard, in a clinging smell of burning, had the sinister honour of being the first to discover this inhuman landscape. The band led the way; the fifes, the drums, and the bells flourished on their handle by a tall, sad African, echoed around, like anachronisms, their music only partly drowning out wolves' howls and birds of prey's cries. Every ten metres a grenadier detached himself to take up a position on the road the Emperor would take to the Kremlin, which had been saved by its walls. General Saint-Sulpice rode in front of his four bizarrely-uniformed, dysentery-depleted squadrons; he bowed his head and slouched forward in the saddle, overwhelmed by fate. D'Herbigny cast a sidelong glance at his general's black horse, a Turkish mare with its tail braided with ribbons and secured by a gold-tipped pin. Ruins didn't make an impression on him anymore, not since the capture of Saragossa.

The infantry of the Guard was going to be quartered in the citadel, but what about the others? The cavalry's senior officers were to join Marshal Bessières, who ordered them into a wing of the Kremlin; it was up to the squadrons to fend for themselves. So d'Herbigny set off amongst the ruins with a hundred or so dragoons. They passed houses without roofs, doors, or windows; the first habitable palace had already been occupied by Captain Coti's moustachioed chevaux-légers. They had to push on further into the livid landscape; they could spot intact buildings a long way off, their walls only blackened by smoke and their statues fused into strange blocks, a head, a marble hand, the pleats of a friable coat. The Muscovites who had gone to earth were emerging from their cellars now, darting out from between piles of fallen masonry; they were collecting twisted sheets of iron to construct shelters and scrabbling with their fingers for wilted roots in what used to be vegetable gardens. They were in rags, leaden-skinned, fearful. Groups of them kneeled, mumbling prayers at the foot of gallows spared by the fire; they devoutly kissed the dirty rags covering the incendiaries' legs and sang hymns of an unbearable melancholy, believing that the hanged men would rise again on the third day. Other Russians dived into the river where the barges with cargoes of grain had sunk; they crawled out onto the bank on all fours, dripping and skidding in the muck as they hauled out waterlogged sacks of fermented wheat. Oh yes, thought the captain, I'd better feed my rascals as well.

At that moment the dragoons met a resupply team led by Comptroller Poissonnard. Piled on the platforms of their drays, which were drawn by old plough horses with withers as broad as oaks, were carcasses, in varying stages of disintegration, of horses, cats, jaundiced dogs, swans with tousled feathers and rotting crows.

'Where are you going to bury that carrion, you old swindler?' the captain called.

'Carrion? My meat?' bristled Poissonnard. 'You'll be happy enough when it's simmering in front of you, you freebooter! Get a good fire going and the maggots'll hold their peace.'

'And you keep the best bits for yourself, is that it?'

'Everything's negotiable, Captain, everything . . .'

The comptroller was setting up his butcher's shop in the Church of St Vladimir. He pointed out, in the vicinity, the Convent of the Nativity, which the flames had merely grazed; a few hundred metres on they could see its pinnacle turrets, cracked but standing, the verdigrised dome of its chapel and its surrounding wall, on which the ivy had shrivelled and its leaves turned a charcoal grey. The dragoons rode there at a slow trot. The charred gate stood open; a push and it would have come away from its casing.

Inside, a rough stone well with a rusty iron coping stood in the middle of a grassy court surrounded by a vaulted arcade; under this portico with rounded pillars, a flock of nuns in brown habits were taking to their heels.

'Bonet!' the captain laughed. 'You go and catch me those angels from heaven, seeing as you can't be parted from your soutane!'

Bending his neck so as not to scrape his head on the arch, Bonet urged his mount under the gallery and grabbed one of the runaways by the sleeve. Her companions scattered, chirping, into the low rooms to reappear as clusters of faces at the barred windows. The nun who Bonet brought back to his captain had her cheeks smeared with soot to spoil her looks and keep men away, an idea of the Mother Superior's, a sour-tempered old matron with a nose and chin that almost touched. Other dragoons had dismounted and were holding her in the courtyard; she spat scornfully on the ground, yelling incomprehensible words, cursing the strangers.

'Chantelouve! Durtal!' ordered d'Herbigny. 'Draw some water from this well and wash these pretty little faces!'

It became a game, without cruelty, to catch the young nuns, pull off their veils and rub their little faces with cloths; some of them were excited by this unprecedented experience, the men could tell by their hot cheeks. The bucket made a muffled splash as it landed at the bottom of the well, but troopers Durtal and Chantelouve had trouble bringing it back up; the rope stretched to breaking point, they pulled, their faces turning purple, their boot heels digging into the grass.

'Can't you get that flipping bucket back up?' shouted the captain.

'Oh, I see,' Trooper Durtal said, leaning over the curb stone.

D'Herbigny got off his horse and bent over. Down below, the bucket had caught on a body lying face down, a French soldier pushed down the well.

'By the colour of his jacket, sir,' Chantelouve declared knowledgeably, 'that must be one of our friends from the artillery . . .'

*

Stretching along the Kremlin's corridors in single file, servants in periwigs, gloves and white stockings were carrying buckets of steaming water which they spilled a little each time they shifted under their weight. They were going to refill the bathtub in which the Emperor had been steaming for over an hour, yelling that the water was never hot enough, even though Constant, who was scrubbing his back with a brush as stiff as a currycomb, was drenched in sweat, the long room was so full of steam that visibility was reduced to three paces and beads of condensation were streaming down its panelling. Doctors Yvan and Mestivier, who recommended His Majesty take hot baths to relieve his bladder problems, couldn't understand why he wasn't boiling alive, and they mopped their foreheads with already damp handkerchiefs that they then wrung out on the parquet floor. Berthier chose the worst moment to appear; choking, he stepped into that Egyptian hammam, wiped his gleaming face with the back of an embroidered sleeve, approached the bathtub and was immediately insulted.

'What disaster has he come to inform us of now, this scourge of our bathing?'

The Emperor splashed the major general with a gush of

hot water, soaking his impeccable uniform from top to bottom.

'We've found the messenger, sire . . .'

'What messenger?'

'The man who can take your dispatch to the Tsar in person.'

'Who?'

'A Russian officer. He is called . . .'

Berthier put on his misted-up spectacles, which he rubbed with his finger to read the name scribbled on a piece of paper. 'He is called Jakovlev. We've taken him out of the military hospital where he's been lucky not to roast like so many other wounded.'

'Where is he, your Jacob?'

'In the column room, sire. He is waiting.'

'Let him wait.'

'He is a brother of one of the Tsar's ministers at Cassel.'

'Well, go and keep him company, then, he'll adore your refined conversation. Is that hot water coming? Did I tell you to stop scrubbing, Monsieur Constant? Go on! Harder! Like a horse!'

The meeting with the envoy chosen by Berthier took place that evening. The Emperor smelled strongly of eau de Cologne and grumbled to himself, clasping his hands behind his back under the turnbacks of his colonel's coat. Jakovlev got to his feet, leaning on a cane; his full moustache hid his lips; with his puce trousers and white spencer, he presented a rather curious, half-military and half-civilian appearance. Napoleon began on a conciliatory, sorrowful note before flying into a rage against Rostopchin and the English, whose baleful influence he denounced.

'Let Alexander ask to negotiate and I will sign the treaty

of peace in Moscow as I did before in Vienna and before that in Berlin. I didn't come here to stay. I shouldn't be here. I wouldn't be here if I hadn't been forced! The English, it is their fault! The English have dealt Russia a blow she will suffer from for a long time. Is this patriotism, these cities in flames? No – it is a maddened frenzy! And Moscow? Rostopchin's fever has cost you more than ten battles! What is the good of this fire? I'm still in the Kremlin, aren't I? If Alexander had said a single word I would have declared Moscow a neutral city, Ah, how I waited for that word, how I longed for it! And look what we have come to. So much bloodshed!'

'Your Majesty,' Jakovlev replied, sensing that the monologue was finished, 'perhaps it would be for you, the victor, to speak of peace.'

The Emperor reflected, walked round the room, and then returned to the Russian's side with a bound. 'Do you have direct access to the Tsar?'

'Yes.'

'If I write to him, will you take my letter?'

'Yes.'

'Will he receive it in person?'

'Yes.'

'Are you certain?'

'I give you my word.'

All that remained was to compose the letter. In what terms? Anger, no; supplication, no, even less so. How to get through to Alexander? How to make him yield? How to move him? Napoleon went out alone onto the terrace from where he towered over the decimated city. Through his theatre glasses he saw, sparkling in the night, church chandeliers hanging in the few palaces still standing, which were serving as barracks; bivouacs in the palace courtyards, bivouacs in the plain, points of light, echoes of drinking songs. He went back inside to sleep, got up in the middle of the night and sent for his secretaries. Pacing up and down the large salon, he mumbled his way through his missive to the Tsar. The secretaries took notes of the snatches they could hear and stifled their yawns.

'Mon frère,' said the Emperor very quietly. 'No, too familiar ... Monsieur mon frère, that's it, Monsieur mon frère ... I want him to prove that deep down he still feels some attachment towards me. At Tilsit, he said, "I will be your second against England." ... Lies! Don't put that word. At Erfurt I offered him Moldavia and Wallachia, which would extend his borders to the Danube ... Monsieur mon frère ... Then say that the brother of one of his ministers ... a minister of Your Majesty's ... Write Your Majesty ... I sent for him, I spoke to him, he promised me ... no ... I *recommended* he make my feelings known to the Tsar ... Stress *feelings* ... Then the burning of Moscow has to be deplored, condemned, the blame put on that swine Rostopchin! The incendiaries? Shot! Add that I am not waging war on him for my own pleasure ... that I waited for a word from him ... One word! A word or a battle. One word and I would have remained at Smolensk, I would have rallied the armies, assembled the supplies from Danzig, the droves. One word and I would have organized Lithuania. I already held Poland ...'

When Sebastian went over Baron Fain's half-drafted notes to combine them with his and write up a version in ink, he added some figures (*Four hundred incendiaries have been arrested in the act*, and *Three-quarters of the houses have been burnt*) and took the liberty of inserting a remark of the Emperor's he'd heard earlier that day, about Ros-topchin, that seemed to him to reinforce the message (*This conduct is atrocious and utterly purposeless*). The Baron reread the final copy of the letter, appeared satisfied and submitted it for Napoleon's mechanical signature. Sebastian was especially proud of his conclusion: *I have waged war on Your Majesty without animosity; a note from him, before or after the last battle, would have halted my march.* He expected congratulations but received none.

*

In the Mother Superior's cell, which he had commandeered for himself, d'Herbigny stood up with an aching back. Bare-chested, in buckskin undershorts, he rubbed the small of his back; that wooden bed was confoundedly hard, even with the mass of cushions he'd brought from a canteen-woman who owed her business to pillage from the bazaar. 'I'm getting rusty,' he said, opening the window. He shivered. The air was damp and cool. Below, in the courtyard, horses were noisily drinking Moskova water that had been brought up to the wash-house in hogsheads. Two dragoons were cooking soup, their cauldron hanging from the beams over a brazier.

'What is it?'

'Cabbage, sir.'

'Again!'

Grousing, he went to the oratory, where Paulin had laid out his straw mattress. Assisted by a young nun with downcast eyes, he was treating the captain's uniform for lice, the Muscovite welcome, as their infestation of every scrap of clothing was known. Dressed in a coarse canvas shirt, with chestnut-brown hair cut very short, long-lashed eyes that she kept half-closed and slow movements, the sister had turned the breeches inside out and was pressing them with a stone. Paulin was singeing the seams with flint and steel to kill any survivors.

'Nearly there, sir.'

'She's charming, this little girl. I wonder if I shan't take your place!'

'She's lucky, is what she is, sir. Lieutenant Berton's have been getting different treatment.'

They had locked the cantankerous Mother Superior and the oldest, most wizened nuns in their chapel; the troopers had shared out the others amongst themselves to wash and mend their linen. The evening before, Lieutenant Berton had organized a dance; d'Herbigny had heard laughter and crude songs most of the night. Berton had dressed up some of the nuns as fine ladies, got them drunk, and forced them to dance, laughing at their silent tears, the looks on their faces, their awkwardness. Bah! the captain thought to himself, those girls are better off than if they'd fallen into the clutches of a Württemberg regiment; they would have given them a good going over, those brutes.

'It's ready, sir,' Paulin said, checking the deloused uniform one last time.

'Then nip along to the robber's and bring back something for a decent stew.'

The robber was their nickname for Comptroller Poissonnard, who reserved his best cuts to exchange for icons from the convent, the silver from which he melted down into ingots.

'I'll get you dressed and then run off there, sir.'

'No need. The little one will help me; look at her fingers, those aren't peasant's hands, she's the daughter of

an aristocrat who's been shuffled off into a convent ...
What is she called?'

'I don't make small talk in Russian, sir,' said Paulin
with an offended air.

The servant heaved a long sigh, took another icon out
of their cabinet, went down to the ground floor, heard a
woman's moans as he passed Lieutenant Berton's cell,
crossed the refectory, which had been converted into a
stable and set off towards St Vladimir's, pulling his donkey
behind him.

The church was filled with a stale, nauseating, cloying
smell. Hung from scaffolds by butcher's hooks, animal
chunks rotted in midair, their blood dripping into sticky
pools, running off in gutters and congealing on the flagstones. Paulin left his donkey tethered under the porch; he
walked down the middle of the filthy nave, blowflies
buzzing around him, and blocked his nose as tightly as he
could, but the fetid atmosphere still seeped in through his
mouth. He cleared his throat and spat. How could Poissonnard live here? Very happily, as it turned out. He was
buoyed up by the idea of profit; in this cesspool, he breathed
easier than he would have at two thousand metres' altitude
with no hope of a fortune. Cheeks blue but shaved with
care, he had set up his office in a confessional; the door,
torn off and laid across two barrels – there was his desk;
files were stacked on the penitents' prayer-stools.

'Ah, good day, my dear Paulin,' Poissonnard said
unctuously.

'Comptroller. What can you offer me today for this
work of art?'

He held out the silver-grounded icon.

'Let's see, let's see,' said the crook, adjusting his spectacles on his florid nose. He appraised the icon expertly, and, scraping it with his fingernail, estimated it at three hundred grams of silver; he thought for a moment and then led Paulin, who was still ill at ease, to the sacristy he had converted into a storeroom and his lodgings. They passed a hundred or so skinned cats piled up in a chapel. Butchers were carting the heads away in tubs; they were going to join a mound of bones, oozing muzzles and hooves at the bottom of a crypt; thrown out, even buried, this waste would attract the wolves.

Paulin looked away from a group of workmen from the commissariat; their red fingers were prising ribs apart with a cracking sound and throwing soft things into buckets overflowing with offal. Others, on ladders, were hanging garlands of dead crows on lines strung between the pillars. 'Will this church ever return to normal?' the servant wondered. Stones have a memory, the old priest who had taught him the alphabet used to say. In Rouen, you could still see holes in the pillars in the church of St Ouen: during the Revolution, the zealous new recruits of the armies of the Republic had set up forges in its aisles to cast bullets; the choir's copper grille had ended up as a cannon. But this wasn't the same. Blood was going to stain the stones and tiles of St Vladimir's.

'I've kept the best for our dear captain,' said Comptroller Poissonnard, taking a mare's liver — which glinted olive green when it caught the light — out of a chest, and wrapping it in a Russian newspaper.

'Is that all?'

'Ah yes, Monsieur Paulin, that is all, but it is oh so tender.'

'Just a little more effort, Monsieur Poissonnard.'

'A bottle of Madeira, then, there you go! Do you think you're going to find beef after eight days' pillaging? Our regiments have swiped the lot!'

Even dried vegetables were running out. Squads went out marauding every day, but they had to go further and further afield and brave the peasants' hostility. Fresh meat was growing scarce and Poissonnard was reaping the benefits.

'Captain d'Herbigny should try and bring back a drove,' he joked.

'I'll tell him,' answered Paulin, recoiling at the sight of the high altar, his heart racing. The non-believers in army stores had nailed a wolf to it.

Poissonnard smiled. 'They're not squeamish, those wolves. My goodness, they're fond of my meat – too fond, even. Talking of which, ask the gendarmes out there to see you back safely. Those beasts could easily attack you, on account of that choice piece you're leaving with.'

*

Time passed and the Tsar didn't respond; Kutuzov's troops, it emerged, had disappeared down south, as Berthier had predicted. The Grande Armée settled in for winter in the ruins of Moscow. The Emperor made numerous arrangements to that end: he wrote to Maret, the Duke of Bassano, who had remained in Lithuania, for fourteen thousand horses; he considered raising new regiments, organized parades, pestered his Parisian bookseller for the novels of the moment; he had the Kremlin fortified, the convents likewise. Caulaincourt had stepped up the post; the mail arrived every day from Paris, bringing wine and parcels. The couriers took fifteen days to travel between the two capitals; the service functioned punctually by way of post stages. A rumour spread that reinforcements were on their way with winter clothes; they would throw the Russians into the Volga.

And then, suddenly, the incidents began. Soldiers were found murdered. The Cossacks, whom Murat claimed to have won over, turned hostile. One day they fell on some artillery wagons from Smolensk and burnt them; three days later, on the same road, they killed and wounded a party of dragoons of the Guard. The next day it was a whole squadron, and they seized two trunks of mail that were returning to France.

Sebastian was watching the first snow; big, slow-moving flakes were melting as they landed on the roofs. In the courtyard, the soldiers had constructed huts using pictures from the palace walls. An aide-de-camp from headquarters entered the secretaries' office; in his Hungarian-style uniform, with gold silk belt and red trousers, he cut a very elegant figure.

'For His Majesty, the text of the 22nd Bulletin.'

'Monsieur Roque,' said Baron Fain, 'instead of watching the snow fall, read that and take it to the Emperor.'

He returned to drafting a promotion, a new general who was being sent to Portugal.

'My lord . . .'

'Take it, I tell you.'

'There is a problem.'

'What?' said the Baron, looking up from his paper.

'Do you think that allusions to the incidents on the Smolensk road are necessary?'

'Certainly not!'

'I can excise them?'

'Of course.'

'And also . . .

'What else?'

'This dispatch lacks any favourable news.'

'If you can find anything favourable to add, then do so, in your most florid style.'

'I need your approval.'

The Baron took the piece of paper and Sebastian, standing at his side, made certain suggestions. 'After *The fires have entirely ceased*, why not add *Warehouses of sugar, furs, linen are being discovered every day . . .* '

'But no meat.'

'No, but this will be published in the *Monitor*; it's better to be reassuring. See, there as well, after *The greater part of the army is in cantonment in Moscow . . .*'

'What am I supposed to see, Monsieur Roque?'

'In the same positive spirit, I would add *where it is restoring itself after its exertions.*'

'Add away.'

'This young man is right.'

It was the Emperor. He had entered silently and was listening to them. The secretary and his clerk got to their feet.

'Watch out for this lad, Fain, he has ideas. Where is Méneval?'

'In bed with fever, sire.'

'What's this lad's name?'

'Sebastian Roque, sire. I employ him as my chief clerk, because he has a good hand.'

'Perhaps we could use him at Carnavalet. What do you think, Fain?'

'He is well read, it's true . . .'

In the Hôtel Carnavalet, the censor's office altered the texts of plays that had been authorized to be performed. Just as Pisistratus used to have Homer rewritten in Athens, so bookish civil servants cut any allusions from *Athalie*, however oblique, that might be disagreeable to His Majesty; they toned down the classics for the continuing peace of the empire and transposed overly contemporary comedies to the age of the Assyrians.

Flushed with happiness, Sebastian clasped his hands together to stop them trembling. Napoleon quizzed him, 'Do you like the theatre?'

'In Paris, sire, I went as often as my work at the Ministry of Defence allowed.'

'Would you be able to revise a tragedy?'

'Yes, sire.'

'Comb the classics for situations and words with double meanings in which the audience would see allusions to the Empire and my person?'

'Yes, sire.'

'If you were submitted a play about Charles VI, how would you react?'

'Badly, sire. Very badly.'

'Explain.'

'In that case, sire, there's nothing to rework, the subject itself is damaging.'

'Go on.'

'One does not show a mad king on stage.'

'*Bravissimo!* And would you be able to add classical material to plays that are too contemporary?'

'I think so, sire, I know the Greek and Latin authors.'

'Fain, when we get back to Paris, send your clerk to Baron Pommereul, he's in great need of assistance. Don't pull such a face! You'll find another secretary to copy out your notes.'

To show his satisfaction, the Emperor either pulled your ear until it practically came off, or slapped you as hard as he could. Sebastian had the pleasure of feeling all five imperial fingers on his cheek, which was equivalent to being decorated.

*

'Durtal! On reconnaissance.'

The dismounted dragoon began slowly crossing a long, narrow footbridge suspended over a ravine; he held his horse's bridle between thumb and index finger, as instructed, so as not to be dragged down with it if the animal stumbled and fell. The others watched him. D'Herbigny had taken thirty or so of his men south, into country beyond the desert of yellow sand. Comptroller Poissonnard's remark had nettled him and he had vowed to capture a drove. They had left Moscow before dawn, in the rain, their boots stuffed with straw because there had been frosts overnight. It wasn't raining after four hours' ride, but the wind was gusting sharply, their damp cloaks floated on their shoulders and their helmets' manes fluttered. On the other side of the gorge, they could see houses made of fir and moss. Smoke was rising from the wooden roofs. These peasants had fires going, they hadn't fled, they had provisions, forage – maybe even livestock.

'Durtal!'

The footbridge had given way, as the dragoon was halfway across: the man, his mount and the logs of the roadway crashed to the bottom of the stony ravine. D'Herbigny averted his eyes. Durtal's screams died away.

Now they'd have to go round the ravine, which seemed to grow shallower before the horizon, and work their way back to the huts under cover of the forest, if it wasn't too dense. They rode into the wind in single file, didn't risk a second footbridge which they suspected was fragile or sabotaged and found a way over by late morning. As they were climbing the other slope, they heard hurrahs – the Cossacks' battle cry – and saw a small troop in flat caps charging at the gallop, lances and pikes levelled to run them through. The captain thought he was back in Egypt; the Arab horsemen used the same harrying tactics: they'd appear from nowhere, strike, scatter and then return from another direction.

'Dismount! In position!'

The dragoons knew the drill. They took cover behind their horses, brought their guns to their shoulders. The Cossacks bore down on them; when they were ten metres away the captain gave the order to fire. After the smoke of their musketry had cleared, they inspected their bag: two horses and three men; the third horse was grazing the parched grass on the side of the ravine. The rest of the Cossacks had turned about and disappeared into the forest. The dragoons reloaded.

'Any wounded?'

'Not one, sir.'

'We've been lucky.'

'Except Durtal.'

'Yes, Bonet, except Durtal.'

D'Herbigny had planned to spend the night in the hamlet he had seen a little while before, but entering the forest or pitching camp were now out of the question. Regretfully, he gave the order to fall back, and they rode their exhausted horses as hard as they could. Returning empty-handed, the captain at least had the consolation of having picked up a sturdy horse and a pair of bearskin boots, with the fur on the inside. They were too small for him; he would give them to Anissia the nun, his protégée with short hair whose name he had found out.

In driving rain, the marauders returned to the Convent of the Nativity before nightfall. Water spurted off the roofs, streamed from the gutterless porch; d'Herbigny had to take a running jump to get through the waterfall and into the dry. Inside he took off his soaking cloak and his water-logged bearskin, which sprayed him in the face. In the middle of the vaulted room that had previously been a parlour, some dragoons were sitting morosely in front of a mountain of bags.

'What's happening?'

'We've got our pay, sir.'

'And that's not enough to gladden your hearts, you bunch of no goods!'

'Well...'

The captain picked up a bag, opened it and took out a handful of yellow coins.

'Are they copper?'

'They're only worth their weight.'

'You'd rather some false *assignats*?'

Large amounts of copper currency having been found in the cellars of the courts of justice, the regiments had drawn their pay. As the first in line, the Imperial Guard had been entitled to these bags of twenty-five roubles. The captain sneezed.

'First I'll get dry, then we'll see.'

He left his troopers to their disappointment and ran up

to the first floor. Paulin was sitting on a stool, in the captain's cell, at the sleeping novice's bedside.

'Anissia, Aniciushka . . .'

'She hasn't got up all day, sir.'

'Sick?'

'I've no idea.'

'You didn't call Monsieur Larrey?'

'I don't have that authority.'

'Idiot!'

'Anyway he's a surgeon, Monsieur Larrey, what part of her is he going to amputate, poor little thing?'

Without listening to his servant's mumblings, d'Herbigny knelt down by Anissia. She looked like a madonna that he had stolen from a Spanish church once, because he found it touching; later he had sold it to treat himself to a blow-out.

*

It was still raining the following day. Sent to the Kremlin by his master, to the Guard's special infirmary, Paulin, on his donkey, was holding a Pekinese parasol that he had picked up in the bazaar as an umbrella. Without a cockade in his hat, the sentries hadn't let him into the citadel; nothing had swayed them, not even the letter dictated by d'Herbigny and signed with his left hand. Paulin was slowly making his way back; he was going to feel the captain's anger again, but he was used to it. In a spirit of conscientiousness, he made a detour via a military hospital on the banks of the Moskova; there he found overwhelmed doctors, rushing through high-windowed rooms between rows of fifty beds. They took a dead man out in front of him, wrapped in his sheet, while the dying looked furtively on. Paulin left without having even been able to talk to a medical orderly. Drifting through the ruins, he caught sight of a crowd of Muscovites in Nicolskaya Street, where an impromptu currency market had sprung up. A handful of official buildings were still standing and soldiers were changing their copper coins at trestle tables. For ten kopeks, then fifty, then a silver rouble (the demand for legal currency kept pushing the prices up), the poor people took away a bag of them. There were women, urchins and old men in rags who seemed reinvigorated in that scrum. Sabres in hand, the infantry of the Guard were trying to maintain order; some fired into the air. But the press of the crowd was too great. They trampled and pummelled one another, those Russians, punching and elbowing their way through to the moneychangers' counters. A tall moujik grabbed a bag which a woman had managed to get hold of; she scratched him, he drove his knee into her stomach, but she clung on to his grimy tunic; he battered her with the bag to make her let go and finally she fell down, shouting abuse, and the people behind walked over her. The soldiers, meanwhile, had retreated inside the building, and were throwing their bags through the open windows, which only inflamed the crowd and made them even more brutal. A boy in a cloak with an oilcloth wrapped round his head had managed to get the wretched woman out of the mêlée. Under the cloak, Paulin recognized the blue-black coat with crimson velvet facings; this lad was part of the medical corps. He called to him. His voice couldn't carry in that din; he urged his donkey on until he was beside him. 'Are you a doctor?'

'Yes and no.'

'An orderly?'

'Junior assistant to a medical officer.'

'My captain needs you.'

'If it's for an officer . . .'

'It's to stop him shouting at me.'

'I know a little about powders and ointments, I've seen some bleedings . . .'

'That's the spirit!'

The junior assistant seemed a bit simple but willing enough; besides, the colour of his uniform indicated his occupation, so that would probably do for the captain. Which it did. The boy took off his cloak and headgear, bent over the novice, took a small mirror out of his double bag and put it in front of her mouth. D'Herbigny watched him, scowling; he liked quick results.

'I think . . .' began the boy.

'I want certainties!'

'I think she's dead, well, she seems dead, look, her breathing, the mirror's not misted up.'

'When I'm asleep, I don't mist up any mirrors! What you're saying is impossible! What would she have died of, since you're so knowledgeable?'

'We could take her to the medical officer . . .'

'Get her back on her feet or I'll wring your neck.'

'If you wring my neck, that will make two deaths.'

There was logic to what the simpleton said. He bent over the bed of furs again, studied the whites of her eyes, her complexion: 'It looks as if she's been poisoned.'

'Haven't you been watching her the whole time?' the captain asked Paulin.

'Yes, apart from when I made her lunch.'

'What did you give her?'

'A piece of the mare's liver.'

'That's the last thing you should have done! That meat was half rotten!'

'We didn't have anything else . . .'

'Where there's poison, there's antidote,' the simpleton added.

'Administer your potion,' the captain whispered in a broken voice.

'Ah, you'd need a priest for that. They know those things, secret herbs, healing prayers, icons that work wonders, it was my medical officer who told me so.'

For a moment d'Herbigny began to believe that the dead could rise again, that magic did have power, that sickness dissolved in incense smoke. The Emperor had authorized the resumption of religious worship to mollify the Russians who had remained in Moscow. Orthodox priests were conducting services again. When the captain went downstairs to order his men to find one of these clergymen officiating in a church not taken over by the army, he learned that all the nuns had died of poisoning. It wasn't the mare's liver that had killed Anissia.

*

Along the interminable corridors of the Kremlin, sentries guarded every door, although *guard* is probably an exaggeration. These grenadiers in fur-lined coats had swapped their belts for cashmere shawls and their bearskins for wrinkled Kalmuk caps; the least inebriated of them leant against the wall, the others sat and fished around in crystal vases with long wooden spoons, eating exotic jams which gave them a thirst and taking swig after swig of a robust brandy. Their weapons lay about amongst the jars and empty bottles. Sebastian no longer paid any attention to this everyday sight. As he was making his way towards the staff mess, he met some Russians in civilian clothes with armbands of red and white knotted ribbons; a semblance of organization was being put in place: the Emperor had re-established a town council, distributing posts among the merchants and townsmen who had refused to flee with Rostopchin.

Aides de camp, officers, doctors and paymasters now met for meals in an immense room with walls hung with red velvet and a central pillar supporting the arches that divided it in four.

'Monsieur le secrétaire!'

Henri Beyle, a steaming plate in front of him, waved to Sebastian to join him. 'I've kept you a place next to me.'

'What are you eating?'

'A fricassée.'

'Of what?'

'It tastes like rabbit . . .'

'It must be cat.'

'It's not so bad cooked in spices and with a glass of Malaga.'

Sebastian helped himself to beans but declined the fricassée. The two men discussed the merits of *Letters to my Son* by Lord Chesterfield, the book stolen from a library in Moscow, and then turned to Italian painting, of which Beyle admitted to be writing a history. They argued about Canaletto.

'I know why you like Canaletto, Monsieur le secrétaire. His Venetian cityscapes resemble stage sets and, I might add, with his father and brother, when he was young, he did paint backdrops, balustrades and breathtaking perspectives. On canvas, I find the result a little stiff.'

'Monsieur Beyle! Stiff? There is a perfection . . .'

'Yes?'

Sebastian had fallen silent, his eyes riveted on a group of new arrivals, who were being shown in by Bausset, the prefect of the palace.

'Those civilians appear to captivate you.'

'I know them a little . . .'

'What are they doing within our walls?'

'They are a troupe of French actors. They were performing in Moscow.'

'The girls, well I do declare! Not bad, *mon cher*. Hasn't a theatre lover like you, even to the extent of Canaletto's pictures – haven't you tried your luck?'

'Oh, Monsieur Beyle, I leave the floor to you.'

'Thank you, but I've spent a good deal of time with that sort, and in a few days I have to leave for Smolensk to set up reserve stores there. Then Danzig. I'm not exactly thrilled by the prospect.'

'Well, I envy you. Why stay in Moscow?'

'My toothaches plague me unexpectedly, especially at night, I sleep badly, I have fevers . . .'

'But a hearty appetite!' Sebastian answered laughing, hardly knowing whether this laughter applied to his friend Beyle or to the troupe's having reappeared safe and sound.

When they had finished their meal, they got up together. The actors' table was close to the door, but Sebastian assumed a detached expression and pretended not to see them.

'Monsieur Sebastian!'

Ornella had called him, he couldn't slip away now.

'Mystery-maker,' his friend whispered in his ear. 'I'll leave you to bill and coo, but this time I'm the envious one.'

Sebastian held his breath, turned around, pretended to be surprised, went over, took a chair and sat down, smiling. He had to listen to Mme Aurore recount their misadventures, the looting of their chalet, how they'd escaped death by fire, then by thirst and then how, by a pure stroke of luck, the King of Naples had saved them and put them up at his headquarters in the Razunonski mansion. With a feigned air of distraction, Sebastian observed Mlle Ornella. She had let down her curly black hair, which fell to the shoulders of her satin dress. When it was her turn to talk, he noticed that she lisped slightly, just enough for it to be charming.

'The King of Naples adores the theatre, Monsieur Sebastian. He behaves as if he's always on stage.'

'He has uniforms slashed with gold,' continued Catherine, the redhead, 'diamond earrings, a whole wagon for his perfumes and his pomades, another for his wardrobe...'

The Great Vialatoux, who was wearing a Neapolitan uniform, couldn't contain himself anymore; he interrupted his colleagues to give his impersonation of Murat.

'He told us,' Vialatoux adopted a swagger, '"In my palazzo in Naples, I used to have all Talma's parts performed solely for me and I'd declaim them— El Cid, Tancred..."'

'So why have you come back to the Kremlin?' Sebastian interrupted.

The Emperor wanted life in Moscow to return to normal. He was sending for opera singers, famous musicians, and, since he had actors to hand, he was asking them to perform their repertoire to divert the army.

'What are you going to play?'

'*The Game of Love and Chance*, Monsieur Sebastian.'

'I'll be there applauding. I can see you as Silvia, and your friend as the maid.'

'And then we will put on *The Cid*,' said the juvenile lead, '*Zaire, The Marriage of Figaro* . . .'

Prefect Bausset had offered them a genuine auditorium, minus its chandeliers, in the Posniakov mansion. They had only three days to organize costumes, but the military administration had gathered together all sorts of fabric, hangings, velvet and gold braid in the Church of Ivan in the Kremlin, which promised to be enough, draped or sewn. So they had come to the palace to choose. Sebastian had to get back to his office; when he left, Ornella and Catherine laughed as they recited some Marivaux which they thought apposite. '*I have noticed that a handsome man is often vain*,' Ornella said as Silvia.

'*Oh, he is wrong to be vain but right to be handsome*,' Catherine answered as Lisette.

The Great Vialatoux, his nose buried in a plate emblazoned with the Tsar's coat of arms, greedily tucked into his cat fricassée; he went back for second helpings three times.

*

A detachment of dragoons was escorting a line of tumbrils loaded with the bodies of the nuns, who had been sewn into canvas bags. They almost looked like shadows, the cold fog clogging up the early October morning was so dense. Captain d'Herbigny led the way to the cemetery. He hadn't wanted to mix Anissia up with the other sisters; he'd wrapped her in Indian silk and was carrying her in front of him, on his horse's withers. He was as pale as the novice, sadness etching new lines in his weather-beaten face. Where did the poison come from? Who had procured it or used it? And how? These women's religion forbade suicide, so what then? Cossacks had been sighted in Moscow; they were on the prowl, gathering information, watching, confident of support. But poison wasn't a weapon they used, this didn't seem like them, and they wouldn't have been able to get into the convent either, let alone the former Mother Superior's cell. D'Herbigny couldn't make head or tail of it. No ready explanation? Well, it couldn't be helped. He stuck to the facts. He had so often killed with his own hands, but the brutal death of this Russian girl, who he knew nothing about, had hit him hard. He'd planned to take her to Normandy, since they were bound to leave this filthy city one day or another. He would have taught her French and treated her like a daughter, there, that was it, like a daughter; she would have watched him grow old peacefully.

They reached the cemetery. Fires glowed red through the now-thinning fog. Large numbers of poor, homeless Muscovites had taken refuge among the graves, cobbling together shelters and lighting puny fires to cook roots, warm themselves and ward off the wolves and stray dogs that were turning vicious with hunger.

In silence, the riders began digging a large pit in an alley. The captain laid Anissia on a moss-covered gravestone. When the pit was finished, which seemed to take an eternity, they tipped up the tumbrils; then they shovelled back the earth. D'Herbigny had sat down next to Anissia's body. He uncovered her waxy face, undid the gold cross she was wearing round her neck and clenched it in his fist. After a while, he realized he couldn't hear the shovels anymore; his troopers had finished filling in the pit and stood waiting, in silence. The captain contemplated the muddy ground for a long time, and then looked up. 'Bonet, and two others, lift that for me.'

He pointed to a white marble tombstone.

'It's already occupied, Captain.'

'You don't really expect me to chuck Aniushka in that pit, do you? She'll be better off here. It's horribly cold in winter in this cursed country, nothing's as good as a nice vault.'

Bonet obeyed, thinking his superior officer was cracked in the head. They cleared away the earth, until the iron of their shovels struck coffins.

'That's enough,' said the captain.

He took Anissia in his arms. Bonet helped him lay her gently in the grave. With his boot, d'Herbigny replaced the earth; he told them to put the slab back.

'Anyone remember any prayers? No?'

He tightened his saddle girth and mounted up.

*

In the evenings, an usher lit a pair of candles on the Emperor's desk. 'He never stops working!' the soldiers would exclaim, enraptured, when they looked up at the illuminated window. In fact he spent large parts of his days asleep, or lying on a sofa, browsing through his volumes of Plutarch. He often took up Voltaire's *Charles XII*, a little gilt-edged morocco volume, which he would close, sighing, 'Charles was determined to brave the seasons...' He shut his eyes, dozed. What did he dream about? The news was unfavourable: a coalition of Russians and Swedes had just forced Gouvion-Saint-Cyr to evacuate the city of Polotsk, their wait was growing longer and longer, the Tsar was holding his tongue. Caulaincourt had refused to go to St

Petersburg to solicit a peace in which he had never believed. Lauriston, more biddable, had managed to contact Kutuzov and extract a verbal armistice from him. Would he keep his word? The Emperor was wavering, giving impossible orders: 'Buy twenty thousand horses, have two months of forage brought in!' Buy the horses from who? Bring in the forage from where? Another time he told Count Daru, the Intendant General, of his plan to attack Kutuzov.

'Too late, sire,' said the count. 'He has had time to re-form his army.'

'We haven't?'

'No.'

'Well?'

'Let us retrench ourselves in Moscow for the winter, there's no other solution.'

'But the horses?'

'Those we can't feed, I shall have salted.'

'The men?'

'They'll live in the cellars.'

'And then?'

'Your reinforcements will arrive as soon as the snow melts.'

'What will Paris think? What will happen in Europe without me?'

Daru had bowed his head without replying, but the Emperor seemed to take his advice. The investment works were stepped up; labourers demolished mosques to leave the ramparts clear, gunners set up thirty guns on the Kremlin's towers and drained the ponds to recover a hundred thousand cannonballs dumped there by the Russians; surgeons were sent for from Paris. One morning, at around two o'clock, Napoleon was dictating instructions for

Berthier: his mind was clear and he spoke fluently as he strolled back and forth, his hands clasped behind his back, wearing his white flannel dressing gown. He demanded of the major general that the men have three months' supplies of potatoes, six of sauerkraut and six of brandy. Then, as if he had a very detailed map of the city and his forces in front of him, he said, 'The depots in which these will be stored are, for I Corps, the convent of the 13th Light Brigade; for IV Corps, the jails on the Petersburg road; for III Corps, the convent near the powder magazines; for the artillery and the cavalry of the Guard, the Kremlin … Three convents have to be selected on the roads out of Moscow to make entrenched posts . . .'

The Emperor knew the country but still he refused to believe that his army was short of provisions. Little matter. Next day the weather was mild, all his go had returned and he took lunch with Duroc and Prince Eugène.

'Berthier?'

'In his apartments, sire,' replied Duroc.

'Isn't he hungry?'

'You warmed his ears this morning: *Not only are you a good-for-nothing but you actually do me harm!*'

'Because he is incapable of finding any bloody sauerkraut in the land of the cabbage. Can't he stand being hauled over the coals anymore, the old girl? Old girl, that's it! It's no coincidence he took the Tsarina's apartments!'

The two guests forced themselves to smile as the Emperor laughed until he cried. He wiped his eyes with the corner of the tablecloth and became serious again; gulping down a mouthful of beans, he abruptly changed the subject. 'What is the most glorious death?'

'Charging the Cossacks!' Prince Eugène cried passionately, holding his cutlet by the bone.

'Which is what awaits us,' added Duroc.

'I would like to be carried off by a cannonball during battle, but I shall die in my bed like an idiot.'

Then they spoke of the great deaths of Antiquity, those who took poison, who died laughing, who committed suicide by holding their breath, who were stabbed. His Majesty often looked for forebears in Plutarch; he shuddered at the death of Sulla, that general without fortune, rank or land, who, with the army's support, lived to govern Rome and command the world. Like Napoleon, he had to control an immense empire; like Napoleon, he interfered in his citizens' private lives, legislated heavily, struck coins bearing his own likeness. His wife Caecilia belonged to the aristocracy, like the Empress Marie-Louise. The parallels impressed the Emperor, but Sulla's end, no, not at any price: 'Can you see me rotting like him? Can you see me surrounded by actresses and flute players, drinking and gorging myself as swarms of maggots ooze out of my corrupted flesh until it bursts? Puoah!'

'Plutarch's account is very exaggerated, sire,' said Prince Eugène.

'My destiny is so like his . . .'

'Or Alexander the Great's,' suggested Duroc, who knew the Emperor's inclinations and dreams.

'Ah! India . . .'

Ever since his ill-starred campaign in Egypt, Napoleon had dreamed of reaching the Ganges, like Alexander. He saw resemblances there as well. The Macedonian had launched himself eastwards with several thousand barbarians, Scythian and Iranian horsemen, Persian infantry, Illyrians from the Balkans, Thracians, untrustworthy Greek mercenaries, each with their own dialect just like the Grande Armée. He likened the Agrian javelin-carriers to his Polish lancers, the Bulgarian bandits to the Spanish battalion, the Cretans with goat's horn bows to his regiment from eastern Prussia . . .

'We could march on India,' he went on, looking at the ceiling.

'Are you really considering it, sire?' Duroc asked anxiously. 'How long will letters from Paris take?'

'How many months to get there?' wondered Eugène.

'I've consulted the maps. From Astrakhan you cross the Caspian and reach Astrabad in ten days. From there, a month and half to the Indus . . .'

*

The auditorium set up in a wing of the Posniakov mansion was like a genuine theatre à l'italienne, with two curving rows of boxes, stalls and an orchestra pit. Chandeliers from the Kremlin hung over the stage without a set; the troupe would play against a backdrop of tapestries, with a few pieces of furniture for props. A row of paper lanterns served as footlights. The bandsmen of the Guard, sitting on chairs, were preparing to improvise pieces of their choice to emphasize theatrical effects or provide links between scenes; admittedly they weren't used to this sort of music, but it passed the time between parades. The officers and civilian staff filled the boxes; the soldiers sat in the stalls or stood, leaning against the pillars. Drums rolled to drown out the hubbub, and the Great Vialatoux stepped forward dressed as an aristocratic fop, his face powdered with talc; he gestured, silence fell, and he declaimed:

'Behold the French within your gates
Bow your head, Alexander, capitulate!
This is no children's game that meanders on and on.
You swore us false, you breached our trust
We'll settle your hash in the Russian dust.
March on St Petersburg? We'll march beyond
A Grande Armée against your petty, lowly one.
For tell us, pray – where is your Napoleon, Napoleon?'

An ovation prevented him continuing. He spread his arms, bowed as low as possible and basked in his triumph, until, judging the applause was abating, he straightened up. 'Gentlemen, Mme Aurore Barsay's troupe of French actors has the honour this afternoon to perform for you *The Game of Love and Chance* by Monsieur Marivaux!'

The band struck up an imperial march, then, by the light of hundreds of candles, the comedy began to the sound of clarinets. Mlle Ornella emerged from the wings in the role of Silvia, resplendent in a braided, striped velvet skirt and a bustier cut from a chasuble which set off her bosom and naked shoulders. With a slightly forced, simpering manner, she asked: *'But tell me once again! What right had you to interfere? Why did you answer for my feelings?'*

'Because I thought your feelings in this case would be like those of everyone else.' The redheaded Catherine gave as good as she got as the maid, her apron a converted surplice, her hands on her hips and her feet in slippers.

The spectators in the boxes assumed an earnest air; in the stalls they couldn't understand a word but they stared wide-eyed at the stage: stuck-up though she may have been, this Silvia had a very fascinating neckline. At the end of a scene, the characters went behind a large Chinese screen decorated with mother-of-pearl birds, Silvia disappearing round one side, as Vialatoux burst out the other as either Orgon or Dorante – the men were playing several parts and only changing a hat or cloak each time, to the stalls' confusion. Trooper Bonet felt lost. He asked Paulin, at the back of the room, to explain the play to him.

'It's very simple,' Paulin said. 'The mistress swaps places with her maid to test the sincerity of her intended fiancé but meanwhile he's swapped places with his valet.'

'What difference does that make? Even when she's disguised as a marchioness, the maid still talks like a maid.'

'It's for comic effect.'

'Well, it doesn't make me laugh.'

The audience had started shouting and stamping, because Ornella, dressed as the maid now, had just split her blouse at the back.

'Bravo!'

'The blouse! The blouse!' the grenadiers chanted.

'You're much better off without it, my chick!'

Very dignified, Ornella continued saying her lines as if nothing had happened. Equally imperturbable, Vialatoux as Dorante recited, '*I will leave incognito, and I will write a note to Monsieur Orgon that will explain everything.*'

Ornella, aside, that's to say facing the auditorium: '*Leave! That was not in my plan.*'

'*Do you not approve of my idea?*'

'*Well ... not wholly,*' Ornella continued as Silvia, presenting her back to the louts who clapped wildly and heckled.

'Stay like that!' an elite gendarme screamed.

'Rip it a bit more!'

The final scene ended in uproar and Ornella didn't come back to take a bow with the rest of the troupe. In the wings, she burst into tears in Mme Aurore's arms.

'Come now,' said the manageress. 'It's not the first time.'

'I feel ashamed!'

'Go and take a bow, they're asking for you. Can you hear them?'

'Alas, yes . . .'

Mme Aurore pushed her towards the stage. On her entry the applause became louder than ever. Looking at that mocking, bawdy audience, she noticed a pale young man in a stage box who was smiling at her. It was Sebastian Roque. Since the weather had turned out fine, the Emperor had taken the opportunity to inspect the building work he had ordered. Baron Fain had therefore allowed his clerk to work a half-day and he had leapt at the chance to go to the theatre. Reassured by his presence, emboldened in fact, Ornella advanced toward the footlights, tore off her blouse and bowed to the right, then to the left. Amid wild cheers, shakos, bearskins, caps and tartar hats flew into the air, as high as the balconies. The actress whipped those louts into a frenzy, thrusting out her breasts, showing herself off; to a chorus of boos, Vialatoux draped his long cloak over her shoulders, wrapped it around her and led her off. 'You're mad! What if they'd climbed on the stage?'

'Their officers would have stepped in.'

'Are you joking?'

Unaware of the risk that she had taken, Ornella imagined that Sebastian would never have let those oafs come near her or paw her skin. She exaggerated the power of the Emperor's undersecretary. The poor fellow wouldn't have stood a chance of bringing a garrison on heat under control.

*

In the week that followed, Sebastian didn't have the chance to return to the theatre. He regretted not having congratulated Mlle Ornella, who, despite his resolutions, he still had feelings for, but he had been swept out of the theatre by the rowdy crowd and then found himself being whisked back to the Kremlin by officers in a barouche.

Snow fell for three days but didn't settle; Napoleon used this as an opportunity to attend to matters of Empire without leaving his apartments. He displayed terrifying amounts of energy, seemingly much less troubled by his stomach, overwhelming his secretaries with work, not giving them a minute's respite, dictating letters to his ministers in Paris or the Duke of Bassano who, as Governor of Lithuania, secured the liaison with Austria and Prussia. 'Have oxen sent from Grodno to Smolensk, and uniforms.' He re-routed a Württemberg regiment, entirely re-wrote the regulations of the Comédie-Française, established procedures for convoys of the wounded, the first of whom were being evacuated from Moscow in private carriages, and then grew emotional as he wrote to the Empress. 'The little king gives you, I hope, great happiness.' All of which was said in a furious rush, in fragments, different letters to different secretaries who had to guess the recipient from the tone, while he gave orders – the silverware in the Kremlin's churches was to be melted down and the ingots deposited in the Army Treasury – received visitors, listened very little and issued a great deal of commands. As soon as

the weather grew milder, he sent the sappers of his Guard
to climb the dome of Ivan's tower; he wanted to bring its
great gilded iron cross back as a trophy. Sebastian had
watched the dangerous undertaking from his window. The
sappers had looped chains around the cross and pulled for
a long time, until it swayed, buckled and finally fell, taking
part of the scaffolding with it. The ground shook as it
landed and smashed into three pieces. It was Sebastian's
only distraction. Exhausted, he took notes, copied them out,
then copied them out again as fast as his fingers could
move, slept little, dreamed even less and ate in a rush at his
desk. He had been living in Moscow for a month now.

On 18 October, the Emperor was reviewing Marshal
Ney's infantry in one of the courtyards when one of Murat's
dispatch riders appeared, leapt from his horse and ran up
to announce, panting, 'Sire, in the plain . . .'

'What in the plain?'

'Thousands of Russians have attacked the II Cavalry
Corps.'

'What about the armistice?'

'They captured some of the King of Naples' grooms
yesterday.'

'And?'

'The King wrote to the commander of the enemy outposts to ask for their return.'

'In what terms?'

'Very strong.'

'Be specific.'

'If the grooms were not returned, the truce would be
broken.'

'And?'

'The truce was broken.'

'Had no one taken any precautions? Must I be everywhere!'

'The Russians were hiding in a wood on higher ground.'

'And?'

'The moment our men went foraging, they attacked.'

'How have we responded?'

'Badly, very badly, sire.'

'Be specific.'

'General Sebastiani's artillery is destroyed.'

'Prisoners?'

'Probably more than two thousand.'

'Dead?'

'Too many.'

'And Murat? Where is Murat?'

'Leading the charge.'

*

Guiding himself by the muffled sounds of combat, Murat
was galloping on frost-hardened ground, his long corkscrew
curls flying in the wind, a pale sun picking out his diamond
earrings, the gold braid of his dolman, the frogging of his
pelisse slung from his shoulder. He led a detachment of
carabineers. Only the brass of their cuirasses and helmets
with scarlet horsehair crests gleamed, flashes of colour that
were all there was to be seen in a blanket of mist that
swallowed up their white uniforms. They shot out in the
enemy's rear, sabres drawn, yelling. The Russians had
operated a circular movement to cut off Sebastiani from the
Moscow road; they weren't expecting this violent attack
from behind. The first in line were sabred before they
could even turn about, the others fled. 'Fire on the rabble!'
shouted Murat. His men let their sabres hang from their

wrists, shouldered their carbines and brought down the runaways closest to them with a ringing salvo, and then gave chase.

Murat didn't think. He attacked. Capable of throwing his exhausted cavalry against ramparts and small forts, he was a man of lightning raids and showpiece actions. His subordinates knew it. At Borodino they had delayed relaying his orders to the squadrons so that he would realize his mistakes and change his mind; this deliberate procrastination had saved a lot of lives. A genuine tactician, cold-shouldered by the Emperor, Davout constantly challenged his decisions and hated him; he accused Murat of leading his troops to their deaths for no purpose, of having lost the cavalry to show himself off to advantage. Yet the Emperor always took Murat's side, his impulsive brother-in-law whose ardour and chaos he loved. The Russians admired him and dreaded him — look at him on horseback, lithe as a Cossack, outrunning bullets and cannonballs, always safe, magical, mad. He thought himself a real king, no different to other kings, this grocer's assistant from Saint-Céré. He tried to forget that the crowns distributed by Napoleon were only toys, that these kingdoms were the equivalent of sub-prefectures in a vast Empire. Murat had wanted the throne of Westphalia, of Poland, of Switzerland, of Spain, but no, he had to be kept in check, and when he was given Naples he fell ill. The very blonde Caroline Bonaparte, his wife whom he mistrusted, always intriguing in her white satin chamber, had also found this crown a size too small for his head, but it couldn't be helped, the Neapolitans adored the pair of them. Napoleon had summoned Murat to Russia, dazzling him with the promise of a hundred thousand cavalry, and the King hadn't known how to refuse. But could he have anyway? It was only on horse-back, in his theatrical uniforms, that he truly felt alive.

Pursued by his carabineers, the Russian cuirassiers were crossing a river, throwing up fans of water. Murat halted on the bank as if at a border. To his left he heard cannon: smoke was rising above Winkovo, where his vanguard was encamped. He led his cavalry there, and saw Asiatic Cossacks in brightly coloured clothes, a great throng bristling with lances.

Murat spurred his horse; the impact was brutal. A pike tore his pelisse, he caught it in mid-thrust, pulled the Tartar in the pointed cap towards him, guiding his horse with his knees, ran him through, slashed left and right, barged riders aside and forced his way past. Again and again he charged until the enemy were driven back towards the woods or the river, leaving behind them a devastated camp, half burnt to the ground, unusable cannon, equipment reduced to cinders, men dead and dying and the wounded being hoisted onto four-wheeled carts with their thighs shattered or their shoulders blown off. Sebastiani had survived. Murat didn't dare accuse him, even if he did spend all his time in slippers reading the Italian poets. He had been just as negligent as his general; he should have ordered patrols, made sure they couldn't be taken by surprise. He had known for a week that Orthodox priests were raising peasant militias, that there was a ring of Russian armies surrounding Moscow, keeping their distance. None of his cavalry was left. It didn't exist anymore.

*

That same day, two baggage-masters appeared at the Convent of the Nativity. They were transporting their heavy registers in a charabanc. One of them stepped down, brushed dust from the sleeve of his frock coat and asked the dragoons guarding the entrance, 'Which brigade?'

'Saint-Sulpice, 4th Squadron.'

'How many able-bodied?'

'About a hundred.'

'Precisely?'

'I don't know. Eighty-eight or seven or six.'

'Saddle-horses?'

'Ninety.'

'That gives us four extra.'

'So you say. You'd better check, at least.'

'No time.'

The second baggage-master, on his bench, had opened one of the registers and was running his finger along the lines. He made a note in pencil. Captain d'Herbigny had heard the creak of cartwheels and came out to ask what was happening.

'We're registering, Captain,' said the first baggage-master.

'We're taking your horses that are of no use to you,' added the second.

'But they will be of use!'

'The artillery is short.'

'These horses don't pull caissons!'

'They will though, sir,' retorted the first baggage-master.

'Have you got any wagons?' asked the second.

'No.'

'Barouches, gigs, britzkas?'

'Those neither. Just baggage carts.'

'Ah, carts! Those have to be declared,' ordered the first.

'And given a registered number,' said the second.

'Why the devil?'

'Every conveyance without a registered number will be confiscated, by order of the Emperor.'

'What's the use of giving these old carts a registered number?'

'To assign you your quota of wounded.'

'I'm not an ambulance!'

'Every conveyance without wounded on board will be burnt.'

'Explain yourselves, for goodness' sake, or I'll whittle your ears to a point!'

'We're going, Captain,' said the first baggage master.

'We're leaving Moscow tomorrow,' specified the second, closing his register.

Four

MARCH OR DIE

THERE WAS BRIGHT SUNSHINE on 19 October. The army was delighted to be leaving Moscow. In ragged columns, their tattered uniforms hidden under Siberian fox furs and silk cravats, Davout's depleted regiments were the first to leave by the old Kaluga road. 'We're going down to the fertile provinces of the south,' the soldiers told one another, and they believed it. Hour after hour the massive exodus readied itself. The fifteen thousand serviceable vehicles in the city had been requisitioned and distributed by rank. There were the generals' new carriages and berlines loaded with their voluminous baggage, the administration's barouches and fourgons, little Russian wagons crammed with provisions, carts stacked with booty, barrows full of jewels, benches on wheels with people astride them, little horses harnessed by ropes to ramshackle little rattletraps, tired old nags pulling the guns or caissons, all jumbled together amidst a tremendous uproar of shouting valets, torrents of abuse in twenty languages, draught horses' bells and the crack of whips. Civilians were swelling the throng by their thousands: women and whimpering children, rich foreigners, peasants on foot, European merchants without a home or business anymore, the usual adventuresses prostituting themselves in an army's train. At the gates of Moscow, the gendarmes were checking the wounded, who had been divided into categories by the medical officers; they were only taking the least seriously wounded and the non-infectious who were expected to recover within a week. The rest were crammed into the Foundlings' Hospital, left to the fate that vermin, dysentery, gangrene and the Russians had in store for them.

Sebastian and Baron Fain were sharing their staff berline with Sautet, the bookseller. He took up a fair amount of space, this character, what with his belly and his family, which comprised a lady with her hair up in a chignon who sniffled constantly behind the handkerchief she held over her nose, a tall young girl and a fidgety black dog. For wounded, they had been allocated a one-legged voltigeur, with his crutches and knapsack, and a broken-down lieutenant who had been propped up on bales of peas. Their baggage rose from the trunk to the roof, secured by straps, and the postilion had had to allow a third wounded up on his box seat, a feverish hussar in a wolf-skin cloak. Wedged against a window in direct sunshine, the bookseller mopped the beads of sweat on his forehead and remarked morosely, 'At least we won't be cold.'

'We will be in Smolensk before winter,' Baron Fain replied.

'I hope so ...'

'His Majesty has planned everything.'

'I hope so!'

'Twenty days' march, that's all, by the southern route.'

'If it doesn't freeze too hard ...'

'According to the records for the last twenty years, I can

assure you that in November the thermometer never goes below six degrees.'

'I hope so.'

'Oh, stop doubting!'

'I shall doubt if I please, my lord. Why aren't we leaving, what are we waiting for?'

'The Emperor.'

'The army has been moving out since five o'clock this morning, a horde of civilians has started after them, whereas we just sit here and rot away!' He looked at his fob watch. 'It is already almost midday!'

'You are forgetting your good fortune.'

'Ah, now there's a subject. I'm ruined...'

'But alive.'

'Oh, thank you.'

'Listen, Monsieur Sautet, you are with your family in the retinue of the Emperor's household, which the Baden grenadiers will protect the entire way. Behind us, after the carriage carrying the maps and my office's documents, are our supply wagons with bread, wine, linen and silverware. Other people are leaving without very much at all, you should consider yourself lucky. However, if you'd rather stay in Moscow...'

'Heavens, no! I am French as well, and the Russians can't be that fond of us any more. What a mess!'

'Stop your jeremiads, if you please, or I shall forcibly set you down!'

They were arguing before setting off. Sebastian scowled in his corner. The bookseller was right; if it hadn't been for this expedition, Moscow would still be the delightful capital city people came to from all over the world. At least he didn't have too much luggage, just the sabre he had bought from Poissonnard, his books, a little linen and a handful of diamonds he had stolen from the drawer of a dressing table in the Kremlin.

At that moment the Emperor got into his berline and sat down next to Murat, wearing the red uniform of the Polish lancers. Finally they were going to leave.

*

From the top of the nearest hill, sitting astride a Cossack horse that was sturdier than his previous one and rough-shod for the ice, d'Herbigny looked bitterly back at Moscow, at the domes mutilated by the loss of their crosses, the towers, the blackened roofs, the minarets rising from a bed of ashes. The Seminov monastery next to the Kaluga gate was on fire; the rations housed in it had had to be destroyed rather than handed to the enemy, apparently, because the administration thought they had enough food as it was, and in a few days they would be resupplying to the south. An incredible throng was pouring out onto the plain and slowly spreading out; a chaotic, massive tribe, barbaric in its variety, weighed down by plunder, streaming endlessly out of the city and overflowing the road on both sides by several kilometres. Amongst the currents in this noisy tide, the captain spotted the chestnut uniforms of the Portuguese cavalry: they were escorting a column of Russian prisoners – townsfolk, peasants, some spies perhaps, a handful of soldiers; they would serve, if need be, as bargaining counters or shields. He also saw the Imperial convoy caught up in the crush, the Emperor's green berline, the fifty carriages of his train, the precisely dressed ranks of the regiments of the Old Guard in parade uniform; to their knapsacks and the straps of their cartridge pouches the grenadiers had attached little bottles of brandy and loaves of white bread baked in the Kremlin, and they were singing.

Closer to, on the hillside, the wheels of the overloaded wagons were sinking into the sand; officers' wives were taking coachmen's places and adopting their repertoire of curses. Gunners were bending their backs to help their emaciated horses pull the cannon to the top. The dragoons' carts had got stuck for the umpteenth time. They were standing about, wasting time, and each separate incident delayed the whole.

Trooper Bonet came up to the captain. Ever since the latter had made him sergeant in poor Martinon's place (Lieutenant Berton having vanished into thin air), Bonet had been looking to take the initiative.

'Sir, couldn't we lighten our baggage?'

'Oaf! You'll be happy enough when you get your share in France.'

Bonet reflected, puffing out his chest to show off the beautiful silk waistcoat he had made from a Chinese dress, and then, as if the idea had just come to him, he suggested, 'What about the tea in the first cart? We've got a whole shipment of it . . .'

'It's my tea, Bonet. It'll fetch a good price and it's not the heaviest thing we're carrying. Honestly, we're not going to dump all our provisions! Nor unload and load up again at every hold-up!'

'The chests of Peruvian bark?'

'They'll come in useful.'

'The pictures?'

'They don't weigh anything rolled up. And that stuff's worth a fortune in Paris! Should we dump the gold coins and all the precious trinkets we found in the churches as well?'

'The wounded . . .' his servant Paulin said distractedly, looking at his donkey, which was tearing at the leaves of a dry bush.

'The wounded?'

'We're carrying a pretty heavy load, that's true,' said the sergeant.

'And we won't be checked any more, sir.'

'I don't value men by their weight!' answered the captain, bright red. 'They need us.'

'We could put them in with the others, couldn't we?'

'They're full to the gunwales, if not fuller!'

'But we just have to tell the civilians it's an order . . .'

'Take down the wounded!' ordered the captain.

Two dragoons climbed up on the wagons to lay hold of the groaning infantrymen squeezed between the chests of plunder. They picked them up under the arms and passed them down to their comrades, who put them in a heap on the ground in full view of everyone. While some of the troopers tried to impose this extra load on whichever civilians they could, others dismantled the sides of the carts and laid the planks in front of the wheels trapped in the sandy ruts. Some pushed, others attached ropes and pulled, and the rest whipped the mules with their leather belts. Not far away, groups of soldiers and merchants in frock coats were trying the same method to free their stranded carriages. A supply wagon tipped over, a library of gilt-edged books was sent flying, which a bawling officer protected from the hooves and wheels. When the dragoons' lead cart was moving again at the mules' exasperating pace, the captain grew concerned about the wounded.

'Did you manage to find room for them?'

'Course, sir.'

'That's a good job.' It wasn't true, d'Herbigny suspected, but he pretended to believe his men. They had to push on. After this there would be no more hills, and less soft sand, but a stony steppe instead and narrow gorges which this horde would have trouble passing through.

*

A thin, cold rain began on the first evening and the multitude settled itself on the plain as best they could. The Emperor took shelter on the first floor of a wretched stone manor house, with the members of his household. Baron Fain and Sebastian left Sautet in the berline.

'And we're going to spend the night in this carriage, are we?' the bookseller cursed.

'Squeeze up to keep warm.'

'What are we to eat?'

'Your provisions.'

'You promised that we would lack nothing!'

'Don't you have any provisions?'

'A little, yes, you know we do.'

'Well, what are you complaining about?'

'Those two! We're not going to get a wink of sleep with their moaning and groaning!'

He was talking about the wounded, the voltigeur and the Dutch officer who were tossing and turning on the bales of peas. The bookseller became more insistent. 'For Heaven's sake, space is not something that manor house is short of!'

'The Emperor's palace? We don't allow entry to civilians.'

'A palace, that?'

'You should know, Monsieur Sautet,' the baron answered irritably, 'that that is always the name given to where His Majesty stays, whether it is a hut, a tent or an inn.'

When Sebastian and the Baron had left, the bookseller looked in his double bags and took out a smoked sausage, a bottle and some biscuits. The biscuits had not weathered the journey too well and were mostly crumbs. The family shared the food in silence. A grenadier knocked at the window and Sautet opened it. A cold breeze made them shiver. The soldier was carrying a cooking pot which delighted the travellers. 'Ah, they are taking care of us after all.'

'Any wounded?' asked the grenadier.

'Two in the berline.'

Another grenadier with a ladle filled two bowls with a steaming, clear broth which he held out to Sautet.

'I'll see to this,' the bookseller said. 'Ouch! It's boiling!'

He gave one bowl to his wife, hunched over the other and drank the broth in long draughts.

'Hey! It's only for the wounded,' the grenadier snapped.

The black dog started barking, which caught the grenadiers' attention.

'Quiet, Dmitry!' scolded Mme Sautet.

'What's wrong with our dog? Why are you looking at him like that?'

'Very tempting,' said one of the grenadiers, and slammed the door to go and deliver his soup to other wounded.

The bookseller gulped another mouthful with a grimace. 'Revolting!'

'No doubt, my friend,' said his wife, 'but it is hot.'

'I wasn't referring to the gruel, Mme Sautet. Didn't you hear that beanpole's remark about Dmitry? Tempting!'

He finished his bowl. She drank some more and then passed hers on to her daughter who inhaled the bitter fumes. It was an unpleasant-tasting barley soup that the wounded didn't get a drop of. Salt being in short supply, the regiment's cook's boys had added gunpowder. The coal and sulphur separated and came to the surface as it boiled, and were then skimmed off with a ladle. The saltpetre that remained was enough to season the concoction, but it left a bad taste in the back of the throat and tied one's stomach in knots. When Sebastian returned soon after to look for a fur in the secretaries' carriages, he found Sautet squatting in the courtyard, his breeches round his knees; he was easing his bowels under a canopy.

'We were so happy in Moscow!' the bookseller complained, surprised by the secretary in that state.

'At Kaluga,' said Sebastian, lighting the fellow with his lantern, 'we'll find herds, orchards and well-stocked granaries.'

'At this speed, my poor friend, we won't be there for quite a while!'

'What danger can we be in, so close to His Majesty?'

'Catching a good bout of diarrhoea, for a start,' muttered Monsieur Sautet.

He got to his feet, pulled up his breeches, and straightened his braces. Bringing his face very close to Sebastian's, who could smell the soup on his sour breath, he said, 'I admire your confidence but I know this country. I know the steep gorges we'll have to get through, and the Nara marshes we'll have to cross – but how in Heaven's name will we be able to do that with these numbers and this disorder?'

Sebastian didn't know what to say. He turned away, shone a light into the baggage coach and, from under the mound of packages and furs, took out a lamb's wool fur-lined coat to wear under his overcoat: up in the house, the secretaries were only entitled to an icy room without panes in its windows; what little dry wood there was was reserved for the Emperor and the Guard's canteens.

They set off again in the morning. Baron Fain and his clerk were sneezing and blowing their noses as they took their places in the berline next to the bookseller and his family. Woebegone, the Sautets were drowsing under some sheepskins. One of the wounded was delirious. That day they didn't see any of the accidents that occurred in the passes – the Emperor's caravan had priority and the civilians couldn't compete with the well-organized soldiers who pushed ahead of them. But many of the carriages behind them broke a wheel and went over precipices with their passengers. Overloaded fugitives began to be seen jettisoning their surplus booty, scattering bags of pearls, icons, weapons and rolls of cloth along the road, which those following trampled on with complete indifference.

*

Crossing the marshes in damp fog took all the subsequent day. Scouts had marked out the route for the army; the baggage train stretched in single file along a precarious road, boggy in places and churned by the caissons and horses' hooves. Indistinct, mud-smeared objects floated on the surface of the quagmires either side of it. A horse kept its head above the ooze for as long as it could; it hadn't the strength to whinny before it was swallowed up. The slightest misjudgement seemed fatal, so most of the travellers had got out of their heavy coaches. Elegant women in long dresses, frightened, advanced with a thousand precautions on loose stones and between the puddles. One carried a child on her shoulders. Grooms led their draught horses on foot. Mme Aurore's actors walked in front of their covered cart on which had been painted in white letters, on the tarred drill, HIS IMPERIAL MAJESTY'S THEATRICAL COMPANY. Ornella and Catherine had covered their hats with waxed silk to keep off the rain; they held up the hems of their skirts as they walked, stumbling repeatedly and clinging to each other so as not to slip off the path. The Great Vialatoux was no longer up to declaiming, but he bewailed his plight at every step, since he was suffering from rheumatism; Mme Aurore admonished him with equal vigour.

Up ahead, just before the fog closed in, a barouche overturned and began to sink. Its passengers, German, shouted like mad for someone to throw them a rope and haul them out onto the road. A lanky figure in a fox-fur coat threw them a roll of canvas he had found in his cart and one of the Germans caught the end. As their rescuer pulled them back towards firm ground, the canvas started tearing, then ripped in two and the man fell back into the marsh.

'It's stupid throwing a bit of canvas,' a coachman said.

'Got a rope, have you?' came the angry response. 'No? We've got to make do with what we've got, haven't we!' The horses struggled in the shafts, but in a second the mud swallowed them and the barouche with a horrendous sucking sound. There were other scenes of this sort, before which everyone felt helpless.

They left the marshes a little before nightfall. The actors collapsed on ground that was sodden from the fog. To warm themselves up, some of the survivors were ripping the benches and seats out of their carriages, setting them alight and crowding round the resulting pyres. Mme Aurore followed suit, adding the wooden trunks emptied of their costumes. In return for their offer of a share of their provisions, two army stragglers were allowed to sit by the fire. They had no regiment anymore, no arms, just big shaggy cloaks that made them look like bears. One of these bears took Ornella by the shoulder and drew her closer to the fire to get a better look at her.

'Are you on the stage?'

'That's what it says on the cart.'

'That was you that burst out of your glad rags that day in Moscow, wasn't it? You don't forget something like that in a hurry.'

'What if you put on another performance just for us?' said his accomplice.

'Leave her alone!' cried Mme Aurore.

'I didn't hear anyone whistling for you, ma.'

The Great Vialatoux and the juvenile lead, curled up under a mound of furs, didn't move a muscle. Mme Aurore planted herself in front of them.

'Get these verminous tramps out of here!'

'This rheumatism has given me paralysis in my legs,' complained Vialatoux.

'They're not asking for anything that bad,' added the juvenile lead.

The manageress furiously grabbed the pan that was on the fire and tipped it over one of the soldiers' legs; he leapt to his feet, yelling, 'You're getting my goat, you mad old witch!'

'Our beans,' groaned Vialatoux.

A gigantic explosion stopped them fighting. Rooted to the spot, they instinctively turned towards Moscow. Having remained behind with the Young Guard, Marshal Mortier had just lit the touchwood fuses of the gunpowder barrels with which he had mined the Kremlin.

*

'You, my friend, will be beside yourself with joy when you see the meadows in Normandy . . .' The captain was talking to his horse and tenderly stroking its neck as he watched it eat a bundle of hay. On the sixth day the heavy rain that had been hampering their progress had stopped, and the men had taken heart again. Cutting across fields, they had rejoined the new Kaluga road, marched past forests, sped through gently rolling country and found forage and cabbages and onions to improve the soup. They had left Borowsk, the city of hazelnuts, behind, and now here they were, on a plain dotted with clumps of trees. Everything seemed peaceful. D'Herbigny saw the Emperor sitting at a table by the roadside with Berthier and the King of Naples. The chef Masquelet had prepared lentils with bacon on his mobile canteen, simmering them for a long time over a low heat. So far, no sign of any Russians or Cossacks. Except — just then two Cossacks appeared, pulled along on a leading rein by hussars taking them to the Emperor.

The captain kept still. He tried to piece together the

encounter from the gestures of the participants. The Emperor, a napkin around his neck, listened to the hussars' explanations. The King of Naples, listless since the loss of his cavalry, continued to eat his lentils with a spoon. Where did these unattached Cossacks come from? How had they been captured? Were there others? How many and where? At the very least, it meant that the Russians knew of the army's march on Kaluga. There was a roar of cannon. The Mamelukes fetched horses. The Emperor mounted up, then Caulaincourt, then Berthier, with more of a struggle, and they were about to hurry to the fighting when a trooper arrived at breakneck speed, one of Prince Eugène's Italians. He stopped in front of the Emperor and they spoke. Napoleon dismounted and went back into the relay, a simple hut where he was going to spend the night.

D'Herbigny made enquiries. Two battalions of the vanguard had taken up position in a small town; built on an escarpment, it overlooked and covered the road the army had to take. Russians, in far superior numbers, had attacked. There was an English officer among them. Would they reach the south? the captain wondered. Could they withstand troops that had had time to raise a line of defences? Candles burned in the windows of the hut. His Majesty received a constant stream of dispatch riders. No one slept. Hands outstretched before their bivouac fires, grenadiers and cavaliers awaited orders. All night, horses galloped in the plain.

A little before dawn, shadows began to move about the hut. Silhouetted in the windows, the captain made out the Mamelukes' turbans topped with brass crescents; grooms brought round saddle horses, which they presented to the grand equerry. The Emperor was outlined in the frame of

the door; he put on his cocked hat and sent an officer of his
suite to the dragoons' bivouac.

'Captain, collect a troop to escort His Majesty.'

'Did you hear that, you bunch of brigands?' cried
d'Herbigny.

His troopers leapt into the saddle. Near the hut, the
captain heard the Emperor arguing heatedly.

'It's still dark, sire,' Berthier said to him.

'I realize that, you idiot!'

'You won't see anything from the outposts.'

'It will be light when we get there.'

'Let us wait . . .'

'No! Where is Kutuzov in all this? I must see for
myself.'

Some Italians of Prince Eugène's guard charged up at
that moment and gave more detailed information. 'The
Viceroy is standing fast, sire.'

'Has he held the town?'

'He has taken it and retaken it seven times.'

'The Russian armies?'

'It looks as if they are falling back.'

'How do you know?'

'By the enemy's camps. There are only Cossacks and
peasant militias left.'

The sky began to brighten. The little band set off in a
half-light. They had barely gone a few hundred metres
before hurrahs rang out. Cossacks rushed at the drivers and
canteen-women; others whirled between the guns of the
artillery park ahead, urging on their horses with their whips;
a third party swarmed round the Emperor's escort, lowered
their lances and prepared to charge. Napoleon drew his épée
with its gold pommel in the shape of an owl. The generals

surrounding him formed a line in front of him and drew
their swords as well. D'Herbigny and his dragoons rode for
the attackers, who were so hard to make out in the panic
of that dawn. They threw themselves into the mêlée; the air
rang with the impact of sabres on the wood of the pikes and
horses clattering to the ground; riders cannoned into one
another, veered out of the way, wrenched their horses aside,
yelled and struck out. D'Herbigny found himself behind a
green-coated rider brandishing a lance; he drove his blade
in under the man's collarbone. Eventually squadrons of chasseurs and Polish lancers came to the rescue, the remaining
Cossacks turned their horses' heads and the French gave
chase. Some grenadiers helped Dr Yvan lay the wounded
out in the grass. D'Herbigny noticed they were carrying the
man he had run through.

'He doesn't look very Tartar,' he said to the acting
stretcher-bearers.

'Oh no, not him.'

'Who is it?'

'One of our major general's aides-de-camp. He'd broken
his sabre off in the guts of one of those fiends and taken a
Russian lance to carry on fighting.'

Full of pride at having saved his Emperor's life, the
captain thought that anyone could make a mistake in the
dark.

*

Around six o'clock that evening, the council of war con-
vened in a barn. Leaning his elbows on the table, his head
in his hands, without having taken off either his overcoat
or his hat, Napoleon gloomily studied the maps unrolled
before him. Murat had thrown himself on a bench by the

wall and put his plumed cap down near the candlestick. The other marshals stood waiting for the Emperor to decide which route to take. He had spent the day reconnoitring the town in which his battalions had fought with fixed bayonets, except that it wasn't a town anymore, it was more like a field after the stubble had been burned off; not a single house had withstood the Russian cannon, nor even the forests flanking them to the top of the hill. The lines of bodies roughly indicated the street plan; only the church was still recognizable, down below, near the bridge over the river. Prince Eugène had shown him the place where General Delzons had been killed by three bullets . . .

Eventually the Emperor said, 'Kutuzov has pulled his armies back, his baggage is slowing him down, he has lost thousands of men, now is the moment to rout him.'

'Perhaps he is merely changing position, sire . . .'

'If we attack now, we will open the southern route.'

'With what troops, sire?'

'We have all we need! I've seen Kutuzov's dead, do you hear! I've seen them! Most are young recruits in grey jackets who've only been serving two months and have no idea how to fight. His infantry? Only the front rank is made up of real soldiers. Behind them? Those youngsters, moujiks, peasants armed with pikes, militiamen levied in the capital . . .'

'Sire, we have just lost at least two thousand men, and how many wounded are we going to take in this pursuit? Let us return us quickly as possible to Smolensk before the cold of winter sets in.'

'The weather is superb,' the Emperor declared. 'It will hold for another week and by then we will be under cover.'

'In Kaluga?'

'We will rest there, resupply, dispatch reinforcements to meet us there . . .'

'Winter can come overnight, sire.'

'A week, I tell you!'

'Let's hurry,' Murat suggested. 'By forced march, we'll be in Smolensk before the week is out.'

'By forced march . . .' Davout echoed ironically. 'Through devastated country and on an empty stomach? Because, naturally, the King of Naples is suggesting we go back the way we came!'

'It's the quickest!'

'What about you, what do you suggest?' the Emperor curtly asked Davout.

'Here, towards Juchnow, by the middle road,' answered the marshal, a pair of round spectacles on the tip of his nose, bending over the map.

'Waste of time!' said Murat.

'This region, at least, has not seen any fighting and we'll find the provisions there that we are starting to run short of.'

'That's enough shouting!' said Napoleon, sweeping the maps off the table with his sleeve. 'It is for me to choose.'

'We await your instructions, sire.'

'Tomorrow!'

They were leaving on this note of indecision when the Emperor detained the major general.

'Berthier, what do you think?'

'We are no longer capable of doing battle.'

'I'm right, though, I know it. Kutuzov! Just one push and he'd fall.'

'A rapid troop movement, sire, would mean abandoning our wounded and the civilians . . .'

'Civilians, what a curse!'

'We have promised them our protection. As for the wounded, we have to take them, otherwise what soldiers we have left will lose faith in Your Majesty.'

'Tell Davout to send out cavalry to reconnoitre his famous route. But what about you, Berthier, what's your inclination?'

'Let's make haste for Smolensk.'

'By that sacked road?'

'It is in fact the shortest way.'

'Send for Dr Yvan, I want to see him immediately.'

The Emperor gathered up the maps he had thrown on the floor, his plans of Russia, Turkey, Central Asia, the Indies. Events were shattering his dreams. He weighed the arguments. Should they shut themselves up in Smolensk and spend the winter there? He was hesitating when Dr Yvan entered the barn.

'Yvan, you damned charlatan, prepare that thing of yours.'

'Tonight?'

The Emperor was asking for the poison that Cabanis had invented for Condorcet, and that Corvisart, the Emperor's doctor in Paris, had recreated: opium, belladonna, hellebore . . . He would carry the mixture in a pouch under his woollen waistcoat. If a Cossack chief had identified him that morning, he would have tried to capture him and then what? Send him to St Petersburg in a cage? It could happen again; he refused to fall into Russian hands alive.

*

And so it was that the convoy turned northwards to rejoin the road that it had followed in the opposite direction at the start of autumn. A wind blew colder and colder and everyone bundled up as best they could. D'Herbigny wore his fox-fur-lined coat under his cloak; Paulin had unearthed a red cape with an ermine trim, which he wore with the hood up and his hat squashed down on top of it; it made him look like a prelate. They rode their horses at a walk through the firs and birch trees.

'Sir,' the servant called out, urging his donkey alongside his master's horse. 'Sir, I've got a feeling we're going round in circles.'

'Oh, do be quiet! Do you think you're cleverer than the Emperor now?'

'I'm trying to understand what he's up to, sir.'

'He has his reasons.'

'We've been marching for ten days and we can't be more than ten or twelve leagues from Moscow.'

'What would you know about it?'

'I recognize this countryside . . .'

The road came out onto a river whose icy waters rolled over a ford. The artillery were already halfway across; the cannon wheels were spinning on the muddy riverbed, blocking the way; the soldiers, water up to their knees, were trying to help the draught animals haul the mud-clogged gun carriages up onto the bank – a waste of effort in some cases and then they had to unhitch the guns and surrender them to the current.

D'Herbigny recognized the place too: they were approaching Borodino. He saw the stunted, buckled trees, mutilated by constant shelling, the battered hills, the scene of utter havoc. He saw the line of flat-topped rises where the Russians had built their redoubts, the broken palisades, the parapets that had collapsed on the dead or dying in craters like mass graves. The green wheat had come through but it barely hid the marks of the battle. The standards' shoes constantly struck a helmet or a cuirass or a drum case and these iron sounds rang out in the cold air. When the captain decided to carry on on foot, to lessen the chances of his horse missing its footing, it felt as if he was walking on twigs; but it was bones beneath his feet, not wood. The rain had disinterred thousands of bodies and the crows were eating them; the birds progressively flew away, cawing, as the cortege advanced. High up, looking down from one of the redoubts, a group of skeletons greeted the survivors as they passed. One of them, nailed by a lance to a birch tree, clad in the tattered remnants of a grey greatcoat, still had his boots and a horsetail helmet on his death's head.

No one wanted to linger.

They marched with lowered heads.

As he marched along, the captain thought he could hear reveille being sounded and in his mind's eye, the landscape reverted to how it had been before that battle at which the Emperor had husbanded his Guard. They'd had the sun in their eyes, that morning. He remembered the smoke, the explosions, the cuirassiers' lethal charges up the slopes, the roundshot falling around Napoleon and him, sick, kicking them away like balls to follow the movements of the troops through his theatre glasses. Shots rang out; the captain started. Bonet and the troopers had brought down a brace of crows and were running to retrieve them from amongst the corpses that were beginning to freeze in the cold.

'It's only us, sir!'

'We're thinking about soup, sir!'

They brandished the plump black birds, holding them by the feet.

'Are you going to eat those rot-eaters?'

'If they'll stay down . . .'

'Hey!'

'What is it, Bonet? Have your soup birds been pecking one of your old barrack mate's guts?'

'Come and have a look, sir.'

The column continued on its way but the captain broke off for a moment to look at his sergeant's discovery. Something vaguely human, without legs, was squirming between the stalks of wheat, its face encrusted with blood and earth. The dragoons shrank back from the monster.

'He's not dead,' said Bonet.

'He's come out of the open stomach of that dead horse,' said Trooper Chantelouve. 'He must have kept himself warm in there and eaten its insides and drank rainwater perhaps.'

'Impossible!' said the captain roughly to disguise his terror.

'No, look, he's even opening his eyes . . .'

*

Standing on a hillside, protected by a close-planted birch wood, the Kolotskoi abbey resembled a fortress with its battlemented grey walls, towers and stark belfries; poking through a long plank fence, cannon were trained on the valley through which the Moskova flowed. The Imperial suite spent a night there without getting out of their carriages, since the rooms were full of wounded, nearly twenty thousand of them who had been looked after since the horrific battle; it had also been used as an arms depot. A snowstorm blew for part of the night. In the secretaries' berline, Baron Fain and his passengers disappeared under an avalanche of greatcoats and furs. Sebastian was delighted with himself for having bought a pair of velvet boots lined with flannel for two diamonds from a canteen-woman. By morning the snow had stopped but it covered everything. Shaking the handle of the frosted door he was sitting next to, Sautet the bookseller fretted and fumed, 'I feel certain, absolutely certain, that we can find something edible in this cloister!'

'Have some more white wine from the crate,' Baron Fain said without opening his eyes.

'Get drunk in front of my daughter? Heavens, no! A fine example that would be!'

'Eat the peas.'

'Raw?'

'Eat your dog.'

'Are you mad?'

'I'll go and see what there is,' offered Sebastian.

'No, no,' the bookseller puffed. 'I'm cold and I'm ankylosed and I jolly well want to lose my temper!'

'Leave him be, Monsieur Roque,' said the baron. 'The exercise will warm up our friend.'

'I am not your friend.'

The bookseller hazarded a step outside, skidded and crumpled in the snow, squealing, 'My leg! My leg! I'm wounded! I'm entitled to the wounded's hot soup!'

Sebastian got out to help the fat man, but he had trouble standing up himself and slipped every time he took a step.

'My leg, I tell you!'

'There isn't a single person in the entire world who gives a damn about your leg.'

'But . . . Where are the horses?' asked the bookseller.

The postilion, after covering the wounded lying on the roof with a tarpaulin, had got in a canvas sack the night before. Now he shook the snow off his cloaks and sleeping bag, drank some grain alcohol and answered, 'In the stable, they're having a feed.'

'Oh, bravo! The horses are eating. What about us?'

'Do you want some straw?'

The forage in fact consisted of unripe wheat harvested by the abbey's garrison, a pittance which had been supplemented by straw from the pallets of the dying – they, at any rate, wouldn't have to endure this life for longer. When the horses had finished, they were put back between the shafts, and the vehicles of His Majesty's household rejoined the main body of the convoy. Württemberg chasseurs had stowed more wounded on the roofs of the carriages, on limbers, wherever they could, sometimes tying them on with ropes if they were too weak to hang on to the hood or the check straps.

The coaches in front set a course for those following but, apart from those that had been rough-shod for the ice by the farsighted Caulaincourt, most of the horses slipped constantly on the rolling ground covered with black ice; many fell from exhaustion and were abandoned. Nose pressed to the window, impassive now by force of habit, Sebastian studied a group of voltigeurs, blue with cold, whom the berline was passing. The soldiers cut open the belly of a mare that still had steam coming from its nostrils and sank their teeth into its flesh, blood running down

their chins and onto their shabby clothes. A band of
skirmishers were looting barouches that had become trapped in a ditch beside the road; they were tossing candelabras, ball gowns and fine china into the snow while they
loaded up with liqueurs. One of the barouches was on fire
and surrounded by skinny, bearded ghosts; they were
grilling chunks of dubious-looking meat on their sabres.
Just at that moment Sebastian saw a body fall from the
berline's roof, one of the wounded they'd taken on at the
abbey, who'd been poorly secured and knocked off balance
by the jolting of the carriage. The young man opened the
door and shouted at the postilion, 'Stop! We've lost one of
the wounded!'

'Close that door, Monsieur Roque,' said Baron Fain.
'Unless you're too hot?'

'Very well, my lord.'

He glanced at his fellow passengers. The lieutenant and
the one-legged officer weren't moaning anymore, or drinking, or eating: living, were they still doing that? Mme
Sautet and her daughter were curled up in each other's
arms, frozen stiff; the bookseller was clasping his black dog
to him; the dog was panting. Baron Fain had wrapped a
woollen scarf round his head. Their provisions had almost
run out but they were still confident; in His Majesty's
entourage they couldn't die of hunger; when they stopped
they'd go to the canteens. From time to time an explosion
rocked the berline; the gunners were setting fire to any
caissons they couldn't pull, so that at least the enemy
wouldn't get their hands on the powder. Suddenly a more
powerful explosion, closer to, smashed one of the windows
by the two wounded who were huddled together on the
sacks of peas. Sebastian climbed up the baggage piled

against that inaccessible door to try to cut off the icy wind. That was when he realized that the carriage had stopped moving and that the one-legged Dutchman was dead.

This time it was Baron Fain who got out to enquire about the latest setback. Sebastian followed after wrapping a cashmere scarf round his ears and nose, like him. Outside their eyes smarted, their hands turned white at the joints and they had to cling to the berline with numb fingers not to slip on the sheet ice. The postilion was stretched full length on a heap of snow at the side of the road; as it exploded the caisson had shot bits of wood into the air with the force of missiles; a splinter had split open his skull. They saw carriages with all their windows broken which the occupants were trying to board up. Barouches and supply wagons, impatient to pass these unfortunates block-ing their path, were venturing into thicker, more unstable snow, sometimes tipping over. The Baron had crouched down next to the postilion to check he was dead. Sebastian offered to take the man's place.

'Do you know how to drive these contraptions, Mon-sieur Roque?'

'I have driven my father's charabanc in Rouen many times.'

'I'm sure you have, but we're not travelling by cart here; we have, thank heaven, two horses shoed with frost-nails.'

'Do we have a choice, my lord?'

'Get us out of here and then let's catch up His Majesty's carriages as fast as possible, they've left us behind.'

'Very well, but you should know that one of our wounded is as dead as this postilion.'

'I'll get him out, you take care of the driving.'

Fain climbed back into the berline while his clerk took

off the postilion's cloaks and put them on; he relieved him
of his fur gloves, picked up the whip, perched himself on
the bench and took the reins. Barely had he sat down
before some army stragglers had stripped the postilion and
the one-legged officer, whom the Baron had pushed out
into the snow. They were in no danger of losing their way:
they just had to follow the trail of hundreds of naked,
frozen corpses, male and female, lying on the ice, the burnt
carriages and the mutilated horses that stained the snow
pink.

*

The cold and the monotony of the journey numbed the
stand-in coachman. Sebastian just gave the horses their
head, letting them follow the supply wagons without any
chance of going faster or hope of catching the other
carriages of the Emperor's household, which he had lost all
sign of; they must be far ahead by now. There were too
many corpses, too much carrion — how could one still feel
pity? If one of the wounded fell from a carriage he let the
berline drive over him; he couldn't stop at any price or lose
their place in the convoy. Many of these unfortunates died
crushed by hundreds of wheels; the carriages jolted from
side to side, other wounded fell off and were crushed in
turn, to complete indifference. Sebastian sometimes actually
envied these mutilated wretches their lot; that was them
shot of it all, at peace somewhere a thousand leagues away
from this endless plain. At other moments he conjured up
happy memories of the time when, with a few other lucky
fellows, he'd worked in the attics of the Ministry of War
in the Hôtel d'Estrées. His days had been spent copying
out duty sheets, notes and dispatches in an office in the

conscription department, hunched over one of the desks that were arranged around the stove. In the morning he'd splash water on the floor to settle the dust and then put his feet up and sharpen his quill with a penknife, or else nip along to the porter's lodge, where he'd had set up a canteen; from eleven in the morning the corridors would smell of the grilled sausages they'd take back to their desks and eat amongst the piles of letters and reports . . . He was hungry. He would have killed for some of that disgusting horse broth. He'd dream about it at the halting place, he knew, when night forced them to stop wherever they were, without a fire, rugged up in their blankets, with that black dog he kept seeing as a roast.

Fat snowflakes began to fall slowly, then thicker and faster, and soon a snowstorm was blowing. Sebastian bent his head so as not to be blinded. He put his trust in the horses, which plodded on into the wind and stopped when it got dark. The stand-in coachman scrambled down from his bench and sank into snow up to his thighs. The silence was total. He knocked on the misted-up window. 'My lord, I think we are lost.'

'Didn't you follow the road?'

'There is no road.'

Baron Fain lit a lantern and joined his clerk. The storm was abating somewhat and the light showed a group of isbas, some sort of barn and a cluster of low houses made out of fir trunks. The hamlet appeared uninhabited but they were wary; Russian peasants attacked anyone isolated from the main body of the army and butchered them with pitchforks.

'Go and fetch your sabre from the carriage, Monsieur Roque.'

'With pleasure, but I've never learnt how to use one.'

'You pick it up in a flash when you're in danger.'

As he turned in the darkness, Sebastian caught a whiff of smoke and warned the Baron. Somebody, they could see now, had a fire going in the furthest of the isbas. They didn't dare move. Suddenly, Sebastian felt something metal pressing into his temple. The snow crunched and he and the Baron were surrounded by men with pistols in their hands.

'Goodbye, my lord.'

'Goodbye, my son . . .'

'*Parlare lé francé?*'

It was soldiers from the Italian army lost in the storm. They weren't very fearsome; they may still have had their weapons, but they didn't have any ammunition. Sebastian drew breath. He hadn't even been afraid. In the isba, the Italians were making the most of a clay stove, which was heaped with crackling logs. They had stabled the horses in the barn and pulled down part of the roof to fill the racks with thatch. The women lay down next to the fire on a broad bench, which ran all the way round the room, against wooden walls that were crawling with bugs. Opposite they put the wounded lieutenant, whose teeth were chattering with cold or fever or both. Because there was no chimney, the room was filled with smoke that caught in their throats. The Italians had looted oats from a village, which they had reduced to flour with heavy stones and mixed with melted snow; they put balls of this paste in the embers and then picked off the ashes that stuck to the bread. It was flavourless and either underdone or burnt, but Sebastian set to ravenously. He wasn't the only one. They all fell asleep dreaming of green, sunlit country, banquets and other improbable pleasures.

The Sautets' dog had stayed in the berline. It woke everybody at dawn with its barking. Well, not quite everybody – the Italians had vanished. Sebastian had a hunch: 'The horses!'

The Italians had cleared a path through the snow to the berline. They had taken the Russian sabre, the sacks of peas, the furs and the wine; disturbed by the barking they'd left the horses. They were running down through the snow to a frozen lake below, on the edge of a forest. A little later, as he was holding a travelling mirror in front of Baron Fain who was shaving, Sebastian decided to let his beard grow. He revealed this to the Baron, who answered in a detached way, 'Are you eager to displease His Majesty?'

*

The army stragglers – dismounted troopers with boots bound up with rags, voltigeurs and hussars as tattered as scarecrows – had bushy beards on which the snow settled. At night they stole horses, which they rode with the intention of eating them later. If a carriage broke a wheel, they set it ablaze and formed a circle under tarpaulins and blankets, makeshift tents which soon grew heavy with snow. Mme Aurore owned a saucepan, which was making her an invaluable companion. On waking and leaving her tent, she went in search of a healthy horse and found several tethered to a clump of trees. Their owners didn't see her coming, their backs were turned as they stood as close to their fire as possible; Mme Aurore took her penknife, slid it between the ribs of one of the animals, gently cut into the flesh and drew off the blood in her tinplate container. Over the dying embers of a stripped wagon which had kept them warm the previous night, she cooked the blood and shared out the sausage, a few mouthfuls each. Before setting off west again in the crowd of shirkers and civvies, three gunners stopped in front of the cook. One of them said he was a non-commissioned officer and opened his fur-lined coat to show a semblance of a uniform. 'The horse harnessed to that cart there, is it yours?'

'Yes,' answered Mme Aurore.

'Not anymore.'

'Thief!'

'We need it for our cannon.'

'You don't need cannon now!'

'Someone's just bled our horse, I don't have a choice.'

'How are we going to get anywhere if you take it?'

'Walk, like the rest of us.'

The non-commissioned officer signalled to the men with him, who were still wearing shakoes. They unhitched the horse and started to lead it away by the bridle. The Great Vialatoux could be heard yelling, then moaning, then begging. Without letting go of her saucepan, Mme Aurore walked towards the cart, her boots sinking into the thick snow. Arguing was no use with these stubborn soldiers, she wanted to tell the juvenile lead, who was furiously holding onto the horse by its tail, but before the manageress could reason with the actor, the non-commissioned officer shot him in the head. The imbecile collapsed, losing what brains he had. 'Just like a Russian prisoner!' said the gunner, which amused his companions. Vialatoux was crying, sitting with his back to the useless shafts.

'Get up!' ordered the manageress.

'You're not suggesting we push the cart, are you?'

'We'll take what we can and follow the crowd.'

'And leave him to the crows?' said Vialatoux pointing to the body of his former stage partner.

In the cart, Ornella and Catherine had watched the murder and loss of their horse, but they had no tears or thoughts or feelings anymore; they obeyed Mme Aurore and bundled up what seemed essential, and not too heavy, in furs – candles and clothes mostly, which they sorted out on the floor of the cart; not the costumes or stage clothes, but caps and shawls. Then they set off on foot, sticking close to a group of skirmishers who were poking their ramrods in the snow at every step because of the ravines that were invisible now. On their left they saw a dead soldier, his mouth open, his eye-teeth buried in the thigh of a horse that was sprawled on the ground, its heart still beating. Further on, around a cold bivouac fire, they saw soldiers sitting, they weren't moving anymore, they had frozen; Vialatoux went up to examine the contents of their bags, found a potato, pocketed it discreetly and promised himself he would eat it slowly later, in secret. The sky was pearl grey, the firs black, the ground terrifyingly white. On a crest, in shadow, the lances and tall astrakhan hats of the Black Sea Cossacks stood out, menacing them from a distance.

*

Baron Fain was congratulating himself on having invited the Sautet family to share his official carriage. The bookseller knew the district and could explain how to plot a route through that vastness without a compass to rejoin Imperial headquarters. The fat fellow had consulted the tree trunks; the side with the browner bark was north. Thanks to this cunning tip, the bookseller was forgiven his cantankerous moods and they reached the ruined chateau where His Majesty was encamped without too much trouble. Napoleon was waiting for his army to regroup and for news to arrive from Paris; Smolensk was only a few days away, with its well-stocked stores which everyone dreamed of when they wanted to raise their spirits. In any case, a convoy of rations from the city had already reached Marshal Ney's rearguard. The news had spread.

Sawn into pieces, the chateau's only furnishings, a billiard table and a lyre, were blazing in the hearth. In private, the Emperor was in a constant fury. Sebastian knew that the bad news outweighed the good. The mail left Napoleon deep in thought. Not only were the reserve troops, who had stayed in the rear, now yielding to the Russians and falling back, not only had Prince Eugène just lost his artillery fording a river, but he had also learnt that there had been an attempt in Paris to restore the Republic.

Two weeks earlier, General Malet had escaped from the mental home where he was interned. Equipped with false documents, he had released his accomplices: they had taken over the police and staff headquarters by starting a rumour that Napoleon was dead; Savary, the Minister of Police, had been arrested in his bedroom in his night shirt. Then the conspirators had demanded the Prefect of Paris allocate them a room in the Town Hall for their provisional government. They had almost succeeded; the capital's garrison was within an ace of giving in. The Emperor couldn't believe it. He read the dispatches and then read them again, overwhelmed. 'They thought I was dead and lost their heads,' he said to himself. 'Malet, an old lag, a madman! What? Three unknowns spread any old story that no one checks and then they take over the government? What if they had tried to restore the Bourbons? Who thought about swearing an oath to the King of Rome? Who thought of the Imperial dynasty? Once the shout was, "The king is dead, long live the king!" But this time there was nothing. That is what happens when I'm away too long. Everything depends on me. On me alone. Will nothing that I undertake survive me?' He waited for further couriers, agonizing over the affair constantly with Caulaincourt or Berthier. Sebastian and the Baron didn't dare leave their travelling desks, but the Emperor didn't dictate a line. He drummed his fingers on the armrest of his chair, stuffed his nose with snuff and refused to sleep.

The following morning an intense cold added to the freezing fog. There was no time left to waste: they had to get to Smolensk and restore their strength there.

'My boots!' said the Emperor.

At this signal, a murmur went up amongst the valets, secretaries and officers in the draughty salons with their broken windows. Sebastian and the Baron left it to the other clerks to fold up their equipment. The Emperor hadn't moved from his armchair. A major-domo brought him his cup of mocha coffee and Roustam ran up with his boots, crackled under the polish. The Mameluke knelt down in front of Napoleon, who was holding out a leg, put on the first boot but then received a great kick in the chest; he fell over backwards, short-winded.

'This how I am served!' stormed the Emperor. 'Didn't you notice, you cretin, that you put the left boot on the right foot? You're no better than those cowards in Paris who let themselves be tricked by a lunatic escaped from an asylum!'

Malet's failed conspiracy continued to obsess him. What

was Europe going to say of this ludicrous adventure? How would she turn it to her advantage? From now on the Empire was at the mercy of a handful of militants. It grieved him sorely.

*

Choked by a thousand carriages and by cannon covered with sacks, on emerging from a forest, the road followed the course of the Dnieper. D'Herbigny's squadron had been reduced to a dozen or so mounted troopers; the others were on foot; their horses hadn't held out against the hunger and thirst and the men had resigned themselves to eating their stringy flesh before it froze solid. A sheepskin muffling his ears under his imposing cap, the captain inhaled the cold air; the steam from his breath froze on his walrus moustache and the tangle of beard covering his cheeks. The fog hadn't lifted until midday, when it was replaced by a raw wind. They were pushing blindly on, taking care not to lose one another.

Paulin reined in his emaciated donkey at a bend. 'Mfffyuhh,' he said to the captain.

'If you have something to tell me, at least lift your cape! You look like a mummy from Cairo!'

'Monsieur,' his batman repeated, obeying. 'One doesn't notice when one's nose starts freezing and the next thing you know, it falls off, you should . . .'

'Did you stop to give me advice?'

'No, sir. I am just wondering if we are going to get across. It gets dark so early.'

Past the bend, the icy road fell steeply to a bridge, which spanned the river, and then rose just as sharply the other side. Grenadiers, their fingers soldered to their muskets, were posted at the bridge's entrance to regulate the flow of traffic, but what could they do? Horses with worn shoes skidded down to the river's edge and did not get up again. They neighed deafeningly as heavy carriages crushed them, broke through the thin layer of ice and sunk into the grey water; men yelled and pushed and shoved, others hurtled down the slope or used the carcasses like the steps of a staircase, sometimes tumbling to the bottom with their bags that burst open; those behind caught their gaiters in samovars and bracelets and teapot handles.

'The carts, sir, none of them are getting down in one piece.'

'Unfortunately you're right, Bonet.'

'And even the horses we've still got . . .'

'We'll leave the carts,' ordered d'Herbigny. 'We'll make for the bridge by the thicker snow on the bank, leading the horses.'

Some ingenious civilians were managing to lower their carriages by a system of ropes strung between birches, but even using that method the carts would have broken up, so the dragoons set about unloading them; they shared out the gold coins and the precious stones unset from icons; the wine had frozen, but they broke the bottles and set off again sucking Madeira or Tokay icicles. New arrivals, very unprovided for, divided out the rest of the carts' contents. Sighing, d'Herbigny had hung packets of tea from his saddle and strapped them across the backs of their mules, who were glad not to have to carry their full load any more. The squadron managed to regroup at the start of the bridge in order to force their way across in the throng.

'Is that thunder?' asked Paulin.

The captain hadn't time to answer before a cannonball

smashed into the ground a few metres from them. In the distance, Cossacks were training light guns mounted on sledges on the bridge, shaking their whips and howling like wolves. Another cannonball fell in the river. That was it, stampede.

'Keep calm!' the captain shouted, unsure of his authority. 'It won't be any safer on the other bank!'

The wooden bridge moved under the wheels and hooves. If there hadn't been a parapet, many of them would have fallen in the Dnieper. On the other bank, d'Herbigny noticed that he'd collected some pearl necklaces on his boots while he'd been walking. Getting up looked as if it would be trickier than getting down. The horses' smooth shoes couldn't get a grip on the black ice, only the mules and horses with frost nails could manage it without slipping; even Paulin's donkey heeled over and after a dozen metres of hard going, slid back down to the river with the portmanteau, to the servant's despair.

'Don't pull that face!' said the captain.

'I was in charge of your uniforms.'

'I wouldn't have worn all my coats, would I? When we're in France . . .'

'Will we see Rouen again, sir?'

'Of course!'

Paulin looked over his shoulder. Near the congested bridge, a woman had pushed back her sable hood; on her knees, she was cutting open his donkey's stomach with a knife and plunging her head in to take a bite of its liver while being berated by a burgher in a fur-lined coat who wanted his share. Cannonballs rained down. When he regained level ground, after that cursed slope, d'Herbigny wrapped rags round his battered boots and tied them in place with the necklaces. Then he resumed command of his squadron, which was now on foot, apart from four troopers who had got on the mules. Sergeant Bonet was giving them a rocket; if rank still commanded any respect, he was entitled to a mule, but discipline was breaking down and Bonet protested in vain.

*

Their eyes were strained by a freezing wind, they were blinded by the glare from the snow, but at noon on a November day, the fugitives still recognized Smolensk's spires rising up in the midst of a range of mountains that blocked off the horizon. There it was, salvation: shelter, a fire, clothes to replace their lice-infested rags. As they drew near the walls, even the most exhausted found new energy. Yet this caravan of tramps found the city gates closed to them, and groups pitched their tents in the bastions and snow-covered ditches.

D'Herbigny urged on his Cossack horse. Sentries in grey capes were barring entry to the city and roughly questioning anyone who claimed to have a right to enter it.

'Who are you?'

'D'Herbigny! François Saturnin d'Herbigny, captain in the dragoons of the Guard.'

'And where is it, your squadron?'

'Here!'

With a great sweep of his arm, the captain presented the thirty or so dismounted troopers still with him, in their weird get-ups, white with hoarfrost, with long mops of hair, shaggy beards and faces blackened by the smoke of the bivouacs and dirt.

'That's a squadron?'

'4th Squadron, Saint-Sulpice's brigade. The missing are under the snow or in a wolf's stomach.'

'How can you prove it to me?'

The men had formed up in marching order to show a more military aspect and impress these lumbering dullards. At an order from the captain, they stood to attention and identified themselves,

'Sergeant Bonet!'

'Trooper Martinet!'

'Trooper Perron!'

'Trooper Chantelouve!'

'Yes, fine, fine, it's fine,' one of the sentries said, a corporal in the chasseurs.

The gates opened a chink and they were able to enter Smolensk in quick time, despite their chilblains and the wadding of rags bound round their feet. Partly burnt by the Russians in August, Smolensk had not been restored by the occupying troops. The dragoons dropped their act. Without witnesses, without sentries to win over, they lost their martial aspect when they saw the streets. The houses had no roofs; all they passed were carcasses of horses, ridden to death and then picked clean, and piles of rotting corpses that stank even in the bitter cold. Lying at the base of a wall, a frozen Spaniard had gnawed his wrists; another wretch was crawling towards them on all fours, too weak to beg. Near the citadel, ambulance men were carrying their patients into a stark building. The sick were drenched in sweat, their dry, black tongues lolling from their mouths; they were being given snow to drink. From one of the ambulance men, d'Herbigny learnt that typhus was raging, that the Emperor had arrived the day before and that the distribution of food had begun, but initially only to the

Guard. 'Good timing,' he said with delight. 'We are the Guard. Where are the stores?' The ambulance man pointed out the warehouse and added that the supply officers were asking for a receipt signed and stamped by the military administration before giving out the rations. Which is how the captain found himself in the citadel facing Comptroller Poissonnard, one of the officials in charge of supplies: at least he wouldn't have to prove his rank or his unit. He planted himself in front of the comptroller, who was as plump and hale as ever, swathed in furs and ensconced behind his desk.

'Sign a receipt for me, you old scoundrel!' said the captain.

'Are you an officer? Which regiment?'

'What! You don't recognize me?'

'I don't think . . .'

'D'Herbigny, you thieving swine!'

'Wait . . . Ah yes, perhaps . . .'

'What do you mean, *perhaps*?'

'With your beard, you know . . . But the nose, yes, as long as ever.'

'Hurry up, so we can get our rations.'

'How many men in your command?'

'Twenty-nine.'

'Whoah! In Moscow you had a hundred.'

'Get a move on!'

'Horses?'

'Just one, mine, and four mules.'

'The oats are only for horses.'

Poissonnard filled out a form in his careful writing, signed it, dried the ink, stamped it and handed it over.

'Convoys from Germany have brought fresh supplies of flour and vegetables; there's even beef.'

Imagining himself settling down to a rib of beef, the captain led the remnants of his squadron to the magazine. An equally well-fed and clothed employee produced their rations from several chests: peas, rye flour, three pieces of beef, and flagons of red wine which they immediately shared out amongst themselves. In the street leading to the citadel, already buoyant at the thought of their first real meal for weeks, the dragoons ran into a band of hollow-cheeked, raggedy men, carrying bayonets and clubs studded with nails.

Unmoving, the two groups stared wild-eyed at each other. One wanted to save their rations; the other wanted to eat. The dead horses were frozen so hard that they couldn't cut them up. Once allies in battle, the soldiers were turning savage now over a little bag of flour. The dragoons in the front rank drew their sabres; behind them their comrades loaded their muskets. The two groups observed each other. As the captain cocked his pistol, Paulin suggested, 'Sir, we have a few ribs of beef, why don't we give one up?'

'Give up part of our rations? Never! Faith, do you think we have too much of them?'

'These skeletons have nothing to lose.'

'We do.'

'They're dangerous.'

'If they want to get themselves sabred, there's nothing we can do.'

'When you're surrounded by wild beasts, sir, it's better to throw them something. That keeps them busy and while they fight over the spoils, you make your run for it.'

The captain searched through his bags, took one of the quarters of beef by the knucklebone, pushed through the ranks and tossed it over the heads of the starving men. Paulin had anticipated correctly. Fists flailing, they started tussling in the snow over the piece of meat, jabbing each other with their bayonets, cudgelling and falling on top of one another. Taking advantage of the fight, the captain and his men slipped off towards the citadel where they would probably find the rest of their brigade, and having stuffed themselves and wet their whistles, then re-form some manner of regiment at the Emperor's side.

*

The code of every man for himself that had prevailed before Smolensk now changed into an enforced fraternity. Self-interest alone united the shipwrecked in some sort of alliance. Little bands had formed at random on the march, on the principle of strength in numbers, to have a better chance of staving off hunger and cold and other people. These tribes brought together disarmed soldiers (who'd preferred brandy to their muskets) and civilians of all classes without a scrap of feeling, capable of stripping a dying man of his boots before he'd taken his last breath. Survival jealously, viciously, went about its work in the heart of these miniature societies outside which people were condemned to a quick death. Ornella, who had caught the eye of the head of such a band, shared the lair of a strange crew in a partly burned house in the suburbs, by the Dnieper. There were seven or eight of them wrapped in blankets, squatting like Indians around a fire of planks. A horse's heart was cooking in a helmet. These men spoke little and barely understood each other when they did; their leader may have been French, but the others were from Bavaria, Naples or Madrid; they communicated basic information by gestures. A big fellow with a beard like a hedgehog wore a cuirass over women's clothes; he skewered the heart with his dagger and put it on the ground to carve it. His neighbour, in a black silk skullcap, had taken off his shako on which he was lining up scissors, a razor, thread and needles; then, his mouth full, he started darning the shawl which he had wrapped round his chest. All that could be heard was the crackling of the fire and eight jaws chewing innards. Suddenly there was a scratching sound from the palisade which acted as their door.

The chief stood up, pushing away Ornella who was curled up against him, opened the bundle that never left his side and picked out a scalpel. His name was Dr Fournereau; a man in his forties with hard brown eyes, he had a fraying beard and hair down to his shoulders. He exercised a natural authority over the youngsters who constituted his pack. Ornella trusted this disillusioned doctor; she had told him her life story, how her mother sold feathers and trimmings from a milliner's stall on the quai de Gesvres. 'We have all been ground into the dirt,' he had replied. The Empire did not trouble itself much about surgeons; the faculties of medicine had closed their lecture theatres; medical students climbed the railings of cemeteries at night to exhume fresh cadavers, which they dissected in their attics where ten of them lived together; the corpses' fat kept them warm through winter. Fournereau did his work with no money and no authority. He was at the mercy of the commissaries of war, loathsome souls who stole the rations from the hospitals. Fournereau could never act during the fighting, he had to wait for days before treating a battle's wounded; headquarters took priority, collecting spare arms and munitions.

Holding his scalpel like a weapon, the doctor stopped and listened. Something was softly scratching the wooden palisade, then there was a yap.

'A dog?'

What a godsend, he thought. Our pittance is jumping into the pot of its own accord. They had already eaten crows baked in the fire and horse's tripe, so why not roast dog? He opened the palisade enough to let the animal in. An icy wind gripped him. The fire threw only a poor light. He couldn't make anything out in that starless night. The snow crunched. He sensed the animal at his feet, touched it, and opened the palisade a little more to let in a huge ball of furs, which, once it was in, shook the snow from its coat. It wasn't a dog. It was a man. Frozen beneath his furs, he was crawling on his knees and elbows, trembling and yapping like a lapdog.

The rest of the band concentrated on chewing their food by the fire, which had been stoked with more planks. The doctor stopped the arrival getting close to the flames, which outraged Ornella. 'Oh, Doctor, you're not going to deny him a little warmth?'

'No.'

'Let him warm himself, please.'

'Go and fetch a pile of snow.'

She obeyed without asking questions and pushed a heap of fresh snow inside those ruins that protected them from the wind.

'Do you see his fingers?' the doctor said to her. 'White, no sensation, they are in the process of freezing. If you expose his hands to the flames, they'll puff up, become bloated and then gangrene will set in in a flash. Help me get him out of these rags . . .'

They helped the man out of his cloaks, which were heavy with ice, his cap and his boots and then rubbed him with the snow. As she was massaging his face, Ornella recognized Vialatoux.

'Do you know who it is?' asked Fournereau.

'An actor from my troupe.'

'Keep on scrubbing hard, so that the snow is burning.'

The Great Vialatoux, emaciated, tufts of grey beard on his chin and cheeks, breathed jerkily; he was almost suffocating, but the rubbing did him good; he spluttered and eventually said in a very low monotone,

'I call no longer Rome that walled enclosure
Which his proscriptions fill with obsequies.
Those walls whose destiny once seemed so fair
Are but her prison – or rather tomb.'

'Is he delirious?'

'I don't think so, Doctor.'

'Do you understand what he's serenading us with?'

'He's reciting *Sertorius* by Corneille, a banned play which he used to dream of performing.'

'Funny time to think about the theatre, but at least his brain's working better than his fingers. Rub, my girl, rub and say something back, get some sort of conversation going.'

Mlle Ornella took some more snow and rubbed the actor's fingers, whispering in his ear,

'Only fall into hands that know their duty
At least I know my goal and you know yours . . . '

The Great Vialatoux opened his eyes, which had been unstuck by the heat from the fire, turned without any surprise towards his former stage partner and replied, very solemnly, '*And yet, my lord, you serve like another man . . .*' Fournereau interrupted the scene to pour a little of the hot red water that they had used to boil the heart between Vialatoux's chapped lips.

*

In the four days he had been in Smolensk, Napoleon hadn't once left the house on New Square, which he had chosen for his quarters. It was undamaged and comfortable. The victuals from Paris for the Emperor's household accumulated in its cellars and kitchens. Did he really understand the situation? He didn't appear affected by his army's tribulations. When they were moving, he barely got out of his berline and ate his fill of the same things he ate at the Tuileries. His entourage did nothing to dispel his illusions. Berthier looked well, as did Daru, and if Prefect Bausset was hobbling on crutches, it was only because he had gout. Caulaincourt was having shoes with three crampons made for the saddle and draught horses, the regiments were getting their strength back, furs and meat were going to be distributed amongst them. Tomorrow the Emperor would leave Smolensk with his Guard. The Minsk road crisscrossed by ravines and, in places, narrowed by gorges, so they had to avoid congestion and march faster. After him would come Prince Eugène, then Davout, and then Ney with his rearguard . . . Sebastian appeared; he had the text of the 28th bulletin: '*Since the bad weather of the 6th, we have lost three thousand draught horses, and almost a hundred of our caissons have been destroyed . . .*' The Emperor glanced through the text, which ended with the line, '*The Emperor's health has never been better.*' He signed it on the writing desk which a valet drew up in front of him. Then he called for Daru, his Intendant General, to inquire about the distribution of supplies.

'The Guard have already had their rations, sire.'

'Good. And the others?'

'Not yet, sire.'

'Why the devil not?'

'The stores are not sufficiently stocked.'

'Liar!'

'Unfortunately, sire, I am not lying.'

'Come now, Daru! We have two weeks' rations for a hundred thousand men here.'

'Barely half that, sire, and the meat has run out.'

'How many men to feed?'

'Fewer than a hundred thousand, far fewer . . .'

'The Guard?'

'Five thousand able-bodied.'

'The cavalry?'

'Eighteen hundred mounted troopers.'

'The regiments?'

'Roughly thirty thousand.'

The Emperor walked round the room, his lips quivering; he took a great pinch of snuff, then threw his snuffbox on the floor, and bawled, 'Bring me the criminal in charge of provisioning!'

Napoleon stayed alone with the commissary responsible for Smolensk's stores. For a long time the secretaries, valets and grenadiers on guard heard His Majesty's yells and threats and the sobs of the guilty man.

Five

BEREZINA

'This year a group of mallards had their feet frozen to a pond's surface, and now a bald eagle busies himself swooping in and tearing off their heads.'

Jim Harrison, *Just before Dark*

IN THE SHATTERED HOVEL in the suburbs of Smolensk, there were no planks or beams left to sustain the fire their survival depended upon, so they had to set off again, keep on walking, find better shelter and food. Dr Fournereau, Ornella and the rest of their wretched band were gathering together their possessions when one of them, who had pushed back the palisade to look outside, grabbed Fournereau by his black bearskin cloak. '*Mira! Mira! Las puertas!*' The doctor put on his gloves. Hordes of men and women were climbing from all directions towards the open gates of the city; if it weren't for the fact that they sank into the snow at every step, the doctor and his troupe would have run to get ahead of the crowd. The bitingly cold air cut to the bone. Keeping close together, they planted their feet in the snow mechanically, their brains switched down, moving on instinct, like hunters. The Emperor had just set off towards Minsk with his Guard; his headquarters staff was packing up and the servants were selling Bordeaux from the Imperial cellars at twenty francs a bottle. No officers were able, or inclined, to bring the chaos under control. The soldiers, stragglers and fugitives wouldn't listen to anything but their stomachs. They were besieging the stores where the supply commissaries had barricaded themselves whilst they waited for hypothetical orders.

The snowstorm had veiled the piles of bodies, studding the road that climbed towards the citadel with white mounds. Halfway up, Fournereau and his dependants merged with the thousands of people hanging furiously on the massive shutters of the main warehouse. From a first-floor window, Comptroller Poissonnard was haranguing the crowd. 'Wait! There'll be some for everybody!'

'What are we waiting for?'

'We have to get the rations organized!'

'We'll organize them ourselves! Open up!'

'Wait . . .'

'Shut up, little piggy, or you'll end up on a spit.'

A barouche whose horses had been taken by the artillery cleared a path, drawn by voltigeurs, and with the crowd helping to push it, smashed into the door; a leaf started cracking, which fifty hands tore clean away. Slats went flying to make the opening bigger. Then without a word, with the force of a torrent, the crowd surged into the building and fanned out. Fournereau held Ornella by the arm; the rest of his band followed him. They let themselves be swept into a room full of crates that a big uhlan in a tricorne was hacking open with an axe. Held aloft on outstretched arms, two-handled baskets were passing over people's heads; those at the front looted the beans and bags of flour and rice; those behind bounded up the staircase. On the first floor, the commissaries had jammed the doors shut with bars, but they couldn't withstand the massive pressure. The besiegers discovered a new stockroom where Poissonnard was preparing to flee. He had fixed a ladder to one of the windows and two of his associates had already climbed down it; wagons were waiting for them at the rear of the building. Fournereau grabbed the comptroller by the skirts of his blue coat, as he stepped over the windowsill. 'What are you taking away in your carts?'

'His Majesty's Service!' Poissonnard answered in a hoarse voice.

'Where's the meat?'

'The droves never arrived!'

The doctor bent forward. Catching the comptroller by the throat, he half-strangled him. Below, the man's quarter-master colleagues were waiting for him; the wagon drivers were on their seats, reins in hand, looking around for the signal to leave. Poissonnard moaned, 'Let me go, I'm no use to you.'

'No, you're no use to anyone. Go and join the other lickpennies!' With a hard shove, Fournereau unbalanced Poissonnard, who toppled from his ledge and fell, scream-ing; he smashed onto a vehicle's oilskin hood. The drivers instantly whipped up their horses and the wagons disap-peared round the bend of the snow-covered street. In the warehouse, the systematic pillaging was continuing; every-thing was vanishing into pockets, sacks, double bags and caps; even the wooden crates were being taken for the next campfire. Fournereau knelt down next to Ornella. She was stuffing her bundle with dry vegetables. 'Looks like we're not going to paradise today either,' he said.

'Then it'll be tomorrow,' she answered with a distracted smile. They heard a cannonade in the distance. No doubt one of Kutuzov's armies was attacking the rear-guard.

*

The baggage train followed the route taken by the Emperor and his Guard, across twenty-five leagues of flat country to Krasnoie, a small town where they would be joined by Davout's, Eugène's and Ney's army corps, who were going to leave Smolensk in stages. The secretaries' berline and their department's wagons had spent the night under cover in a birch forest, surrounded by campfires lit by skirmishers of the Young Guard who were commanded by a beefy captain, loudmouthed but attentive to his men, named Vautrin. Before dawn he was poking those who were asleep with his stick, chivvying them along; they were stretched out in the snow, their cloaks stiff with ice. 'Up you get! Up you get! If you sleep now you won't wake up again!' They sat up and got to their feet, one by one, blinded by the smoke from the glowing fires that the non-commissioned officers had watched over all night, constantly breaking branches to keep them stoked. 'Up you get! A plague on any fool who sleeps too long!' His bellows echoed in the silence. Sebastian opened an eye in the berline he'd been sharing with Fain, Sautet, who was snoring open-mouthed, and Sautet's family since Moscow. 'Up you get! Up you get!' Captain Vautrin repeated, belabouring one of his men. The officer stuck his stick in the snow, shook the sleeper and bawled at the survivors of the 2nd Battalion: 'On your feet! Otherwise you'll end up like your friend Lepel!' Sebastian left his travelling companions and went over to

the fires. The soldiers of the Guard were the only ones
wearing uniforms that more or less matched, with grey
greatcoats, albeit frayed, and shakos with chinstraps in
place; despite the furs over their ears and the rags round
their gaiters, they had retained a soldierly bearing.

On the tip of a bayonet, Captain Vautrin offered the
secretary a piece of grilled meat that he took with his
gloved fingers and bit into. It wasn't easy to swallow, but
he didn't even ask what things were anymore, he just
chewed the blackened, stringy flesh — what difference did
it make anyway? He'd gladly have turned cannibal if there
were no other way to hold out till Paris.

The skirmishers collected their muskets from the piles;
one of them slung the strap of a drum over his shoulder
and started playing. Sebastian resumed his position on the
berline's box. He sensed similar stirrings in the carriages
behind. Day was breaking in a milky white sky, but now it
had fallen twenty degrees below freezing, the snow had
stopped. Glancing at the hindquarters of their two horses
before touching them with his whip, he noticed that the
one on the left was covered in blood, black blood, congealed
and crusted. He jumped down from his seat, wincing;
during the night, some rogues had cut slices the size of
large steaks from the thighs of the animal, which hadn't
felt anything in the bitter cold.

'My lord . . .'

'Are we setting off?' mumbled Baron Fain under his
covers, screwing up his eyes.

'That is going to be difficult, with only one horse.'

'What are you telling me, Monsieur Roque?'

'Come and see.'

'Oh, goodness, what horrors have you in store?'

'What is it?' the bookseller asked anxiously, emerging from the berline.

'You'll find out soon enough,' muttered the Baron as he walked with Sebastian towards the mutilated horse.

The driver of the maps and archives wagon had come to have a look; he was shaking his head.

'That's not pretty, not pretty at all . . .'

'Keep your comments to yourself,' snapped the Baron, exasperated by this serious reversal.

'What shall we do?'

'First, Monsieur Roque, take this poor animal out of the shafts.'

'That will only leave one horse, and he won't be able to pull the berline, even if he did have his share of oats in Smolensk.'

'Ah now, for a coach that size,' the coachman said, 'you'd have to have a team of four put to.'

The Baron thought. The 2nd Battalion of skirmishers had marched off behind their drums and rolled colour, of which only the eagle showed above the shakos.

'I'll ride the second horse,' decided the Baron. 'We'll pack it with a modest load. And you, Monsieur Roque, will follow with our wagons, on this driver's box.'

'And the Sautets?'

'Let them walk like everybody else. After all, Dr Larrey recommends walking to prevent numbness. You will explain the situation to them.'

The horse that had been butchered alive fell in the snow, jerking spasmodically; the steam pluming from its nostrils quickly turned to ice, like that tear Sebastian thought he could see at the corner of its staring eye. The Baron chose necessities, which he stuffed in a satchel. When he was ready, he mounted the unharmed horse without either saddle or stirrups, clasped its neck with both arms, and pressed his face into its mane. He squeezed the flanks of his mount with his knees and trotted off after the battalion, telling his clerk, 'I'll find a saddle on the road, no one would have thought to slow themselves down with one of those.'

'You follow me then, right?' the coachman suggested to Sebastian.

'Yes, but I have to warn the passengers first . . .'

'Well, get a move on. We don't want to go wasting any time.'

It was a delicate mission. Sebastian loathed being the bringer of bad news. He was trying to become more callous, and it was easy enough in His Majesty's entourage, but in this case, how was he to explain to the bookseller that they were leaving him in this forest a long way from the city? At least, by a stroke of luck, they had entrusted the last of their wounded, the lieutenant with the fever, to the doctors in Smolensk. He opened the door wide.

'Are we setting off or not?' demanded the bookseller.

'The truth of the matter is that everyone, from now on, is making their own arrangements to continue their journey . . .'

'What's this nonsense you're telling me, young man?'

'There are no horses to draw the carriage.'

'That means . . .'

'That you gather up what you think will be useful.'

'And then set off on foot?'

'I fear so, Monsieur Sautet.'

'Well, I dread so! At my age, what an idea! What about my wife? And my daughter?'

The two scared women were biting their lips. Emboldened by a sudden flash of courage, the bookseller asked Sebastian to take his daughter in the map wagon.

'What about you two?'

'Mélanie and I shall stay in the carriage.'

'Be reasonable, Monsieur Sautet . . .'

'Are you invoking reason, in circumstances like this? Come now, there is only the one road. A barouche will have room for us. There are other former inhabitants of Moscow, acquaintances of mine, in this wretched cortege.'

'Very well,' said Sebastian. 'Mademoiselle . . .'

He helped Mlle Sautet down onto the slippery footboard, took her in his arms to prevent her falling and found as best a place for her as he could between the piles of files and scrolls filling the wagon. The dog Dimitri was barking. Sautet leant out of the door, a book in his outstretched hand. 'Monsieur le secrétaire, this volume fell out of your bag, it would be a pity to lose it.'

'Thank you, sir, thank you.'

Sebastian took the book, Seneca's *On the Tranquillity of the Soul*, from which the bookseller, either mockingly or pretentiously, recited a passage: '*When one believes that whatever can happen is about to happen, this always cushions the shock of the misfortune.* But take care of Emilie . . .'

'I promise, Monsieur Sautet.'

The wagon left. As they passed the stranded berline, Sebastian saw the bookseller and his wife clasped in each other's arms. He lowered his eyes. The barking hadn't stopped; the little black dog was scampering along next to the wagon. The secretary bent down, stretched out a hand, picked up the animal by the scruff of its neck and settled it on his lap under the wolfskin cover. The coachman rolled his eyes heavenwards.

*

The reality of what was happening tormented Sebastian Roque. No one had prepared him for such cruelty. He kept telling himself that the secretariat's wagons were full to bursting, fuller, even; it just wasn't possible for them to take the bookseller and his wife; he'd already contravened regulations as it was, by fitting their daughter in amongst the ragtag assortment of maps and administrative documents, maybe he'd get into trouble for that in itself. What was going to happen to the Sautets? No carriage would stop to save them; the bookseller had used this argument to salve the young man's conscience, it was elegant, brave and false. They would die of hunger or cold if peasants didn't massacre them first. Sebastian despised himself and exonerated himself in equal measure as he stroked Dimitri the dog, who gave off a little heat.

'We're there,' the coachman said.

'Where?'

'Krasnoie, probably.'

With his whip he pointed to a jumble of shacks in the distance whose roofs were sagging under thick snow. An unbroken line of regiments and berlines was heading there. Dead horses still lay everywhere, and corpses frozen like statues on the roadside, which they looked at wearily, as one would boundary posts. They hadn't quite arrived, however. First the road dipped down into a defile with sides of sheet ice. At the entrance to a narrow bridge, carriages and wagons were snarled. One of the Treasury's caissons burst open as it fell and unleashed a rain of gold coins. Exhausted soldiers stopped at the edge of the ravine. Sebastian wanted to see as well. Unable to move, the coachman grumbled, 'You're too curious, sir.' When Sebastian pushed back the cover, the black dog bounded down into the snow.

Down below the gold coins had fallen on a drove of oxen. Hundreds of the beasts had been frozen, their eyes open, in a welter of horns and muzzles set in ice. The leaders of the drove had left the road, blinded by a storm perhaps, and their kin had followed, pushing and jostling, until they were at the bottom; unable to get back up, they must have lowed and thrashed about and gouged each other for a long time. The ice had frozen them in ghastly or ludicrous poses.

Some soldiers were letting down ropes to have a closer look at the oxen sprinkled with gold. They walked on the ice, holding onto the horns as if they were handles. A giant fellow brought down a sapper's axe on one of the beasts, but the blade didn't even cut its hide, it was so hard. Under Sebastian's feet, Dimitri the dog barked with impunity at the dead oxen that terrified him. He went too close to the edge and slithered down a few metres. Sebastian went after him, clinging to outcropping rocks, and scooped the dog up against his chest; hands reached out to help him. A modicum of fraternity still existed amongst the men of the Imperial Guard.

Then the wagons crossed the bridge.

It was night when they entered a Krasnoie brightly lit up by bivouac fires. The drivers unharnessed in front of the rudimentary headquarters buildings and Sebastian checked to see how his passenger had taken the journey. She was completely still, curled up on the cardboard boxes of records. He slapped her hands and cheeks, but couldn't get any blood circulating under that transparent skin.

'Take her to the doctors, Monsieur Roque.'

Baron Fain, told that the wagons had arrived, didn't appear surprised to see Mlle Sautet. He even offered to help his clerk take her to the Guard's hospital, where Dr Larrey was practising.

'Don't go to all that trouble, my lord.'

'Oh, but I shall! What if you come a cropper with your load on this slippery snow? If you sprain your wrist? I need your quill hand, you know.'

The hospital proved to be a barn full of wounded and frostbitten grenadiers, who were being massaged by medical orderlies and exhausted voluntary nurses. Sebastian recognized Mme Aurore from behind; she was bustling about a sergeant in a bed, pulling off his boots; his feet were frozen and their skin, which had stuck to the leather, was peeling off in strips. Catherine, the red-headed actress, was going up and down the rows with a flask of brandy. After leaving the bookseller's daughter with an apprentice surgeon, Sebastian questioned Mme Aurore, who was bandaging her sergeant with strips torn from a shirt. Where was Ornella? She didn't know. She had fallen in with a group of stragglers. When they had left their cart, the troupe had split up; the manageress and Catherine had found refuge with some gunners and hitched a lift astride a gun carriage.

*

That night, shirkers had stolen Captain d'Herbigny's Cossack horse; all he had found was the cut bridle. Everyone had to sleep at some time or another, but thieves took advantage of it. How many men no longer left their knapsacks and took it in turns to watch their horses? A cavalryman reduced to an infantryman's state, the captain felt disgraced by his misfortune. When he had discovered the theft, he hadn't even had time to go looking in town: the Emperor was assembling all the able-bodied divisions of the Guard on Krasnoie's main square. Grenadiers, dismounted dragoons, skirmishers – they were all there stamping their feet, snow on their hats and their beards. The Russians were trying to cut Napoleon off from the rest of his army. Davout's I Corps, so staunch and so depleted, was coming under the fire of an army ten times its size but fortunately poorly commanded. The Tsar's generals still feared Napoleon; even in the midst of a rout, his name was enough to make them tremble. Knowing this, he had decided to lead his elite troops into action himself, relying on his presence to push back the enemy and rescue the hard-pressed units trying to reach him. He came onto the square on foot, dressed in the Polish style with a green pelisse with gold frogging, fur-lined boots, a marten-fur cap edged with fox fur tied on with ribbons, and holding a baton made of birch in his hand. He gave a speech, phrases of which were repeated through the ranks. D'Herbigny only remembered one, but it electrified him: 'I have been an emperor long enough, now I'll be a general again.'

The grenadiers of the Old Guard formed square around His Majesty. With the band at their head, three thousand soldiers and horsemen made ready to leave the town. Crowded in doorways, the administrative staff and the servants wondered anxiously whether these last-remaining, well-ordered troops would come back; if not, they would all fall into the hands of the Russians, who would exterminate them. Paulin found himself one of the people having such thoughts. The captain didn't turn his head toward him; he got his dragoons in step, shivering with cold, or joy, it was hard to tell.

Raising fifes to their chapped lips, bandsmen struck up 'Where can one be happier than in the bosom of one's family?' – the irony of which was not appreciated by the Emperor, who preferred a martial air more suited to their situation, and so it was to the strains of 'Let us watch over the Empire's safety' that the divisions emerged shortly after from the sunken road where they had been sheltering. The veterans, Napoleon's old grumblers, spotted the Russian army on a hill, drawn up by a fir forest. They jeered mockingly. They marched straight ahead through the snow, in step, to join up with Davout's soldiers, who were surrounded by hordes of Cossacks. Confronted by the eagles, the unfurled tricolour battalion flags, the music and the famous bearskins of the Imperial Guard, whom they had saluted in so many battles, the Russians were stupefied. The Cossack cavalry fell back in disorder without daring to attack. D'Herbigny deployed his troop as a shield on the grenadiers' flank. He observed his Emperor, very sure of himself, invincible again, just as he used to be. The enemy avoided engaging. Then its artillery positioned on the ridges went into action.

Safely out of reach, the Russian cannon concentrated their fire on the column, an easy, slow-moving target they could take good aim at. The grapeshot and roundshot opened breaches in the dense mass of the battalions. When one man fell to the ground, his knees shattered or his head blown off, another replaced him to close up the ranks and present a wall of bodies to the enemy. They stepped over the fallen without a glance, a gesture, a word of comfort or feeling, deaf to their screams and supplications and oaths. Sergeant Bonet was marching on the captain's right; he stooped forward convulsively, his stomach torn open by a shell splinter, fell to his knees, holding his entrails with both hands, and as he collapsed in the snow, he beseeched d'Herbigny, 'Sir! Finish me off!'

'We can't stop, Bonet, we can't! Do you understand?'

'No!'

As Bonet moaned, his friends set one bandaged foot in front of the other in the reddening snow; after the dragoons came others and they passed by in their turn, inhuman, mechanical. The grumblers marched on, on towards the unbowed Davout; they left comrades from the bivouacs behind them, they heard the report when a wounded man managed to put the barrel of his pistol to his temple and, with a feverish hand, pull the trigger. They marched on. They may not have been able to look down at the dying, but the men's prayers and abuse would stay in their memories for a long time, unless, that is, they joined them within the minute or the hour. They marched on to their graves but the Emperor was with them.

*

General Saint-Sulpice had been hit by a burst of case-shot in the calf, and by another in the hip. Pale, fighting back the pain, he was delegating command to his subordinates as he was being carried off on a stretcher to the infirmary's barouches in Krasnoie. 'D'Herbigny,' he said, 'I'm entrusting the remains of the brigade to you.'

'Don't you think me capable, General, of serving as part of the Emperor's close escort?'

'I do.'

'Perhaps my fellow officer Pucheu is more competent?'

'He has both his hands.'

Having made his way through the Russian lines and escorted back the remainder of Davout's army, His Majesty had given the order that officers who still had their horses should form a sacred squadron for his protection. Generals would serve as lieutenants and colonels as sergeant majors in a new hierarchy of modestly titled ranks that were all the more prestigious for the duties they entailed. D'Herbigny had come through the attack without a scratch and offered to look after his general's Turkish mare, a raw-boned but wiry creature. He would have liked to strut on a proper horse close to the emperor, but Saint-Sulpice had chosen Pucheu for that and now this braggart would win all the glory instead of him. D'Herbigny protested, 'I don't need both my hands to sabre!'

'I'm sure you don't, but Pucheu has less hold over my men than you do.'

'I shall obey your orders.'

'Our profession is not always glorious, Captain.'

'I know.'

'Maintain discipline.'

'I will try.'

'Don't try, succeed.'

'Farewell, sir.'

'Until we meet again, Captain. I'll see you're promoted in Paris.'

'Paris is a long way away.'

D'Herbigny dutifully went off and melted into the rank and file. His record of service meant nothing. Aboukir had been brushed aside, Saint-Jean-d'Acre, Eylau, Wagram –

all of them brushed aside. Pucheu put his foot in the stirrup and swung himself up onto the general's black mare, saying, 'My fellows are all yours! Put them together and you'll have almost a half-squadron of poachers.'

'I'll keep your ruffians in check, even with just one hand.'

'Ah yes, I've got two hands, but for how much longer?'

'*Vaya con dios!*' The captain had heard this expression so often in Saragossa, that it sometimes occurred to him at difficult moments; he translated it oddly as *Go to the devil!* Pucheu set off at a slow trot to join the sacred squadron, about sixty officers of all ranks and regiments in capes, plumed bicornes and fur caps. The emperor was preparing to take the road to the little town of Orcha, through marshes and over a series of wooden bridges. Prince Eugène was already herding the stragglers and the civilians in that direction with his Italians. Davout was staying at Krasnoie to wait for Marshal Ney, of whom there was no news. The cannon boomed again. Drawn up in line, a ravine at their backs, Mortier's Red Lancers and Portuguese were checking Kutuzov's advance. D'Herbigny envied them their part in the massacre. Why did the cannon-balls always spare him? Why must he keep on fighting and always obeying? He imagined himself galloping after Mortier, Duke of Treviso, a tall fellow with a pinhead on an outsize body, not very smart but loyal just like him, and offering himself up to the Russian cannon. For the first time in his life, the captain was asking himself clear questions. His brains felt as if they had been turned upside down.

Lost in thought, he pushed open a door of his dragoons' hutments. They hadn't had enough rest and they grumbled when they saw him; the ones in best fettle fell into line.

Images ran though his mind: he saw Anissia's face, the novice he had buried in Moscow, her imploring eyes, her gentle smile, her gold cross that he had worn round his neck ever since; then Normandy's hedges, meadows, the valleys that stretched like clouds to the horizon, cows, churns of cream, Rouen market, the inns, his home in the countryside that Paulin always talked about with a quaver in his voice. Where had he got to, that one? 'Paulin!' The dragoons hadn't seen him. He wouldn't be able to manage on his own, that idiot! 'Paulin!' He missed his batman, even though there was hardly anything for him to do in this retreat. No need to polish his boots now; polished boots, there's a joke! Herbigny tightened the pearl necklaces holding up the rags on his legs. Drawing himself up to his full height, he laid about the shirkers to get them into line. The trumpeter burst into hysterical laughter, d'Herbigny snatched his instrument from him and blew into it hard enough to rupture a lung; the trumpet let out a squawk.

*

At Orcha, by the banks of a swollen, fast-moving Dnieper awash with drift ice, the weather grew milder. With this abrupt thaw, the snow melted and filled the streets with a runny black slime that came up to a man's shin. Carriages became bogged down in the cesspool, the fugitives splashed and floundered about, swamping the town that was too small to shelter their numbers and crowding into its isbas. Often they didn't even have room to lie down and the most exhausted fell asleep squatting on their heels, jammed together amid a nauseating stench of mould, filth and musk. Distraught, they were reverting to their bestial state. Only the grenadiers posted as sentries indicated that the

Emperor had taken up his quarters in a row of poorly squared log cottages. Beside them, sappers had demolished a cabin to lay walkways between the coaches and doors, so as not to dirty His Majesty's boots, luggage or archives. Valets were ferrying chests under Sebastian's supervision, when several mud-bespattered gendarmes brought up some sort of Russian merchant, with a heavy moustache and very blond, long hair under a bell-shaped hat. The sentries levelled their muskets.

'I am Captain Konopka,' said the supposed merchant. 'I've come from Lithuania, I have a communication for the Emperor from the Governor of Vilna, the Duke of Bassano.'

'You're not Russian?'

'Polish!'

'I'll go and inform His Majesty,' said Sebastian.

He went into a room that was full of smoke from a stove. Slouched in his travelling armchair, Napoleon was listening sullenly to the major general list the army's strength and losses.

'We have not more than eight thousand combatants, sire. We have recently lost twenty-seven generals, forty thousand men have been taken prisoner and sixty thousand are dead. We have had to leave five hundred cannon on the road . . .'

'Our reserves?'

'Oudinot is still in Lithuania.'

'Have him join us. How many men has he?'

'Five thousand.'

'And Victor?'

'Fifteen thousand.'

'Have him join us as well. Davout?'

'He left Krasnoie this morning.'

'With Ney?'

'No, sire.'

'That unreliable fool, who gave him the order?'

'He did himself.'

'He was to wait for Ney!'

'He is marching on Orcha, burning the bridges as he goes.'

'So Ney is lost?'

Berthier did not answer. The Emperor noticed Sebastian standing in the doorway. 'What does that lump wringing his hands want?'

'Sire,' said Sebastian as Napoleon glared at him, 'a Polish officer is here, he has come from Lithuania . . .'

'Well, send him in, you awkward lump!'

'Sire,' said the captain as he entered, hat in hand, 'a Russian army is advancing on Vilna.'

'What of the Duke of Bassano?'

'He is concerned and sent me to inform you.'

'Let him stand fast!'

'Will he able to?'

'He must!'

'The situation is perilous, I had to disguise myself to cross enemy lines.'

'So those barbarians are everywhere, are they?'

'Everywhere.'

'How far to Vilna and the Niemen?'

'A hundred and twenty leagues of wilderness.'

'Which way should we go?'

'The thaw means we have to take the bridges.'

'Cross the Dnieper here?'

'Yes, sire.'

'Then?'

'There is another bridge on a tributary of the Dnieper, at Borisov.'

'How long to get there?'

'A week, roughly.'

'Can the Russians get there before us?'

'Perhaps, sire, but it's the only way out.'

'Is it broad, this river of yours?'

'Not especially, about forty fathoms.'

'Its name?'

'The Berezina.'

*

Two grenadiers of the Guard came out of the convent occupied by the commissariat. Toting a big bundle, they were heading back to their cantonment with provisions for the battalion – keeping clear of the centre of town, where they would have been robbed by the starving even though they were armed – when they saw a tattered, mud-splashed young woman leaning against the wall of a wooden shack. She was giving them the glad eye. She had long, tousled black hair and a face as angelic as her pose was provocative: Ornella made a wickedly alluring picture. The grenadiers stopped in front of her and talked between themselves. 'Do you think she speaks French?'

'If she does or doesn't, what's it matter?'

'Course, you're right, for what we're after.'

'I'm from Paris and I'm hungry,' said Ornella, eyeing them.

'That can be discussed,' said one of the grenadiers.

'That can be paid for,' she answered.

'What are you offering for our biscuits?'

'You won't be disappointed!' she called, disappearing into the shack.

The grenadiers hesitated.

'You go first, you're the sergeant.'

'Keep an eye on our rations.'

'Trust me,' said the other, cocking his pistol.

Then, in a state of high excitement, the sergeant entered a dark room.

'Where are you?'

'Come closer.'

The sergeant groped his way forward.

'Ah, got you!'

He felt Ornella's hair under his fingers.

'Got you too!'

She gripped his wrists as Dr Fournereau slit his throat from behind with a precise movement, without a sound. They conferred in a low voice. 'The one guarding the sack of biscuits is armed,' said Ornella.

'Call him . . .'

'He won't come, he's waiting for his friend.'

'Make him wait, then. Play your part, let's have some groans.'

Ornella started to moan; she lit one of the candles she'd taken when they left their cart. 'Hey, old ham,' the doctor said to Vialatoux. 'You're the same height, or near enough, as that dumb soldier, put on his cap and coat. It's getting dark . . .'

'I understand my character,' Vialatoux murmured professionally.

The others spread out in the semi-darkness; they stripped the grenadier. Striking a variety of poses, Vialatoux put on the coat, jammed the tall bearskin on his head, wrapped his face in the fur scarf, and then regretted not having a brighter light and mirror to check his costume. Fournereau whispered that it was perfect. After some extravagant trills, on Ornella's last scream, he pushed the actor outside.

'Hey, Sergeant, you know how to make that hussy sing!' the other grenadier congratulated him, but as he held out the sack, he suddenly became suspicious and raised his pistol. 'Where's that blood on your coat come from?'

Vialatoux made a sign that it was nothing.

'Have you been struck dumb? Who are you? What about the sergeant? Where's the sergeant?'

Vialatoux jumped at him, wrenched his hand away and the bullet went into the ground. Fournereau and two or three strong men rushed out. The grenadier lost his footing; Fournereau pinned him to the ground, twisted his face into the liquid mud and held him under long enough for him to suffocate. His job done, he went back into the shack where the biscuits and rye bread were being handed out.

'Don't eat it all, think of tomorrow,' said the doctor, dragging in the body of the second grenadier.

They had thrown themselves on the bread; sprawled on the floor, they were devouring it, stuffing their mouths so full they were almost choking. Fournereau joined them.

Suddenly they stopped. A bright light spilled though the door of their refuge. They picked up their share of the provisions and went outside. Carriages were burning in the middle of the street. Gunners were leading horses away by the bridle, others were smashing the windows of a berline; still others were running up with torches. Fournereau and his group went closer; perhaps there would be some clothes to salvage.

'Here,' a soldier said to Vialatoux.

He handed him a torch. The actor was still wearing the grenadier's bearskin and now it seemed he had been enlisted. Why not? The Guard got fed, at least. He seized the chance to join this swirling crowd of incendiaries who were taking delight in destroying half the carriages: they started running, yelling, smashing and setting them on fire with Vialatoux in their midst. The Emperor had set an example by burning part of his baggage on a bonfire: any horses remaining he wanted for the few cannon and caissons that had come this far, not for the useless carriages which only got in the way.

*

Pedestrians and coachmen crossed the Dnieper on two bridges that Davout was going to burn. It couldn't be helped about Marshal Ney; they had to make haste towards Borisov, since the Russians could strike in numbers at any moment and cut off their route home. Oudinot and Victor had been ordered to wait at the Berezina with their reserve armies in winter clothes. After navigating a slushy road marked out by rows of birches, the cohort crossed Minsk's dark forest. In the secretariat's wagon, Sebastian and Baron Fain had cleared a space for themselves by destroying armfuls of archives in Orcha.

'Monsieur Roque,' said the Baron, 'your teeth are chattering.'

'My teeth are chattering.'

'Pull yourself together! And let's walk to get rid of this numbness, otherwise we'll end up like the Sautet girl.'

'I'd promised her parents...'

'Are you a doctor? No?'

'I can see the hospital, the straw, the squalor the sick and amputees were lying in . . .'

'You can appeal to sentiment at the Tuileries. Now then, come on, look sharp, out of this wagon!'

'I realized when the dog ran off howling.'

'A naturalist, now, are we? Conducting a study of dogs' behaviour?'

'Everything's dying around us, my lord.'

'Fiddlesticks! As long as one shaves every morning, there's hope. Come on! Even His Majesty is walking so as not to freeze to the marrow.'

They squelched through the melted snow. In front of them the Emperor was indeed walking, on the grand equerry's arm. They both leaned on sticks. Then came Berthier and the shivering headquarters staff, the canteen, the crates of beef and salt mutton on wagons driven by Masquelet the chef and his cook's boys, and the baggage reduced to their minimum. As the hours passed, a ceaseless stream of dispatch riders informed the Emperor of events. One setback followed another. Minsk had fallen, with its well-stocked stores; the Borisov bridge, the only way across the Berezina, had been taken by the Cossacks; Oudinot's regiments had driven them off, but the bridge had been partly destroyed and three Russian armies were closing on the river in a pincer movement.

'If the cold set in again,' the Emperor said to Caulaincourt, 'we could cross this river on foot.'

'Can the Berezina freeze anew in two days?'

'Berthier!' the Emperor cried without turning round.

'Sire,' said the major general, having trouble keeping his balance in the mud.

'Send word to Oudinot, he must find another way across, a ford, pontoon bridges . . .'

In adversity, the Emperor exhibited impeccable calm; the fact that his plans were being thwarted by circumstances didn't seem to affect him at all. He merely asked Caulaincourt from time to time, 'Marshal Ney?'

'We have no news, sire.'

'He is lost . . .'

The Emperor continued on his way, head bowed, saddened more than frightened by his situation. He had been informed of the mood of the army. Davout had flown into a rage about this "diabolical campaign"; there'd even been seditious talk from some of the grenadiers. When Napoleon had made to warm himself at a bivouac fire, Caulaincourt had dissuaded him.

A lancer riding at a fast trot overtook the carriages and passengers on foot, splashing them with mud. He had come from Orcha. As soon as he saw the Emperor he raced towards him. Sebastian saw Napoleon take Caulaincourt in his arms and shake him, a radiant smile on his face.

'Apparently bad news isn't the only news there is,' remarked Baron Fain.

'Perhaps we've captured Kutuzov . . .'

'Why not the Tsar, while you're on the subject?'

Veterans, the first to be told, were raising their muskets and shouting, 'Long live the Emperor!' as at a review. The cry came closer and closer: 'Marshal Ney has reached Orcha!'

'He's alive!'

'He's got a musket in his hand, he's bringing back a handful of men, and he's managed to slip past a brace of Russian armies!'

It was a symbol. They could get through this. This unhoped-for survival revived soldiers who were on the point of rebellion; those who'd been throwing away their muskets a moment ago and talking of surrender now bawled 'Long live the Emperor' loud enough to strike fear into a thousand Cossacks. At the stopping place, amongst the trees, they told each other the epic of Marshal Ney in snatches.

'Peppered with grapeshot from all sides,' a clerk was saying, 'he had fires lit at nightfall, so then the Russians thought he'd attack at dawn at that point . . .'

'You weren't there,' mocked a major-domo.

'I have it from somebody who was!'

'Let him speak,' Sebastian cut in, swigging brandy from the bottle.

'Well, when it was pitch dark, he left without the guns or baggage and fell back by the byroads. There was hardly a hundred of them, and they crossed the rivers on foot, one by one, the ice was fragile . . .'

As far as Borisov, this was the only subject of conversation. They forgot the danger they faced and believed in miracles.

*

It was midday. Bundled up in his green lined box coat, the Emperor appeared stouter than usual. Legs spread, eyes glued to his theatre glasses, he was staring at a white hillock behind which nestled the village of Borisov. There had been shouting in that direction; the major general had dispatched lancers to scout it out. They were coming back. They appeared on a snow-covered knoll, waving their flags. The Emperor drew breath. This signal confirmed that II and IX Army Corps, which had come from Lithuania, were holding the position. He got into his berline and the cortege set off again. An icebound landscape passed by outside the window: bare trunks, fir boughs and brushwood as fine, transparent and tapered as crystal. Napoleon was prepared for everything, even defending himself with his pistol; ready to abandon the remains of his baggage and carriages to make a break across the fields at the head of his Guard. The Berezina was drawing nearer; now it remained for them to cross it. He would stake his life and empire on this campaign but he wouldn't leave his enemies any trophies. Yesterday he had organized a memorable ceremony; since the Bridge at Arcola he had known that men need powerful images, spectacles to stir and intensify their feelings of attachment. The colour-bearers of the dilapidated regiments had been assembled in open country. A great pyre of burning carts melted the snow. One after another they came forward to throw their eagles into the blaze. They kissed the emblem before watching it warp and melt in the flames; many wept. A drummer boy played, while an officer saluted, his sabre lowered in acknowledgement. Later the Emperor told Caulaincourt that he'd rather eat with his fingers than leave the Russians a single fork bearing his coat of arms, and so he had divided out among the members of his household the metal drinking cups and the forks and spoons with which he ate meals from the Imperial canteen.

Napoleon's carriage passed the first houses of Borisov. Vigorous, spotless men, without beards or lice, in new capes and plumed shakos, were greeting the wretched survivors of the Army of Moscow with consternation. They were staggered by such misery. The blind, their eyes scorched by the glare of the snows and the stinging smoke of bivouac fires, held onto one another's shoulders. The wounded limped along, using their muskets as crutches. Their arms in makeshift slings, their fingers frozen, their ears missing, here they came – the herd of cripples, the army of ghosts. Oudinot's soldiers broke ranks to support their brothers, give them coats, food; in the confusion, the survivors flung themselves on the ration bread, ravenous as hunting dogs, sprawling in the soft snow. Until now, the Emperor had seen no one apart from his Guard; he began to realize the lamentable state of the troops he was leading back west. He entered the shack where his campaign furniture was already set up. He sat on a folding stool, but made no move to consult the maps spread out before him. Constant lit his lamp.

'Berthier?' asked the Emperor. 'Berthier, how are we to get out of here?'

Tears were running down his cheeks; he didn't even wipe them away with his sleeve. Murat stamped his feet to get warm; he answered in the major-general's stead, 'With an escort of Poles, since they know the region, we'll follow the Berezina north. Five days and you are in Vilna.'

'But what about the army?'

'They will create a diversion, occupy the Russians.'

The Emperor shook his head, dismissing this suggestion.

'Sire,' continued Berthier, 'you have suggested on numerous occasions that you would be more useful to the army in Paris than in its midst.'

'But not before it's crossed this damned river!'

'It's impossible here. The other bank's teeming with Cossacks. Kutuzov is informed, the hills will soon be covered with cannon. Even if we repair the bridge, it won't be enough, it would take days for everyone to cross.'

'I had given instructions for fords to be found!'

'You have been obeyed, sire.'

'Where? Show me.'

Berthier explained that some of Victor's Poles had caught a peasant's horse. The animal was wet to the stomach, so they knew it must have crossed the river somewhere. They'd found the peasant and he'd shown them the ford.

'It's upstream, opposite this village,' said Berthier.

He stuck a pin in the map.

'Do what's necessary, dismantle the village plank by plank, assemble enough material for at least two bridges so that the pontoneers and sappers can get to work tomorrow at the shallowest point.'

The staff were about to withdraw when the Emperor entered into greater detail. 'Let us make it seem we're installing ourselves permanently in Borisov, so that the Russian spies think we want to repair their bridge.'

Once alone, Napoleon bent over the map and spelled out the name of the famous village: Studienka.

'Monsieur Constant, my Voltaire!'

The valet was getting a fire to catch in the stove. He took the volume from an oblong mahogany trunk in which His Majesty's books were stored in different compartments. The Emperor leafed through it and stopped at a chapter that he had read countless times. It was at Studienka that Charles XII had crossed the Berezina. He had had no more news of Sweden than Napoleon had of France; his army was disintegrating. Once again the Emperor compared these two scenarios a century apart. What Voltaire wrote of the Swedish troops could have been a description of this shadow of the Grande Armée: 'The cavalry no longer had boots, the infantry were without shoes, and almost without coats. They were reduced to cobbling shoes together from animal skins, as best they could; they were often short of bread. The artillery had been compelled to dump all the cannon in the marshes and the rivers, for lack of horses to pull them...' The Emperor snapped the book shut, as if touching it would put a curse on him. Slipping a hand under his waistcoat, he made sure that Dr Yvan's pouch of poison was safely attached to its string.

*

The headquarters and the Guard installed themselves in the castle of a certain Prince Radziwill, a league from Berezina, the farms of whose estate contained forage, oxen and large quantities of dried vegetables. Armed grenadiers stood guard over this treasure, which they reserved for themselves; no one else was allowed into the farms. The other regiments and the flood of stragglers and civilians had to fend for themselves – no doubt they could beg for coats and for flour from Oudinot and Victor's intendants, who would be amply supplied by the storehouses of Lithuania. This, therefore, is how the sentries came to turn away a bearded little chap with dark rings round his eyes, decked out in a red hat and ermine collar, who, on seeing a colour of the Guard nailed to the gate, had left the train of civilians and headed straight there.

'You've no business here!'

'The dragoons of the Guard...'

'You're in the cavalry, are you, flabby chops?'

'I didn't say that, I wanted to know if the dragoons of the Guard were bivouacking in this chateau.'

'The whole Guard's here — and nothing but the Guard.'

'Then you've got to let me in.'

'You've been told to scarper.'

'I am Captain d'Herbigny's batman.'

'He hasn't got much taste, this captain.'

'At least check what I'm saying!'

The corporal in command of the sentries shrugged his shoulders but turned to one of the grenadiers nonetheless. 'Go and see if there is a Captain Derini.'

'D'Herbigny! General Saint-Sulpice's brigade.'

'If you've been spinning us tales, my lad, you'll get a thrashing.'

'And if I haven't, the captain's likely to warm your ribs.'

The grenadier soon came back with a big chap in a Turkoman cap whom Paulin didn't recognize immediately. But by a stroke of luck it turned out to be Trooper Chantelouve; he confirmed the batman's position and Paulin was reunited with his master. D'Herbigny was camped out with the brigade in one of the main farm buildings, on fresh straw. Paulin dropped his bag; the captain lit into him, as usual.

'Where were you?'

'I didn't know where you'd got to, sir, I had to leave Krasnoie with the refugees . . .'

'Chantelouve?'

'Captain?'

'Give this idiot some lentils.'

In this brigade reduced to the size of a squadron, the

few dragoons who still had their horses were combing them. Paulin tucked in and the captain lay down in the straw without closing his eyes.

He got up soon after, when the drums sounded. In the moonlit meadow, staff officers were rushing between the farm buildings, alerting the Guard.

A colonel in a cloak stuck his lantern under Captain d'Herbigny's nose, who received a movement order to go to Studienka and reinforce Oudinot's II Corps.

'At dawn?'

'Immediately.'

'In the middle of the night?'

'You'll follow the heavy baggage train.'

It wasn't a question of understanding the orders, or their urgency, but simply of carrying them out. D'Herbigny rushed his dragoons; they gathered in front of the chateau where lines of vehicles stood harnessed. The cold was closing in again. A battalion of skirmishers were waiting around, not moving; sometimes there was a barely audible thud as an infantryman, not wrapped up well enough, fell frozen stiff into the snow. Paulin shivered, complaining, 'I finally find you, sir, after terrible days and horrendous nights, and now I have to lose you again!' The captain took his valet by the wrist and led him from wagon to wagon to find him a place, but no one wanted him. At that moment a group of administrators and secretaries were coming down the steps to crowd into some covered barouches. Sebastian was part of the nocturnal expedition; as he was passing under a carriage lantern, the captain saw him, called him over, and settled the matter so that Paulin had somewhere to sit this time. Squeezed between the clerks, he was asleep before the carriage had set off. Mumbling in his sleep, he amused the other passengers by proclaiming imperiously, 'Driver, to Rouen!'

*

Transformed into carpenters, Oudinot's men dismantled Studienka's isbas and took them down to the riverbank. D'Herbigny and his dragoons, meanwhile, were assembling two rafts out of joists and doors. Four hundred skirmishers were to take up position on the other bank where, in light woods, they had glimpsed Russians, identifying them by their round hats with a yellow cross at the front. They had to protect the construction of the bridges. Troopers plunged into the river, sending off waves, and the captain watched them swimming at a diagonal, forced downstream by the current; they used their lances to fend off the sharp-edged drift ice that careered into their horses and cut their flanks. Some were thrown from the saddle and disappeared, especially towards the centre, where it was deeper and the animals completely under water. Two-thirds, however, managed to get to the other side, their horses' hooves sinking in the mud.

Once the rafts had been lashed together with ropes provided by an engineer, they were pushed into the water and a handful of Oudinot's skirmishers clambered aboard. The men sat on the joists; navigation promised to be a rickety business. D'Herbigny got on the first raft with three of his dragoons. They were going to cross like this in groups, constantly fearing that a bigger or a sharper bit of broken ice would capsize them.

They set off, rowing with the butts of their muskets to counter the current, but still the craft veered off course; d'Herbigny and the skirmishers, their bayonets in the water, repelled as best they could the blocks of ice speeding towards them. Partly deflected, one of these blocks jammed itself under the planking of the raft, causing it to lurch and spin as if it was on a pivot. The men lay flat on their stomachs, grabbing knots in the ropes and hanging on as sheets of water hit them in the face; they ended up hurtling into the other bank and tried to moor, throwing out ropes to troopers who'd crossed before and could help pull them up. The second raft made land further downstream. There had been no casualties but already rowers were taking the battered craft back to Studienka. Incredulous, the captain exclaimed, 'The carriages and cannon will never be able to move in this quagmire!'

'We'll have to extend the bridges,' a non-commissioned officer replied.

'There won't be enough wood.'

'What about the forest? We'll break off the branches and lay them on the mud so the wheels won't sink.'

There was a crack of musket fire. Bullets crashed into the mire around them. The captain looked up and spotted two Russians under the cover of a clump of trees. He swore furiously, pushed out of the way one of the lancers who had dismounted to help with the landing, took his horse, mounted it without being able to get his feet in the stirrups because of the rags round his boots and rode hard towards the trees. The Russians made a run for it, not having had time to reload. He caught hold of one of them by the cross-belt, picked him with his one arm and, dragging him along like a package, brought him back, out of breath but overjoyed at his catch, who went sprawling in the mud.

'This swine knows things His Majesty will be very glad to hear!'

The Emperor had just appeared on the left bank, which was becoming crowded with people. He rode alongside Marshal Oudinot, Duke of Reggio, an uncouth fellow with a great thirst for glory, thirty times wounded and thirty times sewn back together again. D'Herbigny saw the cannon of the troops freshly arrived from Lithuania, climbing a knoll from where they would cover Studienka. He made out the long-limbed silhouette of General Eblé, whom he had known as a gunner at the siege of Almeida; he was tall, with a bony face and grey hair fluttering under his bicorne. At the head of his pontoneers he was bringing portable forges, wagons of charcoal and caissons of tools and nails found in Smolensk. Unfortunately, for lack of horses, he had been forced to burn his boats, which prevented him throwing a pontoon bridge across the Berezina, but in any case, would he have been able to? The wind was getting up and blowing hard. On the right bank, the captain cursed his spectator's role; he wanted to be useful, manifold, every-where at the same time. The Russians, having moved up from the boggy ground, were encamped on the heights and lighting fires. Opposite, the sappers and Poles were swelling the ranks of the pontoneers. They were nailing trestles together; D'Herbigny heard the mallet blows, the rasp of saws. Studienka was starting to look like a huge stack of wood. Eblé gave instructions for the first trestle to be set in the mud; it sank under the impatient gaze of Napoleon, who was almost unhorsed by a gust of wind.

The captain set off back across the river to deliver his tied-up prisoner. The conditions were as dangerous as before, with only three rowers, the dragoons. The wind blew counter to the current, churning the water into eddies; the raft bucked, drift ice smashed into it, the ropes stretched taut. Several times they almost capsized. In the commotion, the Russian manoeuvred himself until he lay flat on his stomach and, as the captain deflected the ice and the others struggled to keep the raft afloat, he rolled into the black water. D'Herbigny tried to catch him with his one hand.

'Leave him, he'll drag you under!'

'The bastard!'

'Hang on!'

Picked up by the current, the raft rammed into the left bank at brutal speed, temporarily knocking the captain unconscious. His dragoons laid him in the snow, staggering under the weight. One of them smacked him to bring him round; he snarled, 'Is that you slapping me, Chantelouve?'

'No choice . . .'

'Do you want to fight a duel?'

Still dazed, d'Herbigny realized the silliness of what he was saying, extricated himself with a 'Let's not talk about it anymore . . .' and stood up. It was dark and clouds hid the moon. He couldn't see anything but he walked towards the sounds of building. The Emperor had forbidden fires so as not to alert the Russians to the heavy concentration on Studienka; the pontoneers worked by the distant glimmer of the enemy's campfires. They moved forward metre by metre on rafts. Hampered by the high water, which was still rising because of the thaw, they lost the ford countless times. Time and again they were forced to undress and wade into the river up to their shoulders to drive piles into the spongy bed, attach them, nail planks. Some would climb back onto the edifice bleeding, their backs cut by ridges of ice.

*

Crowded together to keep warm on the benches, cushions and floor of the covered barouche, Sebastian and the other clerks of the secretariat had only slept in snatches, woken by the roaring of the river, the shouted orders, the noise of hammers and mallets and the bouts of cramp. They had managed to drowse off when an unexpected cry jolted them all awake. 'Cockadoodle do! Cock – a – doodle – do!'

'Are we there?' asked Paulin, forgetting where he was.

'Where?' a clerk said to him.

'Cock – a – doodle – do!'

'Is that a cockerel?'

'It sounds like it, Monsieur Paulin.'

'Does His Majesty have a travelling barnyard?'

'Heavens, no; his meat is transported in salting tubs. A salt cockerel can't sing.'

'Cock – a – doodle – do!'

Outside, soldiers were laughing and slapping their thighs. They formed a circle around the make-believe fowl, a valet in green livery laced with gold and a powdered wig; he was hopping up and down, his heels tucked in under his bottom, producing very convincing cock-a-doodle-doos. Sebastian asked what game they were playing. A corporal answered, gasping for breath, 'Thinks he's a cock. He's mad.'

'We're going to pluck him,' said another jovially.

Sebastian was not particularly amused. He had been noticing cases of delirium for more than a week, but they took less comical forms – yelling, incoherent speech, cursing. The man suddenly collapsed in the snow and refused to move; he was going to freeze to death. Prefect Bausset, whose gout made every step painful, gave instructions for the hysteric to be carried in the medical orderlies' caravan, and then ordered the major-domos to take a hundred bottles of Chambertin to His Majesty. The first bridge was finished and the Emperor wanted personally to distribute his wine among the shivering workers, who were moving a hundred metres upstream to build a second one.

The coachmen put horses to their carriages, the gunners likewise to their cannon. Stragglers were coming out from the Borisov road, alerted by a rumour that the engineers were throwing bridges across the river; a multitude of vehicles, horses, and tatterdemalions spread across the plain without being able to reach the bridge, which was sealed off by the grenadiers. An angry clamour greeted this obstruction, as if their survival depended solely on crossing this river, the Berezina with its multiple branches and miry islets. Berthier, Murat, Ney exerted all their energies organizing their troops. Oudinot dressed the lines of his impeccably uniformed regiments. The carriages of the Imperial household moved off towards the site of the second bridge, where trestles had already been fixed in the bed.

Sebastian didn't stay in the barouche; he needed to move about. He approached the new building yard, where the Emperor was avidly monitoring the bridge's progress, standing at the start of the barely laid roadway, beside General Eblé who was coordinating the work.

Tied to rafts, pontoneers were nailing road-bearers or, as they had the previous night, stripping to dive into the water and hold piles steady in the muddy bed, or climbing under the trestles, nimble as acrobats, with nails at the corner of their mouths and hammers hanging from strings round their necks. The temperature was falling. There was no let-up in the mass of drift ice being swept downstream, spinning and crashing into wood or bodies. A pontoneer cried out: a piece of ice was pinning him against a thick plank; he opened his mouth, threw his head back and sank. His companions didn't help him – they didn't have time – this bridge for the artillery had to be finished and sturdy before nightfall. Sebastian heard the Emperor say, 'Eblé, reinforce your men with my sappers.'

'They don't know this work, sire.'

'Then explain it to them, we have to hurry.'

'And make something that holds, sire.'

'If you'd kept your boats, it would have made life easier for us.'

'You requested I burn them.'

'This drift ice!'

'If we had had time, we would have built a barricade of tree trunks . . .'

On the right bank, Polish lancers were returning from patrol; their officer was shaking his lance with its multicoloured pennons. As he rode across the first bridge at a slow trot, it wobbled. On the other bank he made his way upstream to the site where the Emperor was standing.

'Sire! Sire! The Russians!'

'They're advancing on us?'

'They have disappeared.'

'They've scurried off to Borisov,' the Emperor said, smiling, pleased with his trick and the mediocrity of the enemy's generals.

*

'There, Chantelouve, you see why the wounds they inflict are so awful?' D'Herbigny had kept the musket of the

Russian who had fleetingly been his prisoner and was displaying the calibre of the bullets he'd found in the cartridge pouch. 'Those are pigeon's eggs, not bullets.'

'What about when you haven't got any Russian ammunition left, Captain?' asked another cavalryman.

'If I run out, that means I've put it to good use! I'll have blown some Cossacks' heads to bits!'

'Or civilians', Captain. Look at that shambles.'

At the entrance to the finished bridge, over which Oudinot's regiments were filing, the grenadiers were endeavouring to keep the hordes at a distance. Their bayonets didn't impress anyone, however; civilians pushed in between horses and wagons, their numbers constantly growing as they massed in the plain.

The thousands of men of II Corps had not yet crossed the river when the other bridge was finished. The vehicles of the Emperor's household waited in line for the order to be given; the artillery readied itself. The Guard regrouped while a division deployed in front of the first bridge; navvies from the engineers, loudly booed on all sides, were digging a broad trench to contain the crowd. The captain and his brigade fell in behind the Old Guard. Caulaincourt gave his instructions to the drivers: 'Drive as slowly as possible and keep a gap between yourselves, the bridge mustn't be overstrained.'

'We'll be at it for hours!'

'We've got all evening and night.'

A barouche made its way over the bridge. Everyone held their breath, listening to the wood creaking; then a berline followed in turn without mishap. Caulaincourt let the infantry of the Guard file by on either side of the vehicles. Soon torches had to be lit and for hours on end, they crossed the Berezina like a funeral procession. Back on the plain, the confused mass of civilians had resigned themselves to waiting; they were setting up their camps around burning carts.

Raising his torch to a barouche's window, the captain caught sight of his batman and seemed reassured. Good old Paulin . . . All in all, they weren't doing too badly: in a few days they'd be resting up in Vilna, a prosperous town where everyone could spend their coins and ingots. The Russian army Bassano thought was a threat had gone away; it must have linked up with Kutuzov's forces. D'Herbigny was about to step onto the bridge when the carriage in front of him ground to a halt; a wheel had slipped through the planks. Pontoneers who were watching on rafts hurried over to brace the roadway. The driver and some infantry-men lifted the carriage and worked its wheel free.

As a precaution, the soldiers guided the horses by hand, which allowed them to control their speed and prevent accidents. As they drove onto the bridge, the vehicles kept their distance from one another, but leaving it they began to pile up; despite the hard frost, the ground was being ploughed into mud, new arrivals were becoming stuck and blocking the forest road. Thus overloaded at one end, the bridge began to grow weaker. Every moment pontoneers were straightening an unsteady trestle or reinforcing a joint.

*

D'Herbigny walked his horse onto the bridge, not even glancing at the black water with its great, circling blocks of ice. Sometimes one hit a strut and the roadway pitched. The captain was halfway across the bridge when, just in front of him, a berline pulled up; one of its horses had collapsed. The driver and passengers cut the girths holding the animal and pushed it into the water, sending up a huge spray of foam.

The creaking of the struts was becoming alarming. The captain took the initiative; going from coach to coach, he ordered the passengers for their own safety to continue on foot. He was about to knock on the window of the secretaries' barouche, whose horses were stamping danger-ously, when the roadway broke in two; the horses caught their pasterns in the planks and the carriage pitched over into the river. Dozens of torches lit up the disaster.

'Paulin!' yelled the captain.

The pontoneers pushed a raft closer to the carriage that was edging sideways, the ice slashing at it; a trestle was the only thing keeping it from being carried downstream; everything was about to collapse. D'Herbigny handed over his torch; supporting himself with his one hand, he leant over the edge to step onto the body of the carriage, now on its side, and broke the window with the heel of his boot. Flattening himself on his stomach, the captain reached in his hand, sprung the latch, opened the door. Inside shadowy figures were scrambling about; hands stretched out. The grenadiers threw down ropes, pontoneers rowed towards the accident. Every passenger they saved was pulled up onto the bridge and relative safety. But where was Paulin? And Monsieur Roque? D'Herbigny groped around with his arm and shouted for a lantern to see inside the barouche. There was no one there.

'Sir!'

Paulin was sitting on the edge of the bridge with Monsieur Roque and some other clerks; warned of the risk, they had chosen to walk behind the carriage. Sebastian leant down. 'Monsieur d'Herbigny, will you have a look and see if you can't spot a brown leather satchel. It's where I keep my books.'

The captain pretended to look but was thinking that this young Monsieur Roque, even if he was his neighbour from Normandy, had a damn nerve.

*

Sebastian and the Imperial staff sat shivering around a blazing fire, at the edge of a little wood from which they could see the whole Berezina. The army was still crossing slowly, column after column, lit by a white morning sky. The artillery bridge had broken a hundred times and, all things considered, Sebastian preferred his job as secretary to the gruelling work of the pontoneers, constantly and uncomplainingly immersed in freezing water, repairing, patching together – and knowing everyone's fate depended on them.

At the bridgeheads the grenadiers were struggling to prevent a vast, seething crowd crossing in the rare moments when there was a gap between battalions. The army had priority and let it be known. Generals forced their way through with sticks or the flat of a sabre or a musket butt. Sebastian thought he could see Davout on horseback, almost crushed by two carriages; he rallied his smoke-blackened, emaciated soldiers, and then plunged into the tangle of vehicles, horses and frenzied men and women. Scanning the heaving mass of abandoned on the riverbank, Sebastian hoped, by some stroke of luck, to catch a glimpse of Mlle Ornella, but what did she look like now? Had she survived? Something told him she had and was struggling in that throng, but he wanted to know for sure. He turned on his heels, and headed towards the hamlet where the Emperor was to stay that night. He heard smothered shouts and calls for help. A voltigeur was moaning, lying flat on his stomach. Misled by the darkness before dawn, his friends had fallen into a deep well that had been dug by peasants and hidden by the snow.

'Aren't you going to throw them a rope?'

'All the ropes are being used for the bridges.'

'Your belt?'

'I can't reach my comrades.'

'Branches?'

'They break.'

'There's nothing we can do ...'

'Yes, there is. Watch where you're putting your feet, make sure you don't fall into these damned holes!'

Lancers wrapped in thick blankets were smoking their pipes around the remnants of a fire. They had tethered their mounts to a clump of fir trees.

'Can you lend me a horse?' asked Sebastian.

'To go where?'

'Down by the bridges.'

'And what if we don't see this horse again?'

'Lend it to me for this ...'

Sebastian held up a diamond between two fingers. The diamonds from the Kremlin were everything he owned. The lancers smoothed their moustaches; they weren't sure, they hesitated. Gold, silver, precious stones: none of it was any use in those frozen wastes. The other day Sebastian had seen an unattached man sitting on the ground like a beggar; he was trying to trade an ingot for bread but people were walking past him without stopping. One of the lancers agreed. He was a lieutenant and he had two horses; he gave Sebastian his servant's horse, a spotted mare.

Sebastian covered the two hundred metres to the bank at a trot. He took the bridge cautiously; the trestles were sinking, the planks nearing the level of the water, constantly battered by the ice. On the left bank, which was jammed solid with vehicles, the press of refugees was so intense that they were no longer moving at all. The wheels of the berlines and wagons were locked, postilions were yelling, lashing about them with their whips, while the dense crowd stamped their feet. Sebastian realized his stupidity. What had he come here for? He had already escaped fire, cold, hunger, drowning and the Cossacks and now he was going back of his own free will to join a crowd of civilians who were never going to cross the Berezina unharmed. He scrutinized the faces of those closest to him, hoping to see a head of black hair he recognized. The Emperor was crossing the second bridge on horseback with the Young Guard, and Oudinot's cannon were dashing down the hill from where they had swept the marshes.

'If you go into that morass, sir, the crowd will swallow you up and who knows if you'll come out whole?'

The officer commanding the picket of grenadiers had noticed the cockade on Sebastian's hat and was anxious to warn him. The young man had no need of that type of advice, however: he saw the extent of the catastrophe but a force, or his bad conscience, was urging him on.

'I'll risk it,' he said.

'That's the word for it.'

'On the Emperor's service!'

'I'd gathered that.'

The ranks parted and Sebastian rode into the chaos. The snarl of carriages and wagons prevented any access to the bridges; overwhelmed, the refugees were preparing to camp for a second night on the white plain. In a hail of insults, Sebastian pushed through the crowd, looking around from his vantage point astride his horse – but nothing, no black hair. Wait, near a berline, with her back to him, there was a woman holding a torch of straw. Sebastian shouted Ornella's name but the woman didn't turn round. With his mare's breast he cleared a path through to the berline, which was starting to burn. The woman finally turned round: it wasn't the actress. He tried to turn back before it grew dark. Snow was starting to fall slowly on the fires.

*

'I don't understand these Russians at all.'

'They are concentrating on Borisov, sire.'

'For goodness' sake! They could have cut us off! Are they blind or stupid? What's left of our army at Borisov? A division!'

'Perhaps they're manoeuvring on our rear . . .'

A booming explosion interrupted them, then another, both very close. Napoleon tied on his cap, went out of the cabin and ordered his staff to follow him onto a wooded rise. The snow was falling in a slow swirl but he could see the red points of the fires flecking the plain. The refugees were burning what they could; through carelessness, through ignorance, they had blown up some caissons of powder. The reckless must have been blown to pieces and plenty more wounded by splinters. The Emperor listened to the clamour of several thousand panic-stricken creatures, the calls of distress carrying a long way. Other sounds, further off, muffled and more rhythmical, were coming from the forest; an aide-de-camp sent by Oudinot allowed them to be pinpointed: a Russian army was cannonading II Corps on the right bank. The Emperor ordered that the Guard be called to arms, hoisted himself into the saddle and, surrounded by his sacred squadron, set off to find the fighting. The sounds of battle revived him; he preferred them to uncertainty. Things were becoming clear-cut.

The forest: didn't seem like trees so much as free-standing colossi, in vast numbers, between which the cuirassiers galloped. Cannon pounded Oudinot's regiments and giant branches, mangled by shellfire, rained on the men's heads, crushing some of them. When the Emperor reached Oudinot's headquarters amongst the trees, the marshal had just been gravely wounded in the groin; skirmishers were carrying him to the rear on a stretcher fashioned out of branches.

'Let Ney take his place!'

'Sire! Our cuirassiers have split the Army of Moldavia in two!'

'Attack! Attack!'

'Sire! Marshal Victor is coming from Borisov!'

Having transferred command to Ney, Napoleon returned to his cabin. Marshal Victor, Duke of Belluno and former Revolutionary general, was waiting for him, one of his sleeves torn, his curly hair plastered to his forehead and temples.

'Have you seen action?'

'Two Russian armies, between Borisov and Studienka, but I succeeded in separating them and here I am.'

'At what cost?'

'Saving four thousand men after enduring hours of grapeshot, but . . .'

'But what, Your Grace?'

'General Partouneaux . . .'

'Killed?'

'No, sire. He remained in Borisov as a diversion and was meant to rejoin me at Studienka, but he took the wrong turning at a fork in the road.'

'Has that idiot let his division be massacred?'

'No, sire, he has surrendered.'

'The coward! If he lacked courage himself, all he had to do was give his grenadiers their head! A drummer would have sounded the charge! A canteen-woman would have shouted "Everyone for himself!"'

'My remaining men . . .'

'Have them cross the Berezina as quickly as possible.'

'They are crossing now, sire, despite the chaos.'

'Let them get a move on! The Russians are at your heels; they won't be long, and as soon as it's light we'll be seeing them appear on the hills of the left bank. Berthier! Tell Eblé to burn both bridges at seven in the morning. Caulaincourt! Have someone go and reconnoitre the road to Vilna!'

'It's been done, sire.'

'Feasible?'

'For the moment, yes, sire, but it's not really a road, more an embankment through marshes with narrow bridges and crossings over a mass of streams. If someone set a bunch of gorse on fire, that would be enough to deprive us of this means of retreat.'

*

In the middle of the plain, separated from their companions by the pressure of the crowd, frozen stiff and white with snow, Ornella and Dr Fournereau climbed onto a berline whose driver was whipping his team like a demon; the horses were shaking their manes, rearing in their harness, scattering clusters of fugitives who fell under their hooves. The snow had stopped at daybreak but the cold wind was blowing twice as fiercely. Perched on the roof of the carriage Ornella and the doctor caught sight of the bridges. The one on the left had just broken under the weight of Victor's artillery. Hampered by bodies, the wagons were breaking up between the shattered planks. The river was full of corpses of men and horses; ammunition boxes floated among the bits of ice. Confronted with this wall of carts, baggage and dead, the fugitives made for the other bridge. In these competing tides, many people fell or dived into the water; a sutler sank as she held her baby in her outstretched arms. Desperados leapt onto sheets of ice, which opened up beneath them; screaming, they were picked up by the current and joined the other objects swept along on the surface of the water. Careering down the bank, a cart of wounded smashed into the mud. The berline to which Ornella and Fournereau were clinging broke an axle and tipped over, crushing some stragglers who weren't able to get out of the way in time. Hurled against the frame of a cart, the doctor banged the back of his head and started bleeding. Ornella thought: Don't let go! Don't let go! But her fingers were freezing; she slipped off.

Caught by the floodtide, she had lost the doctor. Already far away, he turned his head to look for her but the momentum was too strong. The fugitives knew the danger without being able to protect themselves from it; they were packed so tightly that they had no choice but to keep moving towards the bridge; they surged forward with the force of an avalanche crushing everything in its way. They trod on charred fragments of caissons that had exploded in the night, severed limbs black with powder, bloody torsos sliced up by wheels, unidentifiable bits of flesh, rags, dented helmets, a lone boot ruined by the snow and without its sole. At the entrance to that famous bridge they turned savage; the roadway narrowed but they all tried to cross at once; deserters, vicious as anything, stabbed anyone who got in their way with their bayonets. Ornella's feet no longer touched the ground; wedged between the shoulders of those around her, she glimpsed the doctor on the overloaded roadway. The bridge had no parapet; Fournereau lost his balance, grabbed the pine planks as he fell, hung down into the water, buffeted by billets of ice; he screamed when a wagon drove over his clawing fingers. German latecomers from Victor's army lashed the wretched with their horsewhips; a woman clung to a horse's tail, until its rider cut it off with his sabre; the crowd trampled her underfoot. On the right bank, engineers were standing by braziers, waiting for the order to set the bridges on fire.

The Cossacks appeared on the hills and Kutuzov's artillery prepared to fire. As shells exploded at random in the helpless crowd, panic mounted. Frenzied figures butchered each other to reach the bridge, the wounded left their ambulances, a sleeve without an arm floated downstream. A brutal surge of the crowd felled a man with a bandaged forehead. Ornella jumped out of the way, her face distorted with fear, her eyes maddened; she climbed up a heap of corpses but when she put her foot down on one of those she thought dead, he grabbed her ankles; she'd have moved away from the bridges if she could have, if the tide of fugitives hadn't been so dense. A roundshot fell on the baggage train. Ornella was dragged back with everyone else, suffocating in the vice-like grip of all the bodies. The wind whistled. The roundshot crashed down. The bridges gave way. When the soldiers on the right bank set fire to them, the choice became simple – burn or drown. Those nearest the bridges rushed through the flames, which caught quickly on the abandoned baggage, the supports, the broken-up carts and the wooden roadway. A tall man in a white cloak caught fire. Croats climbed onto the trestles and started crawling under the roadway; burning planks hit them on the head. Groups threw themselves onto pieces of ice, others swam a few metres before disappearing in the turbid water; still more were trapped between blocks of ice. A current in the crowd carried Ornella back; she stumbled with a hundred others over the carcasses of vehicles and they all fell pell-mell to the ground, lashing out and smothering one another. Ornella lost consciousness.

She came to when she felt someone tearing her furs off; she opened her eyes on her assailant, an Asiatic with a long, thin moustache, in an astrakhan cap. The Cossack pulled her up by her hair. Around her these barbarians were stripping the prisoners and piling their clothes atop their saddles.

Six

THE ESCAPE

THEY HEADED AWAY FROM the Cossacks on the Vilna road, the only one that ran between immense forests and ice-bound lakes, on bridges over countless rivers and streams. At first, leaving the Berezina behind, they had struggled in peat bogs, and although they covered the road with boughs to make it easier for the cannon and transport wagons, the horses had found it awkward, and they had lost more.

Then the temperature fell eighteen degrees; the cold hardened the ground, strengthened the road and helped the Emperor; if it weren't for that, he would have left his entire transport in the marshes. Progress became steadier. There were no more unattached soldiers; instead they marched in close-knit groups, forcing each other to put one foot in front of the other. At night they took turns sleeping, never for more than half an hour at a time on pain of freezing on the spot.

'Paulin, we're getting near Rouen.'

'I can't see our spires this far away, sir.'

'In Heaven's name, what would you rather think about?'

'A good pair of fur-lined boots.'

'We'll buy some in Vilna.'

'You said that before Smolensk and Krasnoie and Orcha, and what happened then?'

'Vilna is in Lithuania, civilization.'

'If the Russians let us get there . . .'

'The Russians? They're a long way behind us and just as frozen as we are, believe me!'

'Sir, allow me to say that I couldn't give a hang and it's not warming me up. I think I'm actually congealing inside.'

After his successful offensive against the Russian Army of Moldavia, Marshal Ney had captured two thousand soldiers in a terrible state. D'Herbigny had seen them, their breeches worn through at the crotch from marching and their thighs exposed to the bitter air. Their guards had let them escape; those buggers could go and die in the woods, for all they cared.

'It's getting dark, sir and I can see smoke.'

They had left the marshlands behind and from time to time they could stray from the road to launch armed raids against peaceable villages. Only a few days previously, the dragoons had returned with sleighs of salt meat and flour. The provisions had been wolfed down and the sleighs, pushed by hand, used to carry the weakest. The captain looked sadly at the fifty troopers on foot whom he called his brigade.

'To the barn, lads.'

Paulin had spotted this barn with its halo of grey smoke. They headed towards it trustingly since the peasants thereabouts were no longer hostile, even if the pillaging they had to endure did not endear the former Grande Armée to them. The barn's occupants had blockaded the door and the dragoons couldn't force it open. Trooper Chantelouve drew his captain's attention to the trunk of a fir tree sticking out of a side window.

'They haven't hung around, this lot, they've felled a tree and set fire to it straight off without chopping it up.'

'Maybe they've suffocated, Captain?'

'Come on, make that window bigger, you pack of surmisers!'

The dragoons busied themselves and the captain was the first to slip through the opening onto what he initially took to be a pile of sacks. Ahead of him, he glimpsed some bearded fellows, their faces flushed by the reluctant fire that had caught on a part of the tree trunk and now gave off a strong smell of resin. Then, through thick smoke, he could make out human forms appearing over the heaps and crawling, like him, towards that pathetic camp fire, the only attraction of which was that it was somewhere sheltered. The mountain of sacks was uneven; d'Herbigny rolled into a gap of sorts and rested his hand on an icy, hard object to lever himself up; he fingered the thing — what was it? A stone shell, no — an ear and the protuberance of a nose, a cold face. He shuddered. This was not baggage or sacks of grain but hundreds of dead soldiers who had frozen stiff before that confounded fire had been lit. They were what was blocking the doors. The least paralysed had been kept warm for a while by these bodies above them and were now emerging from the mounds like reptiles, slithering to the surface. Some managed to set light to another part of the trunk with a burning branch; bark sizzled and pine needles flew like sparks as the men blew on the fire to stoke it. In an instant the flames had reached the roof, which caught like tinder and began to rain down torches of burning thatch. Pulling himself along on his elbows, the captain hurried towards the window he'd come from and pushed back those dragoons that had followed him; the roof beams were already crackling. Outside in the snow silhouettes were approaching the blazing barn; it would warm them and save them – for one night at least – from dying of cold.

*

In their blankets and white fur-lined coats, there was no differentiating generals from the rank and file – or men from women – any more. Everyone walked at a slow, laboured pace and fought the temptation to ride the surviving horses or travel in the carriages: the doctors had been categorical; immobility would be fatal, they had to go on foot and prevent numbness. Sebastian had knotted a handkerchief around his mouth and nose so his breath didn't freeze. The bitter air made eyes smart and water, and tears quickly turned to ice. Baron Fain had to hold him by the arm so he could cover his eyes with a fur scarf and generate some warmth to unstick his eyelids; Sebastian performed the same service for the Baron a few metres on. They passed the gutted barn, stumbled over colourless bodies without boots or greatcoats and found a game-bag containing a crust of rye bread. When they saw His Majesty's olive-green berline outside a sturdy wooden house, they knew they would be able to rest for a moment.

The driver brought out the bundle of hay, which he'd stowed under his seat, and shared it between the four broken-winded horses. On one side, in a courtyard, farriers had lit their portable forge. They were forging shoes through the night, and although they worked in gloves, they still had to keep stopping to rub their hands; the coal burnt white hot without giving off any heat. The Baron and Sebastian followed the other staff into the house, into which the entire headquarters was crowded. The traditional stove was working badly; the wood was damp, the coal reserved for the forge and rationed since Smolensk.

Hung from the walls by string, three lanterns cast a weak light on the dormitory. The Baron and Sebastian lay down next to fellow administrators, officers or valets, on their side to take up less room, between a stomach and a back without being able to scratch themselves or squash the families of lice tormenting them. Sebastian had accustomed himself to the filth and perpetual itching, and he was so tired he was drifting off when a harrowing scream made his eyes snap open. He had recognized Prefect Bausset's piping voice crying, 'Monstrous! I'm being murdered!' In the gloom, a clumsy chap had trodden on his foot − and he had been suffering from agonizing gout since Moscow. Explosions of laughter answered his protest, everyone guffawing at such a mismatch between an event and its description. Bausset himself realized what he'd said and joined in the laughter, as did Sebastian, despite the fact that his chapped lips started bleeding. After this moment of salutary hilarity, everyone sank back into their dreams for a few hours' respite.

The same images, the same voices weaved in and out of Sebastian Roque's sleep. Ornella filled his nights. He gave himself the starring role, elaborating on moments that had actually happened, modifying them to suit his advantage; he was courageous when he slept. He saw himself again in the box of the theatre in Moscow and her, at the front of the stage, scoffing at the raging, yelling, foul-mouthed soldiers. Her blouse undone, Ornella looked them up and down until her eyes met Sebastian's and, without hesitating, he leapt to her side, thrusting aside the baying oafs as they knocked over the candles of the footlights to get to the actress. 'Now you have to get dressed,' he was saying and then without any transition, according to the jerky logic of a dream, he was draping a silver-fox fur around her shoulders, which he had just bought with his diamonds from 'At The Queen of Spain', a fashionable Parisian shop. 'With this creation, you will be simply dazzling!' He put a little hat on her head like a crown, and stroked her black curls. They strolled among the blossoming limes of the Palais-Royal, which stood in rows like feather dusters, and met Mme Aurore on Baron Fain's arm. The manageress was dressed as a canteen-woman, with a barrel of brandy on a chain around her neck and a police cap on her head. 'Leave! You must leave!' warned the manageress. 'The fire has already reached the Solenka!'

'The what?'

'It's the saltfish-sellers' street, Monsieur Sebastian,' Ornella answered, lisping slightly.

'Don't call me Monsieur!'

'Leave! Leave! The Cossacks are going to burst out of nowhere!'

They ran to the Boulevard du Temple, where the crowd of passers-by slowed them down. These people were carefree and laughed when Ornella told them about the Cossacks. Throngs gathered at the foot of a stage: Sebastian and Ornella joined them to shudder at the Incombustible, a juggler who drank boiling oil, the double-headed calves, the bearded lady and the trained fleas harnessed to miniature carts.

'Don't be afraid, Ornella,' said Sebastian. 'These people will easily see off the Cossacks.'

'But they're monsters . . .'

'Ah, we are all monsters, you know,' he said with a studied air of gravity, which he affected in order to make himself stand out.

'Even in the Tuileries?'

'Even in the Emperor's innermost circle, yes, I'll take you to the next ball. Hey! You're scratching me!'

The dream was drawing its inspiration from reality; a mouse was running across Sebastian's cheeks and lips.

*

The prisoners from the Berezina were heading back into Russia in columns. If they weren't officers, and if they hadn't been captured by the regular army, they envied the dead. As was their wont, the Cossacks had stripped them completely, gone through their food, piled the furs and cashmeres on their saddles, filled their holsters with gold and scattered the rags. A band of Kalmuk cavalry flanked a party of captives who staggered, totally naked, over the white ground. An officer in a hat with earflaps, tall and rounded as a shell, lashed them with his whip. Her back and buttocks striped, Ornella no longer felt the blows; her feet were already frozen, her eyes half glued together by tears, there was ice on her eyelashes, her head, the bushy hair at her groin and armpits; she wanted to let herself fall to the ground and sleep, then die, feeling nothing – but any man or woman who fell was instantly riddled with arrows. These cavalrymen had full quivers with their saddlebows and the invaders had no right to a peaceful death from exhaustion or the cold; instead they had to atone for the burning of the holy city. The Kalmuks used their bows for sport as well, to batter around the head those who faltered.

Dimly Ornella became aware of the officer yelling; through the fog of her failing eyes she saw him stretch out an arm and the rest of the Cossacks started shouting in unison. In the direction the officer was pointing, Ornella saw a blurry vision of thickset forms emerging from a forest. They drew nearer, massive, bearded creatures, in sheepskin kaftans. Holding scythes, axes and clubs in their hands or slung across their shoulders, they came closer, until the officer wheeled his horse abruptly around and led his Cossacks away: he was handing the prisoners over to the moujiks.

Instinctively the captives huddled together but the peasants beat them apart and lined them up, seizing a dead baby from its mother's grasp and, as the woman began to howl uncontrollably, tossing it into the snow; they hit her in the stomach with a spade and she writhed about on the ground, leaving a trail of red in her wake. Not stopping to put her out her misery, the peasants forced the prisoners to set off again, thrashing them with sticks and scythe handles to keep the procession moving. They reached the forest and pushed their way through thorny bushes that scratched their bare skin. As she walked, Ornella looked at her legs and the beads of blood forming on them as if they were objects that didn't belong to her.

At the edge of a clearing, woodcutters were toiling over a fir tree, wood chips flying as they cut deep into the base of the trunk, their axes rising and falling in tandem and the blows ringing out in perfect, obsessive, relentless time. What did these Russians want? Were they going to line up their prisoners under this tree and crush them in its fall? A hundred or more villagers crowded into the centre of the clearing, where the prisoners stood waiting to discover their fate. Most of the men had caps over their long hair, canvas patches at the knees of their trousers and rusty old guns slung over their shoulders; the women wore scarves and all had plaited bark shoes tied up with coloured bandages. When the fir came down, the moujiks lopped off its branches with axes. In no time the trunk was smooth and the villagers led the naked prisoners over to it; fifty stupefied, docile, broken men and women. A toothless peasant woman seized Ornella by the neck and forced her down with the back of her head on the trunk, looking up at the sky. All the captives were stretched out in the same fashion either side of the tree. The ceremony could begin.

Ornella thought that lying like that the cold would soon release her from her suffering, but the moujiks built large fires with the cut branches. A sudden pain coursed through her, as if her head was exploding. The trunk was vibrating. The peasant women were roaring songs, keeping time by hitting the tree with sticks as hard as their strength and rage permitted. The blows reverberated along the fir and roared in the prisoners' brains; the women beat and sang like furies and the hammering drilled Ornella into the snow, mute, seeking refuge in this shooting pain that, like the cold, made her whole body shudder. The men watched this bacchanal and smoked their pipes with the serenity of those who are certain they are carrying out God's will. Inflamed against these French by their priests, they were slowly murdering them in the name of Jesus Christ, the Tsar and all the saints of the Orthodox Church. And the termagants carried on hitting, full of hatred – hitting and bawling patriotic songs.

*

At the start of December, despite the intense cold, Napoleon was in cheerful spirits. He'd received encouraging news. Fourteen successive dispatches, held up until then, gave him an idea of the mood in France; Malet and his accomplices had been shot amid more or less total indifference and, lacking independently confirmed reports, Parisians were minimizing the army's disasters. From Bassano, his governor, Napoleon learnt that Vilna's warehouses, two marches away, were crammed with rations and supplies and that, although the Russian armies were approaching, so too were his Austrian allies. The one thing lacking for his peace of mind was the Polish light cavalry, whose presence he'd been requesting for weeks and whose lack of means Bassano had been slow making up for.

In the dark room in headquarters, Constant, Napoleon's valet, was burning bars of resin, which he stood in a block of wood by way of a candlestick; the whole process had to be repeated every five minutes but this was how houses were lit in Lithuania. The light glowed red in Davout's round glasses and glinted gold on Murat's frogging, on Bessières's powdered coiffure and Ney's bushy side-whiskers and red hair; further from it, Lefebvre, a sullen Berthier, the lanky Mortier and Prince Eugène with his balding pate were half-hidden in shadow.

'We are heading towards our reinforcements,' the Emperor was saying. 'The Russians away from theirs. The situation is picking up. Berthier, have you sent one of your aides-de-camp to Paris?'

'Montesquiou set off as planned.'

'Which is to say?'

'Two days ago.'

'Then it's time I went too.' The Emperor explained to

his marshals that he would be of more use in the Tuileries than with the army, to raise new contingents and counter the machinations of a seditious Europe. The men should rest in Vilna, get medical treatment, eat properly and buy themselves decent clothes. A week's rest was becoming possible and desirable. Napoleon then revealed that the 29th bulletin, which Montesquiou had taken with him, was going to be published in Paris; it described something close to reality, and so he would have to go back in order to moderate its effect and reassure his subjects by his presence. He asked Baron Fain to elaborate, and Fain in turn asked his clerk to speak. Sebastian began to read the text, which he had helped draft and a copy of which he carried in his secretariat portfolio. *Until 6 November the weather was perfect, and the army's movement was carried out with the greatest success. The cold weather began on the 7th: since then, we have lost several hundred horses each night.* There followed details on Russian strategy, the fall of the thermometer, the loss of the entire cavalry and a good deal of the transport. The Emperor blamed the winter. He reviled the Cossacks in the harshest terms. The fatal bulletin ended, like the previous one, with reflections on his perfect health, but the tone did not disguise an army put to rout, and it would have a huge impact in France. The marshals were agreed on that.

'When do we leave, sire?' asked Berthier.

'I'm leaving tonight but without you. By his rank, the King of Naples will replace me and you will hold yourself at his disposal. The army needs its major general.'

'The army . . .'

Berthier and Murat had turned pale. The former was missing his income of a million and half, his estate at

Grosbois and his Parisian mansion which he had never had a chance to enjoy; the latter thought only of resuming control of his kingdom from Caroline, who was regent; no doubt she was abusing her position and praying every morning that he would never return from this ill-fortuned expedition. Having made his pronouncement, Napoleon left the room. Murat grumbled, 'I'm to command an army that doesn't exist any more, am I?'

'Obey,' said Davout. 'You are a king as I am a prince.'

'Oh no! Naples is a reality, not your make-believe principality, your hollow title!'

'You're the one who is hollow!'

'Bernadotte was right!'

'He has betrayed us.'

'He reigns over Sweden!'

'He was elected by the Diet of Stockholm!'

'I must think of my people!'

'You think about your throne more than anything!'

'Yes!'

'We're here to obey!'

'Whom?'

'The Emperor who crowned you!'

'That crown is on my head!'

'Ingrate!'

'We hav endured the vorst,' Lefebvre said to stop the quarrel. 'At Vilna we will be safed.'

'Saved? For how long?' sighed a very downcast Berthier.

Constant and the other valets were packing the Emperor's bags; Sebastian helped Roustam the Mameluke stow sixty thousand francs in gold in a silver-gilt chocolate box, which was then secreted in a false bottom in His Majesty's dressing case; Roustam then locked the whole thing up. With that money the grand equerry would pay the journey's expenses at the post stages to which he had already sent messengers. Caulaincourt was hurrying along the preparations for leaving. A troop of chasseurs à cheval of the Guard, with dark green coats and black bearskin busbies, had set off first to open the road; there'd been signs of Cossacks. A sleigh had followed with a Polish count, one of the Emperor's orderlies who would be the interpreter, and an outrider. During the day, Caulaincourt had bought some little Lithuanian horses in town to complete the teams of the three carriages. Napoleon would take the coupé with Caulaincourt; Sebastian and Roustam were stowing provisions in it. Dressed in thick wool, the Emperor got in the travelling carriage, made himself comfortable and slid his legs into a bearskin bag, tiny icicles on his eyebrows and under his nose. 'Let's be off, Your Grace!' he said to Caulaincourt. Roustam perched on the footman's step. Sebastian was about to get out when the grand equerry stopped him. 'Since you're here, Monsieur le secrétaire, stay.'

'I'm to travel with His Majesty?'

'If he needs to dictate a letter, you'll be to hand.'

'I haven't told Baron Fain and . . .'

'It doesn't matter. In a few hours he'll come on in the third carriage, with Monsieur Constant and Dr Yvan.'

They talked; the temperature was so low that as their breath rose, it condensed and covered the hood with a hard frost. Before the coupé had even moved off, during this hushed conversation, Napoleon had fallen into a heavy sleep. Moonlight on the snow lit the way but Sebastian only saw its milky glow through the misted-up windows. The Emperor slept, Caulaincourt's teeth chattered and Sebastian thought about the strangeness of his fortune; he wasn't slow drifting off either.

The aide-de-camp riding in the sleigh in front of the coupé roused everybody in the next town. The Cossacks had raided the previous evening and been seen off by musket fire; now they were bivouacking west of the Vilna road.

'What time is it?' asked the Emperor.

'Two o'clock in the morning, sire. Do you want to wait for it to get light? Do you want the commander of the garrison to send a patrol on reconnaissance?'

'No, that would draw attention to us.'

'The Russians are ahead of us on the left this time.'

'What troops are there at this post?'

'Poles, Germans, three squadrons of lancers . . .'

'Will I have an escort?'

'Lancers, sire.'

'Are they ready?'

'Yes.'

'Deploy the escort around the carriage, we will set off immediately.'

'In the pitch dark?'

'One must always reckon on good luck, otherwise one never gets anywhere.'

The Emperor passed his pistols through the door and said to his interpreter, 'Count, if you think danger is certain, kill me, never let me be captured.'

The sleigh, the coupé and the escort of a hundred Polish lancers set off immediately towards Vilna. Far away, to the left of the road, the Cossacks' fires could be seen but, in the middle of the night and in that cold, they wouldn't think of venturing forth. How were they to know that Napoleon was escaping towards the Niemen? The only sounds came when horses fell, brought down by the ice. They were a hundred when they set off; at dawn there were only thirty-six left. The thermometer showed twenty-eight degrees below zero.

*

For security, the Emperor wanted to travel incognito. He refused to go into Vilna, where, if they recognized him, the inhabitants wouldn't be able to refrain from talking and the rumour of their excited chatter would reach the Russians. He did, however, consent to stop for an hour in a modest house in the suburbs. Roustam took the opportunity to shave him and Bassano, the governor, whom Caulaincourt notified, came to receive instructions. Sebastian caught a powerful smack because the ink had frozen and he could not make a fair copy of the orders he'd written in pencil.

They set off again in the dark with an escort of the Neapolitan cavalry garrisoned in Vilna, where Caulaincourt had prepared the relay posts and halting places, and bought fresh horses and fur-lined boots for His Majesty's travelling companions. Impatient to get back to France, Napoleon had no desire to sleep and Sebastian listened to his long conversation with his grand equerry in the carriage.

'In Vilna,' the Emperor was saying, 'the army will lack nothing, Bassano assures me. The Austrians will keep the Cossacks at bay, and the Poles will never let the Russians cross the Niemen. The Tsar is mistrusted in Warsaw as much as in Vienna.'

'You are more mistrusted than anybody, sire.'

'Come, come!'

'You imposed a military regime on Europe, the peoples complain . . .'

Caulaincourt got a slap on the cheek.

'How ridiculous you are! Our laws are just and we will administer Belgium, or Germany, exactly the same as France. I only do what I think useful, Your Grace. I like peace too, but the English have driven me to incessant wars.'

'The blockade of their merchandise is impoverishing the peoples, sire . . .'

'Stupid! One must take the larger view, Caulaincourt, stop considering one's immediate advantage to think of the general interest. These English! If the Austrians or Germans or Russians want to sell their products, they ask London for permission, and that's the truth. On the one hand there is Europe, on the other the English manufacturers and their ubiquitous fleet; they control the Adriatic, Malta, Gibraltar and the Cape, they hold sway over trade, exercising an utterly pernicious monopoly. The blockade? It must be strengthened! England must be brought to its knees and then – picture it – a federate Europe will know prosperity, industry will be able to develop, the nations will support each other, they will have the same currency, the pound will collapse.'

'Will the reverses of this campaign allow us to impose our views on other countries?'

'If only I hadn't stayed so long in Moscow, I would have won. Winter has defeated us and not those pathetic Russian generals.'

'In Spain . . .'

'You think Spain should have been wound up first? It's

not certain. The English army has been mobilized there. Besides, is there anywhere they would not attack me? Belgium? Brittany? In time the Spanish will understand as well, but they don't realize that we have entered a new era! Their colonies in the Americas, too far from Madrid and too close to the United States, will declare independence one after the other, like Paraguay, like Mexico, and they were what laid the foundations for Spain's power ... You'll see.'

At five o'clock in the morning, still preceded by the sleigh, the Emperor's coupé stopped in Kovno outside a sort of tavern run by an Italian. There had been a heavy snowfall overnight, but servants brandishing spades had already cleared a path from the road to the door. Logs were burning in a tall fireplace, where three cook's boys turned three rows of chickens on spits. Those members of the escort who had been lucky enough not to freeze to death stretched out their bloodless hands to the flames, while Caulaincourt explained in vain to their captain the danger of warming frozen fingers up too quickly. The innkeeper showed His Majesty to his best table; Sebastian, the Mameluke, the interpreter and the outrider sat in a corner but were entitled to the same hot meal, with crusty bread and served on tablecloths, which they had almost forgotten existed for so many months. They heard the birds' fat dripping into the fire, drop by drop, and listened to Caulaincourt questioning the innkeeper on the state of the roads; with such deep snow and ice, was there no way they could get sleighs?

'I know the senatore, he has one,' said the innkeeper.

'What senator?'

'The Polish senatore, squire of Kovno.'

'The Poles are our friends.'

'But I know he no will sell.'

'He'll think again with ten thousand francs in front of him.'

'It a keepsake for him, this sleigh.'

Senator Wybicki, on the occasion of his daughter's marriage, had commissioned a light berline to be built on sleigh runners. He was extremely fond of it, the innkeeper was correct. The interpreter went to visit his compatriot, who refused at first, and then, learning that his enhanced sleigh was intended for Napoleon, agreed enthusiastically, declining any consideration other than that he should be presented to the Emperor, which he duly was that same night. The encounter lapsed into an exercise in mutual admiration; His Majesty spoke of his love for Poland, the senator paid him homage. The outrider, meanwhile, took the opportunity to put the horses to. The travellers took the fur-lined coats and arms and not much luggage because there was not much space; in any case the provisions had frozen and the bottles of Chambertin had cracked in the cold. The interpreter sat opposite the Emperor and Caulaincourt, and next to Sebastian. Roustam and the outrider were to follow in a smaller sleigh. They set off for the bridge and crossed the Niemen, frontier to the Grand Duchy of Warsaw, in an uncomfortable but fast carriage, travelling alone and without escort. No one said anything.

At the sight of the river they all recalled the same event. It was at the very start of the campaign, on the eve of entering Russian soil: 23 June. Napoleon had wanted to reconnoitre the ford in person and had borrowed a black silk forage cap from a Polish chevau-léger. He'd been trotting along, wearing this disguise, when a hare rushed between Friedland, his horse's, hooves; His Majesty toppled off into the wheat, picking himself up moments later, unassisted, very pale. Caulaincourt was there. Berthier too. The story leaked out; it was repeated frequently and people saw an ill omen in the accident.

Six months later, in December, crossing the Niemen in the other direction, the Emperor, curiously enough, was smiling.

*

D'Herbigny and Paulin, with white beards, ragged as tramps, walked up the dark, twisting alleys of Vilna. They had just come from the Old Town with its hundred church towers, where they had passed wine shops without stopping; these would be the first establishments swamped by the army of beggars that stretched for kilometres behind them; even so Paulin, dying of thirst and hunger, had protested.

'Up ahead,' the captain had said, 'there'll be shops and cafes and townsfolk who'll welcome us.'

'How? With cudgels?'

'Don't think like an idiot.'

'Are people going to offer us hospitality looking, and stinking, like this?'

'Maybe not because of our looks, but with the pearl necklaces bound around the rags on my pins, oh yes, I think we'll be able to buy something that will make us look like men again.'

'May heaven hear you, sir.'

'Leave heaven where it is, you old church hen! What hotel-keeper is going to throw an officer out of the room he's paid for?'

'One who's a bit crooked.'

'I still have my sabre.'

'Strength and victory are no longer on our side, sir.'

'Hold your tongue!'

Their breath had frozen on their moustaches and shaggy chins; the situation hardly lent itself to optimism. The captain and his servant were alone in the wreckage of the army. As soon as the Emperor's departure was known, disorder had increased, even in the heart of the Guard, among the dragoons and grenadiers. No one obeyed anyone but themselves. Germans, Croats, Spaniards and Italians scattered. The real vultures disguised themselves as Cossacks to terrify their former comrades and rob them. Across the plain, frozen bodies stretched on and on – but now in impeccable uniforms: those of the twelve thousand conscripts from Vilna who had come to the rescue of the Army of Moscow; with no chance to acclimatize after the warmth of barracks, they hadn't withstood the cold of the bivouacs.

D'Herbigny and Paulin saw the shutters of the houses close as they passed. The captain thought this perfectly normal: 'Civvies are always afraid of soldiers.'

'Sir, on the little square, Neapolitan troopers!'

'Well then, blockhead, let's go and join them.'

'It looks as if they're leaving . . .'

'They're leaving, oh yes, they're all leaving.'

Behind them stood an extremely tall grenadier whose bearskin seemed to make him even taller. He wore a lamb's wool frockcoat and sturdy new boots; his stentorian voice, a little forced but powerful enough, boomed through the fur scarf covering his face up to his eyes.

'Explain yourself,' said the captain.

'They're running like rats, all of them, the Governor, the commissariat, the Treasury, even the King of Naples. We'd be well advised to follow their example – but I know

your voice, I've got a good memory for intonations. You
are Lieutenant d'Herbigny.'

'Captain.'

'You had such a pretty helmet enturbanned in panther
skin.'

'Navy calfskin. Who on earth are you?'

'Can't you hear? The theatre is there, innate, in everything I say, gentlemen!'

'I know,' said the captain, staggered to recognize the
Great Vialatoux's bombast.

'Ah yes,' continued the actor, 'your helmet used to set
me dreaming, I could have played *Britannicus*, with a few
little changes here and there.'

'It wasn't a toy!'

'No, but it was a good part of a costume.'

'Talking of which, you are not very convincing as a
soldier in the middle of rout. Too well kitted out.'

'A long story, Captain.'

'You couldn't tell it to us in a warm tavern, could you?'
suggested Paulin, shaking with cold.

'I can do better than that.'

They disappeared down an alley that wound between
boarded-up houses and the wall of a mosque before coming
out on a small square, where a grocer was fixing shutters
over his windows. Vialatoux knocked at the entrance of a
palace built of heavy, sombre stone; a valet opened the door
and almost fainted at the sight of the captain and Paulin,
whom he took for the living dead freshly risen from their
graves. He understood French, however, and Vialatoux
reassured him, 'These men are close associates of General
Brantôme's, despite their pitiful appearance.' The valet

crossed himself. In a practised authoritarian tone, Vialatoux continued, 'When her ladyship returns from mass, tell her that I am personally looking after the general's friends.' The valet nodded, although concerned about these paupers' disgusting trotters tramping all over his carpets.

Following the actor, they ascended to the first floor, where a grenadier on a gilt chair was guarding the landing and burping; he had eaten and drunk too much. Good sign, thought Paulin, his mouth watering in anticipation. In the vast bedroom, near a faience stove, a table was strewn with dishes and plates. The window was wide open; in front of it sat a human figure covered with a sheet, an arm hanging over the arm of the armchair, a waxy hand, a blue sleeve with gold braid.

'Here is our General Brantôme,' said Vialatoux by way of introduction.

'Never heard of him,' said the captain.

'Us neither.'

'Where's he sprung from?'

'Had to call him something,' groaned a corporal, lying on a sofa digesting an enormous meal.

'Brantôme – where does that name come from?'

'A village near Périgueux; my father is the miller there.'

'Is he dead?' asked Paulin.

'Extremely dead,' confirmed Vialatoux. 'We've left him by the window so he won't thaw too quickly.'

'What's the meaning of this sham?'

'Sit down, Captain, finish what's left and I'll tell you.'

Paulin hadn't waited to be invited, he was already gnawing on a chicken carcass with relish; d'Herbigny began to work his way through a series of small carafes. Standing in the middle of the room, one hand on his hip, the other

outspread to orchestrate his story, the Great Vialatoux struck
a storyteller's pose. 'The company of the Guard I'd slipped
into thanks to a uniform which I'd – how shall I put it,
borrowed, yes, that's the word – borrowed from a sergeant
who had no need for it anymore was marching at the head
of the army. In the panic, I'd been accepted without question.
Anyway, an hour from Vilna, as we were marching past
some abandoned carriages, we saw a bunch of lackeys looting
one of them. We went closer and scared off the scoundrels,
who escaped on a sleigh with their booty. Inside the berline
what do we see? A general. He's completely white and as
stiff as a board. We peer into his face. He's dead, just like
that, sitting on the seat. We try to undress him to steal his
uniform – a general's uniform can always come in handy,
rich Poles give them a warm welcome, so people say. But
he's too stiff. No way of getting the uniform off. The harnessed horses look strong, it's a mystery why they haven't
been eaten or stolen. So we set off with the dead man and
are some of the first to arrive in Vilna, before the flood of
people on foot and the destitute, just after the commissariat.
We look for a palace, find one in the Old Town and ask for
shelter for a poor general. A Polish countess greets us and
she is very moved when I explain, "General Brantôme is
very ill, but he eats enough for ten." The ruse works. We
take the general out of the carriage and link arms to make
a chair for him; his appearance alarms the countess, but his
gold braid sets her mind at rest and we bring him up to this
room. Valets bring us trunks of clothes, boots, water to shave,
razors, soap and best of all, this slap-up dinner. We stuff
ourselves, I leave the palace to purchase some sleighs so we
can get to the Niemen as quickly as possible, and that's when
I bump into you.'

A grenadier in a fox-fur coat opened a trunk and tossed clean clothes on the bed. Vialatoux offered to shave the captain and Paulin, but asked, for pity's sake, could they first get rid of their rags?

'Are you playing all the parts? Even the barber?'

'All the parts, Captain,' said Vialatoux, giving himself airs. 'People say that actors have no character because, by acting so many different roles, they lose the identity nature gave them and become fake, in the same way that a doctor or a surgeon or a butcher becomes callous. But I think that is to mistake the cause for the effect; I think they're only suited to act at all because they don't have a character in the first place.'

'Meaning?' asked the captain, taking off his shirt, in which regiments of lice were frisking about.

'That I am whoever I want to be as soon as I put on their get-up. To emphasize the soundness of these observations, I should point out that M. Diderot is their author.'

'I don't know that comedian.'

A racket was approaching, the square filling with a raucous crowd who were attacking doors and shutters. These survivors had taken over the city; they had stripped shops and cellars, ransacked cafes and stores, drunk the taverns' wines. However, even this pandemonium could not drown out the boom of cannon to the east of Vilna. Kutuzov's armies were attacking.

'Time's run out,' roared Vialatoux. 'We're packing up, everybody to the general's carriage!' Vialatoux threw some clothes at the captain, who shared them with his servant. The others wrapped the general in his shroud and picked him up. 'He can still be useful,' said Vialatoux, excelling in the role of director. 'Good chap that he is . . .'

*

'Thank you, General,' Vialatoux said to the corpse, 'but your journey stops here.'

'Thank you for the boots and furs,' continued d'Herbigny. 'We are in your debt.'

'We've only just got a carriage and now we have to leave it,' Paulin groaned.

'Have you got a better solution, you oaf?'

It was 10 December when the fugitives abandoned their vehicles by the hundred at the bottom of the Ponari hill. With its steep, icy sides and summit obscured by fog, the only way to continue was to climb on all fours, holding on to shrubs and jutting rocks; the guests of the dead general had no choice but to follow suit. Before getting out of the berline, they wrapped more cloaks over the fur-lined ones they already wore and took a last look at the bogus General Brantôme, at his frozen face, his fixed, colourless eyes and the absurd braid at his collar and sleeves.

'Still,' the captain said ruefully, 'I would have liked to know his name.'

'Perhaps he wasn't a general,' Paulin conjectured.

'You're right,' continued Vialatoux. 'The costume determines the role, that's what I've always said. Look, with this bearskin and these epaulettes, I'm brave.'

'Perhaps he was a civilian who'd dressed up to have a better chance of escaping.'

'Either way, the uniform is genuine.'

'How long do you fellows intend to go on about this?'

'We're coming, sir.'

'You first, Captain, you're the most senior now . . .'

Once outside they didn't open their mouths. The cold was fearsome, the slope as smooth as a mirror; even the sleighs were no use. The captain and his band forged ahead into the tangle of empty carriages where men were taking down barrels from three of the Treasury's covered wagons. Each barrel was lifted by several soldiers who smashed it repeatedly on the ice until it burst open and discharged its load of gold louis. They then rushed to pick up the coins, stuffing them into their clothes, double bags and hats. Paulin and the grenadiers, warmly dressed thanks to the Vilna countess, looked at the captain. They understood one another instantly and, without a word, threw themselves into the melee. They climbed onto one of the wagons, tipped a barrel onto the ice, grabbed it, and all seven of them picked it up and dashed it on the ground until the wooden slats finally broke and coins spilled across the snow. Plenty of them joined in the plunder but there was gold enough for them all. Paulin elbowed the captain in the back; with his eyes he indicated that Cossacks were bearing down on the bandits.

Absorbed by the pillaging, which officers were trying to check in order to save at least part of the treasure, most of the soldiers paid no attention to the Cossack horsemen and carried on breaking barrels and scooping up capfuls of louis without looking up; the few that did notice their enemies' approach ran off into the woods. The captain automatically tried to draw his sabre but couldn't as the blade had been frozen to its leather sheath. To die without being able to defend oneself, run through against a barrel of gold, how absurd! They should have taken the other route, longer but not as hilly, the captain thought; it was easily worth another day's march; unfortunately they, like the rest of the cortege, had wanted to reach Kovno and the Niemen by the shortest route. Now, even supposing they managed to escape, they would have to finish the journey on foot.

The Cossacks weren't moving, however, in the face of the snarl of vehicles. They had no intention of charging into that chaos. They stuck their lances in the snow and slid from their saddles.

Then they became a blur of motion. They squeezed between the barouches and wagons, climbing over and under them, working their way in, slipping through gaps until they stumbled over the wagons of the Treasury. D'Herbigny found himself face to face with a burly Cossack. The brute had a white fur cap which he wore pushed back like a Chechen and a broad, curved sabre which he kept sheathed in its shoulder-strap; he didn't need it yet because he was raising a hatchet. A barrel stood between the two men. D'Herbigny was looking for something to defend himself with when the axe fell and split open the lid; the soldiers were of no interest to the Cossacks, only the gold. They plunged their arms into the barrels, shovelling coins out with both hands, not bothering to pick up what they spilled, but just rolling more barrels over and setting to work on them instead. Snowflakes began to fall, rendering conquerors and conquered indistinguishable. The captain had never seen a Cossack so close but now was the moment to leave. Once sated, wouldn't these brigands kill them or take them captive? The burly Cossack in the white cap raised his arms skywards, opened his hands and let a shower of coins fall on the snow. His laugh was deafening.

*

That same day the Emperor was in Warsaw. He had chosen to occupy a ground-floor room at the end of the courtyard of the Hôtel d'Angleterre in Willow Street. Under the name of Reyneval, he was posing as the grand equerry's secretary. The shutters were open slightly. A Polish maid was trying to light a fire of green wood, which wasn't catching; the main room was so badly heated that Napoleon hadn't taken off his box coat and was now walking back and forth to stretch his legs.

'Caulaincourt!'

'Sire,' said Sebastian, coming in from next door.

'I didn't call you! Where is Caulaincourt?'

'The Duke of Vicenza has gone to our embassy to fetch M. de Pradt.'

'That humbug Pradt! I'm going to tear his ears off, that incompetent! An ambassador? What a joke!'

Sebastian wondered about this monarch he was seeing at such close quarters. He couldn't determine what lay behind his terrible temper. Was it callousness or firmness? If he was too kind, would people take advantage of him? At the last relay before Warsaw, Sebastian had witnessed a scene where His Majesty's sincerity could not be doubted. At the postmaster's house, just as at the Hôtel d'Angleterre, a young maid had been lighting a fire to prepare soup and coffee while they changed the sleigh's horses. Sunk in a couch, the Emperor had taken pity on the scantily clad little girl; he'd ordered Caulaincourt to give her an armful of coins so she could buy herself warm clothes, and later, as they had continued their journey in the sleigh, he had revealed himself a little. Sebastian had just carefully written down his words from memory, in the next room. 'Ah yes, Caulaincourt, whatever anyone thinks, I have compassion and a heart, though it is the heart of a sovereign. If the tears of a duchess leave me cold as marble, I am touched by the sufferings of the people. When peace is established, when England submits, I will attend to France. We will spend four months in every year travelling within her borders, where I will visit thatched cottages and factories, where I will see with my own eyes the state of roads, canals, industries, farms; where I will invite myself into my subjects' homes and listen to them. Everything remains to be created but prosperity will be universal if I reign another ten years, in which case I will be blessed as wholeheartedly as I am hated today . . .'

The Abbé de Pradt entered the room; he had a small pursed mouth, a broad, high forehead and not much of a chin. 'Oh! Sire! You have caused me no small amount of worry but I am pleased to see you in perfect health.'

'Save your compliments, Pradt. The people who lauded you to me are asses.'

Caulaincourt pushed Sebastian into the next-door room, leaving the Emperor to his rage and the ambassador to his embarrassment. The grand equerry began dictating a dispatch for Bassano, who he thought was still in Vilna, but even while scribbling, Sebastian missed none of the volley of insults emanating from the salon. The more the Abbé de Pradt sought to justify himself, the more the Emperor yelped.

'Caulaincourt!'

The grand equerry left Sebastian and his correspondence, only to return immediately, throwing down a visiting card, on which Sebastian could read: 'Get rid of this scoundrel!' Behind the door the argument continued.

'Without money,' the Abbé was saying, 'it was impossible for me to raise the smallest troop in the Grand Duchy.'

'We are fighting for the Poles and what are they doing?'

'They haven't a crown piece left, sire.'

'They'd rather become Russian?'

'Or Prussian, sire . . .'

To rescue the Emperor, Caulaincourt announced that his food was getting cold. A moment later the door of the apartment shut. The Abbé had left. Railing against the incompetence of his ambassador to Warsaw, the Emperor dined, and having ascertained that Roustam's sleigh had caught up with them, asked Caulaincourt about the road they had to take. The grand equerry fetched the map he had brought from the embassy and pointed out the stopping places with a finger.

'We are going towards Kutno.'

'Tell me, isn't Countess Walewska's chateau thereabouts?'

'Indeed, sire.'

'Would that necessitate a detour?'

'Don't think of it, sire, we have to get to the Tuileries as quickly as possible. Besides, who is to say that the countess is not in Paris?'

'Let's forget it. I am eager to see the Empress and the King of Rome again. You're right.' The Emperor gave in easily; Caulaincourt's arguments were convincing. Still, he would have liked to have greeted his mistress and kiss the son she had given him.

Caulaincourt resumed his explanations. 'Then, after Dresden, we cross Silesia.'

'In Prussia? Are we obliged to?'

'Yes, for a short distance.'

'What if the Prussians stop us?'

'It would be a terrible stroke of luck, sire.'

'What would they do to us? Demand a ransom?'

'Or worse.'

'Would they kill us?'

'Worse still.'

'They'd hand us over to the English?'

'Why not, sire?'

The Emperor shuddered at the idea – but it was a fit of violent hysterics rather than fear or revulsion that shook his shoulders, 'Ah hah hah, Caulaincourt! I can picture your face in London, in an iron cage! They'd smear you with honey and give you to the flies, hah hah hah!'

They set off again in the red sleigh with its badly jointed windowpanes that let in freezing draughts. Sebastian felt all the same that he'd returned to civilization. His stomach was full; he'd been able to wash and put on new clothes; above all, the mind was reasserting its superiority over the body as he forwent sleep in order to remember what the Emperor said.

'In less than three months, I'll have five hundred thousand men under arms.'

'The ill disposed, sire, will say that equates to five hundred thousand widows . . .'

'Let them talk, Your Grace. If the Europeans understood that I'm acting for their own good, I wouldn't need an army. Do you think I enjoy war? That I don't deserve a rest? As for the sovereigns, they're narrow-minded. Honestly, I've made it clear enough that I want to put a stop to revolutions! They owe me thanks for having stemmed the torrent of revolutionary spirit that was threatening their thrones. I loathed the Revolution.'

'Because it killed a king?'

'On the famous 13 Vendémiaire, Caulaincourt, I hesitated. Oh, I remember it well. I was coming out of the Feydeau Theatre, having been to a melodrama, *The Good Son*; the alarm was sounding throughout Paris. I was ready to sweep the Convention from the Tuileries, but whom would I have had to command? An army of Royalist dandies, students and innkeepers trained by Chouans. In the Royalist sections, they held their muskets like umbrellas! And then, when it started to rain, the downpour dispersed the rioters, who left to find shelter in a convent and talk ... So that evening I reluctantly chose the Directory – the Directory, that nest of swindlers driven entirely by self-interest. I seconded Barras to use his power and establish mine.'

'You would have served the monarchy?'

'Do you want me to tell you who really killed the king? It was the émigrés, the courtiers, the nobility. One does not go into exile. If they had created a real resistance on the nation's soil, I would have ranged myself on their side.'

'You received them later at your court...'

'My duty was to win them over. One must unite every shade of opinion and make use of people whose interests are most opposed. That is the way to prove a government is strong.'

'How many would remain faithful to you in adversity?'

'I hold men in slight esteem, as you know, but am I

wrong, Your Grace? I have no illusions about their behaviour. None. As long as I stoke their ambitions and coffers, they will bow their heads.'

*

The Emperor and his travelling companions were wary of ambushes but over the five following days they suffered only mechanical problems and vexations due to the dilatoriness of postmasters. At Dresden they exchanged the red sleigh, by then almost in pieces, for a berline fitted with runners which the King of Saxony gave them; having been woken at four in the morning, he had come rushing to greet them in a sedan chair without telling his entourage. For want of snow, this new sleigh was in turn replaced by a mail barouche, then by a landau – and this was now in a coaching inn between Erfurt and Frankfurt awaiting fresh horses. Napoleon remained sitting in the landau; no one was showing any signs of urgency.

'Caulaincourt, it's infuriating! Are they putting those horses to?'

'I have ordered them to, sire,' said the grand equerry.

'And what answer does this fool of a postmaster give?'

'He tells me *presently, presently*.'

'He hasn't got horses in his stable?'

'He claims not. We're waiting for some to be requisitioned.'

'We need to leave before nightfall!'

'That would be desirable, sire. The road is difficult in the forests.'

'Help me get out, you graceless idiot, I'm freezing.'

Furious at the delay, the Emperor strode towards the postmaster's house. Once inside, however, he calmed down.

In the salon, a woman was playing a sonata on a harpsichord. She didn't speak a word of French, Napoleon not a word of German. He thought her entrancing and she played with a lightness of touch unexpected for such a place.

'Caulaincourt!'

'Sire?' said the grand equerry, entering at a run.

'You speak their language. Ask for coffee and hurry these flabby lumps along!'

Caulaincourt met Sebastian and the interpreter in the courtyard, which was surrounded with dwelling houses, outhouses and stables.

'Your Grace,' Sebastian said to him feverishly, 'they've locked the main gate as though they are trying to keep us here.'

'Could they have recognized His Majesty?'

'Why delay us?'

'What if they've told German partisans who are now setting an ambush for us in the defiles before Frankfurt?'

'Unless they are in the habit of robbing travellers . . .'

'I talked to one of their postilions,' said the interpreter. 'No one has changed horses here for more than thirty-six hours.'

'Logically, then, they should have horses.'

Caulaincourt gave his instructions. The Polish count was to go to the village to fetch a squad of the French gendarmes stationed in that part of the country. He was to give one of His Majesty's pistols to M. Roque and make haste on an unharnessed horse; the village wasn't far, he should reach it without mishap, even with a tired mount. Where was the outrider? Exhausted, he was snoring on the landau's seat.

Sebastian woke him so that he could hold the gate open with Roustam.

'The stables are this way, Your Grace,' said Sebastian, holding the pistol pointing at the ground.

Inside they heard whispering, the stamping of hooves. Caulaincourt banged on the door with his fist and demanded in German, '*Mach auf!* Open up!'

Tricked by the accent and the firm tone into thinking it was one of his fellows from the post-house, a postilion opened the door. Sebastian and the grand equerry pushed him out of the way and entered the stable. Ten well-rested horses were there at their mangers. 'Filthy liars!' Caulaincourt shouted, very annoyed, and ordered the postilion to harness four of the animals.

At the sound of the altercation the other postilions ran out of the surrounding buildings and began to threaten the equerry. A frenzied figure pushed through them, red-faced, thick brows joining in a line across his forehead. Sebastian didn't understand a word of the curses he spat in Caulaincourt's face like blasphemies, but he knew enough to realize it was the postmaster. The man raised his whip and lashed the air; Sebastian, who had moved closer, caught the blow in his face. A red weal appeared on his cheek. Caulaincourt grabbed the postmaster by the collar and pinned him against the wall. The horses sidestepped nervously. Sebastian, blood running down his cheek, hesitantly threatened the surly postilions with his pistol, while Caulaincourt released his captive, drew his sword and jabbed it against his throat. The postmaster barked orders and the horses were immediately put to the landau.

At that moment the Emperor came out with the panic-stricken harpsichord player on his arm.

'Caulaincourt, tell Madame, in her language, that she is good enough to come and play at the Tuileries.'

'Can I add without her husband?'

'Is she the spouse of that malevolent lout?'

'I fear so, sire.'

'What a pity. Let's go.'

The outrider started the team off at full gallop; Roustam leaped up onto his seat and they were pulling out onto the road when the Polish count returned with a party of gendarmes.

'Count, follow us with your gendarmes!' the grand equerry shouted through the door. In a quieter tone, he added to the Emperor, 'I smell a trap.'

'Don't look on the dark side of everything, Caulaincourt.'

'Isn't there some intrigue behind this? Why should they lie to us?'

'Perhaps they didn't want to spoil their horses on this wretched road,' volunteered Sebastian.

'What if the lad's right?'

The Emperor wanted to tweak Sebastian's ear but, reaching for it under the furs, his fingers touched a sticky liquid and he pulled his hand away quickly. 'What is it?'

'A wound acquired in Your Majesty's service.'

'M. Roque received a blow at the coaching inn,' Caulaincourt explained.

'I see, I see . . .' The Emperor wiped his fingers on the landau's cushions with a grimace of disgust and then retreated sullenly into his corner. Sebastian observed his profile in the twilight, the fine features in a fat face. Napoleon was muttering, 'Intrigues, intrigues . . .' and these words took him back to his dynastic obsession: Malet's conspiracy and what it revealed about the attitude of his minister.

'Malet! So many people in Paris are going to sing their own praises to make me forget their cowardice, but how many were thinking of another revolution rather than a regency? All these marshals around the Empress — are they there to help her? Oh no, certainly not, they are there to stifle her. I can imagine the pressure they put her under, their greed. If I died everything would turn to ashes. They're not up to it, they're jealous of each other.'

'You have often exacerbated their jealousies, sire.'

'You tell me that, do you, Your Grace? My poor friend! If you knew the people who have called for your downfall! You know why? Because your nobility, as a marquess of the Ancien Régime, is several centuries old and they're dying of envy. Duke of Vicenza, fine, not that you could give a hang, but Marquess of Caulaincourt, no. That envious rabble! They will never have the bearing or elegance of true nobility; in ten years they'll be just as uncouth as they are now! I reign for their children.'

*

Behind, far behind, the remnants of what was once an imposing army and now numbered a few thousand beggars at most were drawing near to the Niemen. In a hut which only had part of its roof remaining — the rest having, as usual, been burnt — a dozen of these savages were sitting around the ashes of last night's fire, growing numb.

'Sir,' Paulin stammered through chapped lips. 'Sir, it's light.'

'Don't be stupid! I know it's still the dead of night and the embers are protecting us. '

The Great Vialatoux waved a hand in front of the captain's open eyes and turned to Paulin in silence. D'Herbigny's corneas had been burnt by the cold and the glare of snow. They picked him up.

'Come on.'

'No, no, I can't see anything!'

'It's the frost, sir, your eyelids will come unstuck.'

'My eyes are open!'

'The ice in them will melt. Put this bandage on,' said Vialatoux, tearing a strip from one of the jackets they had taken, with the boots and gloves, from the countess at Vilna.

'How am I meant to walk with this bandage over my eyes – with another over my mouth and a third over my ears?'

'Put your hand on my shoulder, sir, I'll guide you.'

'Where is your shoulder?'

Paulin picked up his pine stick, Vialatoux the bags.

As every morning they passed the previous night's dead, sitting in a circle round their wet bivouacs, their skin black with soot. One had frozen on his feet, carrying branches; he had no fingers left and looked strangely as if he was smiling – but then, as the captain often repeated, dying of cold is not so bad, you just fall asleep, that's all.

The plain was dotted with ghosts moving in the same direction, staggering like drunkards, losing their balance, collapsing and never getting up. Some had nosebleeds that wouldn't stop, the blood freezing on their beards. Splinters of ice blew in the wind. A crow fell to the ground like a stone. A tree cracked apart, its trunk split by the cold. A group of soldiers' bare feet struck the ground with a sound like horses' hooves; the skin was peeling off their legs, the

bones showing through, yet they felt nothing. Otherwise
not a sound, the air was mute, nature inert.

The captain's hand lost its hold on his servant's shoulder;
he tripped over a body, sprawled full length in the snow,
half got up and groped around until he found the body
he'd bumped into. It was Paulin who was mumbling feebly,
'Leave me alone . . .'

'Who'll guide me then, eh?'

'M. Vialatoux . . .'

'No! I pay you to serve me!'

'Not for a long time . . .'

'What about the Treasury coins you stuffed in your
breeches, you swine!'

'Leave me here, I'm falling asleep . . .'

'Don't you want to see Rouen again, you ass?'

'Long way . . .'

'I loathe all this carry-on!'

The vapour of their breath was freezing on the bear
skins over their mouths, making it impossible to talk
further, but the captain gripped Paulin's arm and forcibly
set him back on his feet. Vialatoux whispered encourag-
ingly, 'A village or a town . . . anyway, some houses.'

They joined the bands converging on Kovno. Vialatoux
took the lead, while Paulin rested a hand on his shoulder
and, behind him, the captain did the same in turn, like
those blind men who walk in line, each holding on to the
one in front. In this fashion they progressed; with no goal
in mind other than simply to keep moving, they eventually
stumbled across the threshold of the tavern where His
Majesty had stopped before crossing the Niemen. Sleighs
stood outside, tied to wall rings. Vialatoux steered his

unsteady companions to the door, which he opened to find himself face to face with the Italian innkeeper, who refused to let them in. The heat of the room gave them fresh energy and unwrapping the fur over his mouth, the actor declared haughtily, 'This is an invalided officer and his servant and I am guiding them through this frozen desert.'

'What proof can you give me?'

'We have gold.'

'That is something else.'

Vialatoux threw a handful of coins on the floor. The cook's boys rushed forward as the innkeeper counted them, apologizing, 'I cannot extend my hospitality to everybody.'

'What about him?'

The Great Vialatoux indicated a sick man buried under a mound of blankets at the end of the room, an emaciated, ashen-faced figure whom a maid was feeding a bowl of bouillon. Other men, healthier but with drawn features, were sitting at his bedside.

'It's General Saint-Sulpice, he has been wounded and we are his escort,' answered one of the men.

'Saint-Sulpice?' roared the captain. 'Take me to him!'

He flung his arm out into space, searching for something to lean on, and Vialatoux guided him across the room. Under his coats and blankets the general still wore the embroidered uniform which was his passport: the Cossacks didn't dare kill or rob senior officers; their capture earned more than their effects.

'General,' said d'Herbigny, standing to attention.

'What?' asked the wounded man.

'Captain d'Herbigny, 4th Squadron, at your service.'

'Herbigny . . .'

'You put me in charge of the brigade.'

'Where is it?'

'Here, General!'

'I don't understand . . .'

'I am the brigade!' said the captain, thumping his chest.

In the meantime Vialatoux was making enquiries. Could one easily cross the Niemen? Yes, it had frozen afresh. Could one stay a few days in Kovno first? That would not be prudent; so close to the Duchy of Warsaw, this would be the last town the Russians attacked and they were apparently only two or three leagues away. A sleigh? There were none left. Those outside, the general and his suite's? Didn't they have three places spare? Alas, no.

'Captain,' one of the men of Saint-Sulpice's escort was saying. 'Captain, you've dropped something . . .'

'I have?'

'Wait, I'll tell you what it is . . .'

The man bent down and let out a scream, as if he'd touched something diabolical. The others fell silent.

'What have you found?' roared the captain. 'I can't see anything anymore, nothing but unending night.'

'It's that . . .'

'Tell me! That's an order!'

'Your nose, sir,' said Paulin in a broken voice.

'My nose scares these ruffians, does it?'

'Oh no . . .'

'Well, what is it?'

'It has frozen.'

'And?'

'It has fallen on the ground, sir.'

*

The Emperor's impatience grew as the distance between him and Paris lessened, particularly after he crossed the Rhine by boat and met Montesquiou. Berthier's messenger, who was on his way to rejoin the major general, confirmed that the Empress and his son were in wonderful health and that the fatal 29th Bulletin was to be published in the *Monitor* immediately. Thereafter Sebastian had less to record. Napoleon became more playful and little inclined to confidences. Indefatigable, once again he blamed all the faults of his campaign on the English. That tactic of withdrawing without fighting, burning the crops and towns, wasn't that Wellington's policy in Portugal? Didn't the Tsar have an adviser from London, Sir Robert Wilson? And the fact that the Russians had missed countless opportunities to exterminate them, was that incompetence or because they wanted to keep France strong enough to counterbalance the English? Apart from reflections of this sort, which he barely elaborated upon, the Emperor immersed himself in newspapers and frivolous novels. At Verdun he asked Sebastian to buy him some sugared almonds from a well-known confectioner. At Chateau-Thierry he took a bath and put on the green tailcoat of his Guard's foot grenadiers, keeping his cap and fur-lined coat, not so much because of the cold, which was now bearable, but so as not to be identified too soon. He wanted his sudden return to be a surprise.

After several broken axletrees and changes of carriage, the travellers entered Paris before midnight on 17 December in a sad-looking post-chaise with big wheels.

They came in on the Meaux road. Even though their carriage was closed, they blocked their noses as they passed the huge open-air dump where the capital's rubbish ended up. Near the cursed spot where the Montfaucon gallows stood, they drove past fallow land and fields, market gardens and farms which proclaimed their size by the brightness of their lanterns. They turned to the left, down rue du faubourg Saint-Laurent, then Saint-Martin, reached the quadruple row of limes of the grand boulevards that had replaced the old city wall and dashed through narrow, chaotic, weakly lit thoroughfares, deserted at that hour, the shopkeepers' stalls cleared away. Then – finally – ahead of them was the Tuileries, the Imperial palace. The postilion turned in under the porch of the Pavillon de l'Horloge and pulled up in front of the sentries guarding the peristyle. Caulaincourt emerged first, unbuttoning his coat and show-ing the gold braid of his uniform. As the sentries stood aside to make way for these visitors in fur-lined coats and fur caps, the twelve strokes of midnight rang out.

Caulaincourt, the Emperor and Sebastian climbed the double staircase leading to the vestibule of the palace. They strode along the arcades of a covered gallery and knocked on a door at the end, which led to the Empress's apartments – apartments that were once the Queen's and were then commandeered by the Committee of Public Safety, who filled them with furniture from Versailles and the Trianon, and an armada of secretaries. There was no answer. Cau-laincourt hammered on the door with his fists. They heard footsteps. A Swiss guard with dishevelled grey hair and bleary eyes opened the double door a crack. He was in his nightshirt, like his wife who was looking over his shoulder, intrigued; she was holding a lantern. In the pool of light it cast, she gazed fearfully at the grand equerry's clothes and dirty beard. Once again he showed the braid of his uniform, which was hidden by his fur-lined coat. The Swiss still looked suspicious.

'I am the Duke of Vicenza, Grand Equerry to His Majesty.'

In the adjacent rooms, skirts rustled on the parquet and two of the Empress's lady's maids joined the strange group. The Emperor took off his fur cap and undid his Polish cloak. At last they recognized him, with bewilderment first, then joy. There were tears in the Swiss guard's eyes. The Emperor dismissed his attendants, saying, 'Good night, Caulaincourt. You must need some rest.'

The door closed again. The grand equerry and the secretary, both dressed like Cossacks, found themselves in the shadowy gallery, standing with their big boots on its polished floor.

'Do you know where to go?'

'No, Your Grace.'

'Follow me.'

They retraced their steps and met a valet in the green livery of the court who asked, 'Is it true what they're saying?'

'What are they saying?'

'That His Majesty has returned.'

'Rumours travel, I see.'

'So, is it true?'

'Come,' Caulaincourt said to the valet. 'I need you.'

The grand equerry pushed Sebastian into the post-chaise and the valet climbed up next to the postilion; they were going to Arch-Chancellor Cambacérès's house in rue Saint-Dominique, on the other side of the Seine, to tell him the Emperor had returned. The carriage sped over the new stone bridge in front of the Tuileries and under the porch of the former Roquelaure house, which had been bought and restored, by Cambacérès, who liked to throw lavish and cheerless dinners there. Above the gate, flanked by gothic columns, his title had been inscribed in enormous letters: *Residence of His Serene Highness the Duke of Parma*. The gate opened onto a paved courtyard, there was a staircase at each wing of the mansion; yellow lamps lit the windows of the salons. As Caulaincourt and Sebastian jumped down from the carriage, one of Cambacérès's valets tried to stop them but the servant from the Tuileries explained their business to his colleagues and they were permitted entry. In the large drawing room, bewigged gentlemen from another age, dressed in velvet and satin, rose from their whist tables, their eyes bulging. 'Who let these vagabonds in?' demanded one of them, fixing a pince-nez on his nose.

'On the Emperor's service,' Caulaincourt stated in a loud voice.

'Really, who are you?' asked a marquess in a striped waistcoat.

'Announce me to the Arch-Chancellor,' Caulaincourt told the valet from the Tuileries, who set off down the marble hall towards Cambacérès's office, with his colleague showing him the way.

'This is madness!' protested one of the guests. 'You have got the wrong era, gentlemen. This building was a home to scurvy dogs once, but that was during the Revolution!'

'I am the Duke of Vicenza.'

'You?'

'In that garb?'

'With that lousy beard?'

'And that savage's cap?'

'The Chancellor awaits Your Grace,' announced the valet coming back into the salon.

'Is it really true?' one of the men asked Sebastian, who remained behind when the grand equerry left to report to Cambacérès and make arrangements for the following day.

'Where is the Emperor?' asked another.

'Has he suffered some misfortune?'

'We have been worried since yesterday morning . . .'

'We read the last bulletin in the *Monitor* with horror!'

'Will there be no army left?'

'Why is the Duke in Paris without His Majesty?'

'Speak, young man, speak!'

'Set our minds at rest!'

'The Emperor is in Paris,' said Sebastian, falling into a gilt armchair.

Seven

HEROES

A NEW ARMY WAS making for Leipzig in 1813, where it was preparing to face the coalition of Russians and Prussians. Europe was in ferment against the Empire. Sweden had rejoined England, Austria was wavering, inflammatory pamphlets were circulating in Germany. Napoleon had raised troops, authorizing the early conscription of the very young, the recall of disbanded contingents and the formerly exempt, the enrolment of sailors into the infantry, and the recall of whole divisions from Spain even though the English were sending Wellington reinforcements. All men under thirty were mobilized, except Sebastian Roque, who was well out of it. As Vice-Director of the library at the Hôtel Carnavalet, he devoted his perspicacity and penmanship to the service of Imperial censorship. He approved plays, arranged productions, adapted or cut texts and granted permissions to theatre companies and playwrights. He had a box at the Opéra, a gig with a driver, a generous annuity from the Emperor, which he supplemented with the diamonds from Moscow. He was, in short, the happiest and most serene of men in a tumultuous time.

In the Tuileries gardens that spring, Sebastian climbed the steps of the Feuillants' terrace and entered the portico of the Véry restaurant. He straightened his clothes in front of the long mirrors, checking the shine of his riding boots and the hang of his fashionable cinnamon-bronze kersey-mere frock coat. He'd barely reached the foot of the staircase lined with orange trees in tubs when a maître d'hôtel greeted him. 'The young ladies are here already, Monsieur le vice-directeur.'

'In my usual room?'

'Naturally.'

Sebastian gave him his gloves, knobbed stick and hat and hurried to join the actresses he had invited to supper.

The private room was decorated in the style of Hercu-laneum, with half-columns, imitation Roman balustrades, gilt candelabras and a granite table; the vases of flowers were reflected in the mirrors. 'Dear friends,' he said, seating himself between the chic young girls, 'forgive me. I was detained by Baron de Pommereul.'

Still wearing their ribboned straw hats, the actresses narrowed their eyes, batted their eyelashes, and pushed back their curls as waiters brought oysters and pickled fish, and a sommelier (the word had just been coined) poured the wine.

'Did you know that they have seventeen kinds of white wine at Véry's?'

'We've never been here before.'

'Oh, well, now you can tell people you have.'

'Where did you get that scar on your cheek, Monsieur le vice-directeur?' the more inquisitive of the two asked.

'A wound in the Emperor's service.'

'Did you fight?'

'In Russia.'

'Were you in Moscow?'

'Oh, yes, and I can assure you that the menus there

were not like Véry's! No chicken galantines or champagne truffles.'

The actress studied Sebastian's failings as they encouraged him to talk. To get parts at the Théâtre-Français – for he could cast plays as well as scripting them now – they indulged his conceited tendencies. He was not fooled, but the game amused him and he had his part to play as well. Even if they fluffed their lines, he would still give them what they dreamed of, without demanding anything in return: they were pretty and it was enough that he be seen walking back through the gardens with them on his arm. Tongues would wag. He wanted to make a reputation, for it to be his name that people brought up in salons and at court.

'Over there,' he said between oysters, 'the cold killed fewer people than hunger. Close to His Majesty we managed to survive, but most of the men had nothing to eat except their horses.'

'How dreadful!' said one of the girls, who couldn't care less.

'I have reason to believe that there were even cases of cannibalism.'

'No?'

'I didn't see it first-hand, but it can't be ruled out.'

'They ate the horses, you were saying . . .'

'The horses started to become scarce. They were dying of thirst.'

'Didn't they drink melted snow?'

'We didn't always take them out of harness in the evenings; they needed water but where are you going to find that in the dark? How can you guess where a frozen stream is? Even if we found one, we had to break the ice with an iron bar, collect the water in a pot, bring it back without getting lost.'

The supper passed in this fashion, Sebastian lightening or darkening his tale as his inspiration or the curiosity of his audience dictated. They took their time over the slices of sturgeon on skewers, the cucumbers stuffed with marrow and partridge fillets in rings; glass in hand, they talked of the fire of Moscow, the famine, the cold, the epidemics, the Cossacks and the sound of the cannon.

Sebastian was escorting the young ladies back to their homes in his gig when the driver knocked a pedestrian in crumpled clothes against a corner post. Out of curiosity, Sebastian looked at the individual, shuddered and ordered the carriage to stop for a moment; he jumped down, taking his leave of the actresses. 'My postilion will drive you back. Come tomorrow morning to Carnavalet, rue Sainte-Catherine, ask for Vice-Director Roque. Your business will be seen to.'

Without troubling about his boots in that muddy street with its overflowing drains, he bent over the fallen man.

'Monsieur Roque?'

'Paulin, is that really you?'

'Alas, yes, it is me.'

'Why alas? Is Captain d'Herbigny dead? Have you no job? If that's it I'll take you on in my service, in memory of so many memories.'

'No, no, the captain is alive, but it would have been better if he'd stayed in the Russian snow.'

'Explain yourself.'

'We live near here.'

'You're frightening me with your riddles!'

Near the Marché des Innocents, they turned into an

alleyway and climbed the four floors of a building that was shored up by wooden struts as broad as tree trunks. The stairs were steep and smelled of urine and soap. Paulin puffed and panted as he hobbled up; finally he pushed open a door without a lock and ushered Sebastian into a low, dark, tiled room, which opened onto the well of a small courtyard. In an armchair Sebastian could make out a vague silhouette. When the servant lit some candles, he saw d'Herbigny lying prostrate, his cross pinned to the lapel of a dressing gown; the captain had a leather nose, fixed, milky eyes, wrinkles and white hair.

'Sir!' Paulin said in a very loud voice. 'I've got a surprise for you.'

'Can't he hear anymore?' asked Sebastian, a lump in his throat.

'Oh yes, but he can't see. And I think he left his brain out there.'

'I'm not deaf, you poor sap!' the captain said suddenly, getting to his feet.

He held his riding whip in front of him like a white cane, took three steps, bumped into the table and swore.

'It's Sebastian Roque, Captain.'

'I know! You've been talking together. You should know that that cretin Paulin is as chronic a liar as a teeth-puller! No, I'm not still stuck out there, but what I am is in an absolute fury not to be of any use for anything anymore! A cannonball has just carried off Marshal Bessières, I've been told, Duroc too. I used to dream of that happening to me! But the rest of us, the menials, when we got to Prussia ... Prussia! I know it through the eyes of that blockhead Paulin, those pretty light grey and pink houses, with white curtains at the windows, brown half-timbering, Prussia!

Before allying themselves to the Russians, those scoundrels watched us pass like those bewildered monkeys that are shown on our boulevards, and they refused to give us lodgings, not even a bowl of soup; instead they pelted us with snowballs and stones and robbed us!'

'We reached that country thanks to M. Vialatoux.'

'The actor from Mme Aurore's troop?' asked Sebastian, feeling his heart thump.

'That's the one, he'd got us warm clothes at Vilna through a hoax—'

'The story would take too long!' interrupted the captain.

'What about the other actors?' insisted Sebastian.

'We only saw him,' said the captain. 'And can you imagine, that fool died at Königsberg. Do you know how? You'll never guess, you'll die with laughter. Stuffing himself with cakes in a patisserie!'

'We couldn't take rich food any more,' said Paulin. 'A lot of men died of indigestion.'

'Cakes!' cried the captain.

As one might guess, Sebastian was thinking about Mlle Ornella, whom he was still convinced he would chance upon one day, turning a corner, or on stage even. The picture he had of her in his mind was crystal clear, but already her voice was growing indistinct. In one's memory, it's the voice that goes first. There was no point questioning the two men further, though; instead, he offered to help financially.

'No need,' growled the captain.

'Then why are you living in this rat hole?'

'Because I have become a rat, my young friend!'

The captain broke into a forced laugh. Sebastian thought: In Russia we all crossed paths without ever meeting. The adventure overwhelmed us, we were swept along by the current like the ice on the Berezina, we couldn't bank on anything except luck and egotism . . .

Sebastian gave his address to Paulin and promised to come back. The servant led him downstairs.

'Don't hesitate, Paulin, if I can be of any use . . .'

'He doesn't want anything.'

'Has he no family?'

'I am his family, Monsieur Roque.'

'And the d'Herbigny chateau?'

'Monsieur refuses to go back to Normandy.'

'He'd be better off there than in this stinking building.'

'He says that noises without smells or colours would be too painful.'

'What will become of his estate?'

'Monsieur has bequeathed it to me.'

'Would you be up to running it?'

'On no, Monsieur Roque, I'd sell it if something terrible happened.'

'When that day comes, think of me, Paulin. Herbigny is my part of the world too. Anyway, I only say that to comfort you, let's hope nothing distressing happens . . .'

'What else do you want him to suffer? I've stopped him jumping out of the window so many times.'

Sebastian couldn't think of anything to say and so he left. The following week, as he was inserting some lines of Molière – more animated – into a Racine tragedy, he learnt by a note from Paulin that Captain d'Herbigny had thrown himself out of the window, a little gold cross clenched in his fist. Sebastian Roque, Vice-Director of the Library, scribbled a note to himself on the margin of his copy: Tell Paulin I'll buy the land and the chateau.

HISTORICAL NOTES

'Il neigeait.' Several of my friends, without conferring, suggested this as a title for this novel. It is the leitmotif of a famous poem by Victor Hugo entitled 'Expiation', part of his *Châtiments* [*The Punishments*], in which he evokes the retreat from Russia. Here is the start, followed by Robert Lowell's translation:

> *Il neigeait. On était vaincu par sa conquête.*
> *Pour la première fois l'aigle baissait la tête.*
> *Sombres jours! L'empereur revenait lentement,*
> *Laissant derrière lui brûler Moscou fumant.*
> *Il neigeait. L'âpre hiver fondait en avalanche.*
> *Après la plaine blanche, une autre plaine blanche.*
> *On ne connaissait plus les chefs ni le drapeau.*
> *Hier la grande armée, et maintenant troupeau.*
> *On ne distinguait plus les ailes ni le centre:*
> *Il neigeait. Les blessés s'abritaient dans le ventre*
> *Des chevaux morts; au seuil des bivouacs désolés*
> *On voyait des clairons à leur poste gelés*
> *Restés debout, en selle et muets, blancs de givre,*
> *Collant leur bouche en pierre aux trompettes de cuivre.*
> *Boulets, mitraille, obus, mêlés aux flacons blancs,*
> *Pleuvaient; les grenadiers surpris d'être tremblants,*
> *Marchaient pensifs, la glace à leur moustache grise.*
> *Il neigeait, il neigeait toujours! La froide bise*
> *Sifflait; sur le verglas, dans des lieux inconnus,*
> *On n'avait pas de pain et on l'allait pieds nus.*

Ce n'étaient plus des cœurs vivants, des gens de guerre;
C'était un rêve errant dans la brume, un mystère,
Une procession d'ombres sous le ciel noir.
La solitude vaste, épouvantable à voir,
Partout apparaissait, muette vengeresse.
Le ciel faisait sans bruit avec la neige épaisse
Pour cette immense armée un immense linceul . . .

The snow fell, and its power was multiplied.
For the first time the Eagle bowed its head –
Dark days! Slowly the Emperor returned –
Behind him Moscow! Its own domes still burned.
The snow rained down in blizzards – rained and froze.
Past each white waste a further white waste rose.
None recognized the captains or the flags.
Yesterday the Grand Army, today its dregs!
No one could tell the vanguard from the flanks.
The snow! The hurt men struggled from the ranks,
Hid in the bellies of dead horses, in stacks
Of shattered caissons. By the bivouacs
One saw the picket dying at his post,
Still standing in his saddle, white with frost
The stone lips frozen to the bugle's mouth!
Bullets and grapeshot mingled with the snow
That hailed . . . The guard, surprised at shivering, march
In a dream now, ice rimes the gray moustache
The snow falls, always snow! The driving mire
Submerges; men, trapped in that white empire
Have no more bread and march on barefoot.
They were no longer living men and troops,
But a dream drifting in a fog, a mystery,
Mourners parading under the black sky.
The solitude, vast, terrible to the eye,
Was like a mute avenger everywhere,
As snowfall, floating through the quiet air,
Buried the huge army in a huge shroud . . .

* * *

What did Napoleon look like? It is hard to tell, since the visual record is unreliable. Only the Spanish have produced portraits of their rulers that are realistic to the point of cruelty – debased, monstrous princes and degenerate princesses with black bags under their eyes and huge noses painted by Velázquez or Goya. In the hands of French artists, the portrait becomes a smooth, flattering creation; Gérard and Détaille, for instance, give us a young, thin, alert Emperor when Veretchaguine shows him to be stout and puffy. The only example of truth in official portraiture is Rigaud's portrait of Louis XIV: he painted the aged king's face but then his studio took over and stuck his face onto a young man's body. The finished result looks a bit like an alien; you should go and have a look in the Louvre. As for Napoleon – the question has no real answer. His appearance depends on one's opinion of him.

In many ways, instead of an art gallery one should go to Madame Tussaud's waxworks museum in Marylebone in London, which contains astonishing casts of historical figures. Every morning during the Revolution, Madame Tussaud used to go to cemeteries where the previous day's guillotined were buried. She would wash the blood and sawdust from the severed heads, apply a layer of lead protoxide and linseed oil and, using cloth to secure it, take the impressions that would serve as moulds for her waxworks. Marat, Philippe-Egalité, Hébert, Desmoulins, Danton: the death masks she produced, either secretly or in collusion with the executioners, can never be replaced by portraits. Her subjects weren't posing anymore; they slept, their faces frozen by a brutal death. I was transfixed by the cast of Robespierre's head, which hangs at the entrance to the Chamber of Horrors. The Terror was coming to an end and one senses that Madame Tussaud was finally able to take her time. The portrait is very precise; the most faithful, so it is said, of her collection. And the fact is that this severed head of Robespierre bears little relation to the familiar portraits of him. In it his face is less thickset, his forehead less bulging, his lips less thin and he has an almost sardonic air.

When Marcel Brion writes a life of Lorenzo the Magnificent, he doesn't trust the painters. Gozzoli depicts a blond, curly-haired, vaguely androgynous angel, Ghirlandaio a boxer, Vasari a pickpocket. Instead Brion stops and stares at the death mask: this is the true Lorenzo. He is forty-three years old and there is a whole life etched in the lined, square face, with its crooked nose, toothbrush moustache, broad mouth and non-existent lips; coarse features, which nonetheless emanate an incredible serenity.

Can one form an idea of Napoleon from his death mask? No, not even that is possible. When Napoleon died on Saint Helena, Dr Burton was unable to find the plaster needed for a mould in Jamestown. Gypsum crystals were reported on an island to the south-east, which he sent a sloop to fetch. He calcined them, ground them up and thereby obtained a grey plaster, which he took to Longwood. The previous night an attempt had been made to take a cast using candle wax and tissue paper steeped in limewater. But the results had been inconclusive. When Burton returned, Napoleon had been dead for forty hours. The cheekbones were protruding. The face had altered but a cast was taken anyway, in extremis. As the skin was coming off in places, only one attempt was possible.

Antoine Rambaud, my great-great-grandfather, was thirty when Napoleon camped out in Moscow. What did he think of it? Anything? What did his family in Lyons say? Will the future ever know what we dream of; how we live; that we like Cistercian choirs, or irises, or Peking duck? Will they know our tiredness, our joys, our angers? Only a few avowals will survive us, froth. What does that Merovingian's femur tell us? What do these remnants of a barber's basin evoke? What happened in the caves at night, after the auroch hunt? The scholar deliberates, and then delivers his verdict, which is soon refuted by another scholar's. Honestly – we will never enter the minds of our ancestors; we barely know what they looked like. Paul Morand knew this: 'Those who come after us will be happy to imagine us as we have never been.' In one of its exhilarating publications, the College of Pataphysics gives its response, 'Imagination alone draws crowds to the beetroot fields of Waterloo.' And the imagination is not the province of academia, but of legend and the novel. The musketeers? They will always be Dumas. The jungle, Conrad. The hollow needle of Etretat belongs to Maurice Leblanc and the road to Trouville to Flaubert. The London fog, hansom cabs, Conan Doyle. Besides, Sherlock Holmes still gets mail at 221b Baker Street, now a blockish, unsightly building. History is not an exact science; it rambles, digresses; it should be left to dreamers who can recreate it by instinct.

To return to Napoleon. No historian is objective about him. He began fashioning his legend during the war of pillage he waged in Italy to bail out the Directory. He created and controlled his image by surrounding himself with publicists, draughtsmen and painters. He never stepped onto the bridge at Arcola; he fell in a ditch before he could reach it. In the famous painting one sees him brandishing his standard and leading Masséna's infantry. In fact Augereau played that role. When Parisians came to look at David's *Coronation*, they'd joke, 'Goodness, the Empress is looking young,' and burst out laughing. As for the Emperor's mother, who features prominently, she wasn't even at the ceremony; she was sulking because her son hadn't given her a title. Napoleon invented modern propaganda by detaching official history from facts.

Paintings, drawings and sketches do exist, however, and provide an illuminating record of people's lives. They have been very helpful to me in travelling back through time, as they were before I could read, when I'd immerse myself in the thick volumes of Larousse's *An Illustrated History of France*, published around 1910, with its recreations by academic painters, in photographic detail, of *The Pillaging of a Gallo-Roman Villa*, or *The Excommunication of Robert the Pious*. In the following books, the images are more truthful and in many cases the work of first-hand witnesses:

Campagne de Russie (1812), Albrecht Adam and Christian Wilhelm von Faber du Faur, Tradition Magazine, special edition No. 3, available from 25 rue Bargue, 75015 Paris. Sketches of an unmistakable vividness and immediacy. [1]

Napoléon, 1812, la campagne de Russie, part of the collection compiled by Tranié and Carmignani, Pygmalion, October 1997. A remarkable iconography, containing almost five hundred illustrations.

Then come the participants' accounts. There is an abundance of these and one must know how to navigate one's way through them to identify particular images, scenes and details. I tend to discard the author's judgements and retain the colour. When Castellane makes a note of the weather every day or Bausset describes the Kremlin's apartments or Ali lists the Emperor's tics or Larrey expatiates on the effects of severe cold in his *Mémoires de chirurgie militaire*, why should they be lying?

The works I consulted at the Service historique des armées, Fort de Vincennes are listed with their reference numbers preceded by a V for Vincennes.

[*Publisher's Note*. We have for convenience numbered those works that have been translated into English, and listed them on page 322–3.]

1. Eyewitness accounts of the campaign and retreat

Ségur, P. P. de, *Histoire de Napoléon et de la Grande Armée pendant l'année 1812*, Turin, 1831, chez les frères Reycent et Cie, librairie du Roi. The best-known and most literary account, which one can round out with another Ségur, *Du Rhin à Fontainebleau*, subtitled, '*Personal memories of 1812*'. Gourgaud disagrees with Ségur, devoting an entire volume to his qualifications, *Examen critique de l'ouvrage de Monsieur le Comte Ph. De Ségur*, Paris, Bossange Frères (1825). He also gave us *Napoléon et la Grande Armée en Russie*, V. 72794–98. [2]

Caulaincourt, *Mémoires*, 3 vols, Plon (1933). Meticulous and precious in its wealth of detail, especially concerning the Emperor's flight by sleigh; Caulaincourt accompanied him and recorded his conversations. Incidentally, as often as I was able, I have Napoleon say what those closest to him report him as having said. [3]

Fain, *Manuscrit de 1812*, 2 vols, chez Delaulay, Paris (1827). Baron Fain, secretary to the Emperor, has involuntarily become a character in this novel, whom I have treated with a certain licence.

Méneval, *Mémoires*, V. 9851–53. The other secretary, a more colourful writer than his colleague but who unfortunately fell ill in Moscow. [4]

Constant, *Mémoires intimes de Napoléon Ier*, Mercure de France (1967). The indispensable confidences of the Emperor's valet. He does, however, draw heavily on Ségur for the retreat. Illuminating notes by Maurice Pernelle of the Académie d'histoire. [5]

Marbot, *Mémoires*, tome II, Mercure de France (1983). It is a pity he did not enter Moscow. [6]

Lejeune, *Mémoires*, tome II, 'En prison et en guerre', Firmin-Didot (1896). [7]

Roustan, *Souvenirs*. V. 5931. Reminiscences by Napoleon's most prominent Mameluke.

Louis Etienne Saint-Denis, *Souvenirs du mamelouk Ali*, Payot (1926) recently reissued. This Mameluke and former lawyer's clerk gives us a far livelier and slyer account than his compatriot Roustam.

Fezensac, *Journal de la campagne de Russie*, V. 42037. A lieutenant-general's account. [8]

Bonnet, *Mémoires anecdotiques*, Plon (1900).

Bausset, *Mémoires anecdotiques sur l'intérieur du palais et sur quelques événements de l'Empire*, Paris, Baudoin frères, tome II (1913). [9]

Heinrich Roos, *1812, Souvenirs d'un médecin de la Grande Armée*, Perrin (1913).

Miot-Putigny, *Putigny grognard de l'Empire*, Gallimard (1950).

Rapp, *Mémoires*, V. 73242–45. [10]

Macdonald, *Souvenirs*, V. 42739. [11]

Castellane, *Journal*, V. 9074.

Bourgogne, *Mémoires du sergent Bourgogne*, Hachette (1978). Many accuse him of invention, but acknowledge it is done with great talent. [12]

Peyrusse, *Lettres inédites*, Perrin (1894).

Wilhelm von Bade, *Mémoires du margrave de Bade*, Paris, Fontemoing (1912).

Bourgoing, *Souvenirs militaires*, Plon (1897).

Ernouf, *Souvenirs*, V. 43103.

Jean Jacoby, *Napoléon en Russie*, Mercure de France (1938). Eyewitness accounts.

Roy, *Les Français en Russie*, Mame (1863). As the preceding item.

Labaume, *Relations circonstanciés de la campagne de Russie*, V.72785. Thorough and slightly dull. [13]

Faber du Faur, *Campagne de Russie*, V. 1260.

Stendhal, *Œuvres intimes*, tome I, La Pléiade (1981). Henri Beyle witnessed the fire of Moscow but set off for Smolensk and Danzig before the retreat. Some of his conversations in the novel are those he describes having in his journal. [14]

La Vouivre booksellers, 11 rue Saint-Martin, 75004 Paris, publish a very high quality series of books on the Empire, including:

Jean-Bréaut des Marlots, *Lettre d'un capitaine de cuirassiers sur la campagne de Russie* and Pierre-Paul Denniée, *Itinéraire de l'Empereur Napoléon pendant la campagne de 1812*.

Alexandre Bellot de Kergotte, *Journal d'un commissaire des guerres (1806–1821)*.

Florent-Guibert, *Souvenirs d'un sous-lieutenant d'infanterie légère (1805–1815)* and François-René Cailloux, known as Pouget, *Souvenirs de guerre (1790–1831)*.

Bulletins de la Grande Armée, campagne de Russie.

The two volumes of reports by Sir Robert Wilson, England's representative at the Tsar's court. Among other things, he reports on the atrocities perpetrated by the moujiks and advances the opinion that not all his allies are gentlemen.

Another bookseller also publishing little-known works from the period is Teisseidre, 102 rue du Cherche-Midi, 75006 Paris. I was struck by:

Louis Gardier, *Journal de la campagne en Russie en 1812.*

Bismark et Jacquemont, *Mémoires et carnets sur la campagne de Russie.*

Général comte Zaluski, *Les chevau-légers polonais de la Garde (1812–1814)*

Pelet, Bonnet, Evert, *Carnets et journal sur la campagne de Russie.*

Of collections, *Mémoires d'Empire*, edited by Alain Pigeard, Quatuour, 1997, in a limited run of 300 copies, should not be forgotten.

2. On the Russians and Russia

Schnitzler, *La Russie en 1812*, V. 35845.

Birkov, *Le Mouvement partisan de la guerre patriotique, 1812*, V. 18508.

E. Dupré de Saint Maure, *L'Hermite en Russie*, Turin 1829, 11 vols.

Observations on Russian customs and practices at the start of the nineteenth century.

Godechot, *Napoléon*, Albin Michel, 1969. Contains two important documents, a French priest's account of Moscow and Rostopchin's defence for having ordered the city to be set on fire.

Vassili Verestchagen, *Napoléon Ier en Russie*, Nilsson, 1897. Fascinating testimonies from Muscovites and Russian prisoners.

Grand, *Un officier prisonnier des Russes*, V. 35845.

Désiré Fuzellier, *Journal de captivité en Russie*, editions du Griot, Boulogne. With a very informative preface by a descendant of the author, a historian.

Concerning the mood of occupied Moscow, one may also read *Lettres interceptées par les Russes*, La Sabretache, 1913. V. 59077.

3. On the army

Alain Pigeard, *L'Armée napoléonienne*, Curandera, 1993.

Baldet, *Vie quotidienne dans les armées de Napoléon*, Hachette, V. 17162.

Ferdinand Bac, *Le retour de la Grande Armée, 1812*, Hachette, 1939.

Lucas Dubreton, *Soldats de Napoléon*, V. 61835.

Boutourlin, *Histoire militaire de la campagne de Russie*, V. 72807–2.

'Les Sous-Officiers de la Révolution et de l'Empire', an article by Gilbert Bolinier published in the *Revue historique de armées*, no. 2, 1986.

R. Brice, *Les Femmes et les armées de la Révolution et de l'Empire*, V.4354.

'De Borodino à Moscou', an article by Marc-André Fabré published in the *Revue historique de armées*, 1960.

Masson, *Cavaliers de Napoléon*, V.24811.

Chardigny, *Les Maréchaux de Napoléon*, Flammarion, 1946.

Damamme, *Les Soldats de la Grande Armée*, Perrin, 1998.

4. Life, customs, fashion

Naturally the two volumes of *Vie quotidienne au temps de Napoléon* published by Hachette at different periods, that of Robiquet in 1944 and Tulard in 1988. [15]

Histoire et dictionnaire du Consulat et de l'Empire, Fierro, Palluel and Tulard, 'Bouquins', Robert Laffont, 1995.

'Bouquins', 1998, *Le Consulat et l'Empire*, in the series *'Les français par eux-mêmes'*.

Philippe Séguy, *Histoire des modes sous l'Empire*, Taillandier, 1988.

D'Alméras, *La Vie parisienne sous le Consulat et l'Empire*, Albin Michel, undated.

Bertaut, *La Vie à Paris sous le Ier Empire*, Calmann-Lévy, 1949.

5. On Napoleon

Correspondance de Napoleon Ier, published by order of Emperor Napoleon III, tome XXIV, Imprimerie impériale, 1868. Selected letters which one can consult in the Salle des Archives of the Fort de Vincennes.

Stendhal, *Vie de Napoléon*, Payot, 1969. A new, more complete, edition was published by Stock in 1998. [16]

Bainville, *Napoléon*, Fayard, 1931. [17]

Ludwig, *Napoléon*, Payot, 1929. [18]

Savant, *Tel fut Napoléon*, Fasquelle, 1953. This text was reprinted, with a large number of illustrations, under the title *Napoléon*, Henri Veyrier, 1954. A purely negative point of view, hence often exaggerated or erroneous.

G. Lenotre, *Napoléon, croquis de l'epopée*, and *En suivant l'Empereur*. Two vivid and extremely well-documented collections of articles republished by Grasset in 'Les Cahiers rouges'. I particularly recommend *'Ce qu'on trouve au fond de la Bérésina'*.

Bouhler, *Napoléon*, Grasset, 1942.

Mauguin, *Napoléon et la superstition*, Carrère, Rodez, 1942. Anecdotes and curiosities.

Bertaut, *Napoléon ignoré*, Sfelt, 1951.

Brice, *Le Secret de Napoléon*, Payot, 1936. [19]

Frugier, *Napoléon, essai medico-psychologique*, Albatros, 1985.

Taine, *Les Origines de la France contemporaine*, Tome 11, Hachette, 1907. [20]

Toute l'histoire de Napoléon, Vol. 8, 'Napoléon et les médecins.' I found the formula for Napoleon's poison here.

6. On Charles XII

With regard to the King of Sweden's Russian expedition, I consulted the same Voltaire as Napoleon, namely, in the *Œuvres Complètes*, Baudoin Frères, Paris, 1825:

Tome XXX, *Histoire de Charles XII*.

Tome XXXI, *Histoire de Russie*, first part.

English Translations

Numbers in square brackets correspond to those in the list above.

Faber du Faur, Christian Wilhelm von, *With Napoleon in Russia: the illustrated memoirs of Major Faber du Faur, 1812*, ed. and tr. Jonathan North (London: Greenhill, 2001). [1]

Segur, General, Count Philip de, *History of the Expedition to Russia undertaken by the Emperor Napoleon in the year 1812* (2 vols: London: Treuttel and Wurtz, Treuuttel Jun. and Richter, 1825). [2]

Caulaincourt, Armand-Augustin-Louis de, Duke of Vicenza, *Memoirs of General de Caulaincourt, Duke of Vincenza*, tr. Hamish Miles (London: Cassell, 1935). [3]

Méneval, Claude François de, Baron de, *Memoirs to serve for the history of Napoleon I. from 1802 to 1815 / completed by the addition of unpublished documents* Tr. and annotated by Robert H. Sherard (3 vols: London, 1894). [4]

Constant, *Memoirs of Constant: the Emperor Napoleon's head valet; containing details of the private life of Napoleon, his family and his court*, tr. Percy Pinkerton (London: Hs. Nichols). [5]

Marbot, Jean-Baptiste Antoine Marcellin, Baron de, *The memoirs of Baron de Marbot*, tr. Arthur John Butler (London: Longmans Green, 1892; facs. ed. London: Greenhill, 1988). [6]

Lejeune, Baron de, *Memoirs of Baron Lejeune*, tr. Mrs Arthur Bell (2 vols: London: Longmans Green, 1897). [7]

Fezensac, Raymond Eymery Philippe Joseph de, Duke, *A journal of the Russian campaign of 1812*, tr. Colonel W. Knollys (London, 1852). [8]

Bausset, Louis-François-Joseph de, *Private memoirs of the court of Napoleon, and of some publick events of the imperial reign, from 1805 to the first of May 1814: to serve as a contribution to the history of Napoleon* (Philadelphia, Pa.: Carey, Lea and Carey, 1828). [9]

Rapp, Jean, Count, *Memoirs of General Count Rapp: first aide-de-camp to Napoleon* (London: H. Colburn and Co., 1823). [10]

Macdonald, Etienne Jacques Joseph Alexandre, Duke of Tarentum, *Recollections of Marshal Macdonald Duke of Tarentum*, tr. Stephen Louis Simeon (London, 1892). [11]

Bourgogne, *Memoirs of Sergeant Bourgogne* (London: Jonathan Cape, 1896/1940). [12]

Labaume, Eugène, *1812, through fire and ice with Napoleon: a French officer's memoir of the campaign in Russia* (Solihull, West Midlands, England: Helion, 2002). [13]

Beyle, Marie Henri, *The Private Diaries of Stendhal*, ed. and tr. Robert Sage (London: Victor Gollancz, 1955). [14]

Robiquet, Jean, *Daily life in France under Napoleon*, tr. Violet M. MacDonald (London: Allen and Unwin, 1962). [15]

Beyle, Marie Henri, *A life of Napoleon* (London: Rodale Press, 1956). [16]

Bainville, Jacques, *Napoleon*, tr. Hamish Miles; intr. H. A. L. Fisher (London: J. Cape, 1932; Safety Harbor, FL: Simon Publications, 2001). [17]

Ludwig, Emil, *Napoleon*, tr. Eden and Cedar Paul (London, Allen and Unwin, 1927). [18]

Brice, Léon Raoul Marie, *The Riddle of Napoleon*, tr. Basil Creighton (London: Putnam, 1937). [19]

Taine, Hippolyte Adolphe, *The origins of contemporary France*, tr. John Durand (University of Chicago: Chicago & London, 1974). [20]